The Manor House Murder

ALSO BY FAITH MARTIN

DI HILLARY GREENE SERIES

MONICA NOBLE MYSTERIES

TRAVELLING COOK MYSTERIES

THE MANOR HOUSE MURDER

FAITH MARTIN

JOFFE BOOKS

Revised edition 2024
Joffe Books, London
www.joffebooks.com

First published by Robert Hale in 2016
as *An Unholy Shame* by Joyce Cato

This paperback edition was first published
in Great Britain in 2024

Cover art by Nick Castle

ISBN: 978-1-83526-745-5

PROLOGUE

February

The intruder perched on the edge of a chair in front of an unfamiliar computer and stared at the screen intently. Anyone watching the hunched figure would have noticed instantly the harshness of the figure's breathing and the tense, strained curve of their back. Their eyes glittered with repressed fury as fingers, unused to this particular keyboard, painstakingly picked out the individual letters.

No, no, that sentence just didn't ring true. It didn't sound like the little whore at all.

Do it again. You must get it right . . .

The typist hissed and searched impatiently for the delete button. Hesitantly, the fingers moved over the keyboard once more. Slowly the sinister figure leaned forward, eyes narrowing in concentration as they read the words that now appeared on the screen.

'I feel that I just have to leave all the sin and the deceit behind me. I'm so sorry . . .'

Yes, that's better, the interloper thought, sighing with a small sound of satisfaction and relief. That's just how the

1

prissy little bitch would have put it. Now, just a few lines more . . .

The green-coated figure quickly set about the unnerving task of printing off the forgery, flinching a little as the printer quietly buzzed into life.

But with the study door firmly shut there was little chance that it would be heard by the enemy, and in fact the whore upstairs didn't even stir.

With a cold, gleaming, but satisfied eye, the stealthy figure watched as the missive was faithfully reproduced on paper, then turned off the printer and computer, careful to make sure everything on the desk looked just the same.

Now for the pen, and a few practised forgeries of the rather childish signature on a blank piece of paper. It was easy really, once you'd tried it a few times — all you needed was a little bit of confidence and élan. With a deep breath, the intruder pulled the newly printed letter forward and, careful not to hesitate, boldly forged the name at the bottom. There, it was done. It looked real. It sounded real. And it would convince everyone.

Wouldn't it?

Now for the more dangerous and irrevocable part of the plan. This had to be done just right — the consequences would be dire if any mistake were made now.

But a traitorous little voice wouldn't quite be quelled.

I could always stop now. Just go home and pretend that none of this has happened. I can always go back to how it was.

Except that how it was, was obviously unbearable. To leave things as they stood was too much for flesh and blood to tolerate.

No. No, a thousand times no.

There could be no backing out now.

It was exactly two minutes past midnight as the figure walked noiselessly from the small study through to the kitchen, and stared at the stove.

The gas stove.

How fervently the intruder had prayed that the enemy would have gas. There was no surprise that those prayers had

2

been answered, though. It was as the intruder had always thought.

Anyone would agree: the enemy deserved to die.

To one side of the door there was a rack of what looked like towels. Another sign, surely? Taking one and very carefully walking back to the hallway, the figure in green pushed a towel under the crack of the front door, excluding the draught of life-giving fresh air.

As the interloper passed by the stairs, the hooded head tilted to follow the line of steps upwards. Was she up there dreaming sweet dreams?

Soon, the sleep would become darker. And eternal.

The intruder returned to the kitchen and turned on all four of the gas rings, then opened the oven door and put that on as well, before stumbling to the back door, retching helplessly. Outside, in the dank, cold night, the figure took long, gulping breaths of soothing air. This was no time to panic!

But then, a sudden, awful thought rose shrieking to their brain.

The window! You fool, the window! What if the enemy sleeps with her windows open?

Frantically, the green-clad figure stepped back, neck craning upwards. But no windows were open. Nobody liked to let in the dank, cold February air, did they?

The figure gave a small sigh of relief and satisfaction. Now it was just a question of waiting.

And so they waited, in the cold dark night — as patient and cold-blooded as a snake.

CHAPTER 1

May

The Oxfordshire village of Heyford Bassett glowed smugly under the rays of a gentle spring sun. Its creamy Cotswold stone buildings reflected palely against the soft green fields of barley and the darker oak woods stretching away to one side. It would have made a good addition for a calendar on scenic Britain, or a photograph to go into a tourist brochure.

A two-carriage train on the up-line was just pulling out of the station with a muffled groan of diesel power, upsetting two jackdaws which were resting on top of a nearby telephone pole. A bit further down the road, an old woman walking along briskly, carrying an old-fashioned wicker basket over one arm, turned into the village shop. The scene could have been almost too sweet and comfortably nostalgic, had she not had to pass renovated cottages bristling with satellite TV dishes, and row upon row of parked cars that threatened to clog the narrow lanes and spill over onto the village square.

In the pub, the Bridge and Wagon, the redheaded barmaid-cum-owner June Cowdey was doing a brisk early-ly-evening trade. The real ales, which the establishment was famous for, were going well and so was the well-cooked traditional fare that went with them.

The river that bisected the village glittered in the reddening light of the setting sun, and a pair of yellow and grey wagtails, busy feeding hungry mouths, chinked and flitted along its banks, catching dancing mayflies.

In the vicarage, Graham Noble opened the door to his study and picked up the post that had been waiting there for him all day. Noble, the vicar of many years, had one of the twelve flats that had been created from the original elegant three-storey building.

Monica, his wife of just two and half years, always left the mail for him on the small Victorian side table that stood in the narrow hall, next to a loudly ticking grandfather clock. Despite the perfect domestic scene, Graham Noble looked as unlike many people's idea of a rural vicar as it was possible to imagine.

Although in his very early fifties, he could easily have passed for a man in his late thirties. His hair was still naturally dark and without a hint of silver. He was tall and lean — one of nature's effortlessly elegant men — with the face of a Romantic poet. Needless to say, his church was very popular with the female congregation in the five villages to which he ministered.

That he'd finally married after so many years of being a bachelor was something that many of his female parishioners were still secretly mourning. And, not surprisingly perhaps, something many of the men in the vicinity were delighted about.

Despite these minor complications he remained in everybody's good books simply because he was a very good vicar. People came to him with real problems and were never turned away. He was useful and practical, as well as kind, which were two more factors that kept his church attendance rate higher than any other in the county. He also tried to give interesting and relevant sermons — uplifting, without being sentimental and pithy, but not judgmental. Or so he hoped.

As he shuffled through the envelopes, the door further down the corridor suddenly opened, and a pretty, dark-haired woman looked out, big blue eyes regarding him sympathetically. In her late thirties, Monica's figure was still pleasingly trim, and dressed as it was in a gauzy skirt of sky blue topped with a simple white blouse, she brought an instant smile to his tired eyes.

'Long day, sweetheart?' Monica asked, holding out a glass tinkling with ice and giving it a tempting rattle. 'Fancy a G and T with me?'

'I'd love one,' Graham said, smiling gratefully and walking towards her, glancing down at the mail in his hand as he did so. The ominous brown envelopes had to be bills, of course. And several handwritten letters with cramped, slanting writing were probably from old parishioners who'd long since moved away, but were determined to keep in touch. There was also a large, white, official-looking envelope with an Oxford postmark.

He followed his wife into the lounge, which had been attractively decorated in shades of apple green and rich cream with just a few splashes of turquoise. Monica had been in charge of decorating their flat when the huge house had been converted into its upmarket apartments, and Graham had been more than happy to leave her to it. He was well aware of her artistic talents and trusted them without a qualm, but he was also ruefully aware that even if her taste had run to cherry pink with lime and yellow spots, he'd have gritted his teeth and put up with it. He'd have put up with anything, just to keep her happy.

Before he'd met the widowed advertising executive with a feisty teenage daughter, Graham had been convinced that there was nothing more to look forward to in his life than the inevitable gentle decline into old age. His life would go on just the same as it always had, with nothing to note the passing of the years.

But then, at a party in Oxford, he'd met Monica and everything had changed. Like the proverbial bolt from the blue — or, as he preferred to think of it, divine intervention. In a stroke, his life had altered in so many ways — some of them bewildering, the odd one or two a shade frightening, but all of them delightful. And he still almost couldn't believe it, even now.

'How was the hospital visit?' Monica asked, interrupting his reverie as she made her way to the drinks cabinet and poured her husband a modest gin and tonic. She added plenty of ice and lemon, just as he liked.

'Gruelling,' Graham said briefly. He'd held the hand of a man dying from liver cancer for over four hours, but was reluctant to discuss it.

Monica, glancing into his pale, tired face, wisely said nothing. Instead she handed him the squat glass. 'Here, drink this,' she said softly.

'How was your day?' Graham changed the subject firmly, sinking down onto the sofa and taking a sip. 'Has inspiration finally struck?'

Although Monica had given up her job as an advertising executive in London, as well as her home, to move to her new husband's parish in the Cotswolds, her old boss and best friend had recently persuaded her to take on some easy, part-time work. And Monica had to admit that it was very nice indeed to be working from home with no daily commute. And even better to be able to get back into the swing of things without having the enormous pressure of coming up with a whole campaign before a — usually impossible — deadline.

Luckily Monica was very competent with a computer, a thing that Graham still approached as tentatively as he'd approach a sleeping tiger, and her artistic ability, as well as her quick brain, often came up with stunning concepts and jingles. Her latest assignment was for an advertising campaign for cat food, aimed at women's magazines.

Monica laughed. 'I've been trying to come up with an appealing character which is both feline and mysteriously mischievous, but he keeps coming out as something of a cross between a grumpy Garfield and a more manic-than-usual Tom from *Tom and Jerry*. Apart from that, I've been trying to think up something that even vaguely rhymes with "Harcourt's Cat Munchies."'

Graham grinned. 'Rather you than me,' he said with feeling, and began to open the mail — bills first, which he promptly handed over to Monica with a grimace of apology. Monica, it had to be said, definitely had the better business brain of the two of them, and dealt with all their finances and banking matters.

'From Mrs Dellington,' he said after a few moments' reading, waving one of the handwritten letters in the air. 'Her daughter's just had another baby.'

'What? Another one!' exclaimed Monica, crossing her bare legs and swinging one foot idly. 'How many does that make now?' she asked, draining her drink and contemplating pouring another one.

Then she gave a mental shake of her head. Best not. Although she rarely drank, today had been a particularly hot and frustrating one, and a rare second glass would have been welcome. She was still so new to being a vicar's wife, and she was forced to admit that she was still rather uneasy about falling short of the required mark. While a second very mild G and T would hardly make her even tipsy, just the idea that a parishioner might call in on her husband and then report smelling alcohol on her breath to the rest of the WI made her blanch.

'Five,' said Graham with a grin, interrupting her fretful thoughts and making her laugh.

'Imagine having five children!' Monica had just the one child, and had never considered having more. What if Graham wanted a child of his own? The thought shot through her like an electrical surge, making her go suddenly still.

She shot her husband a quick, assessing look. He'd never mentioned wanting to start a family of their own. Why hadn't they ever discussed that? Had each of them just been assuming that the other wasn't interested, without pausing to think that that might not be the case?

Unaware of the sudden minefield his wife was mentally treading, Graham opened the big white envelope and pulled out a whole wad of information. As he did so, a tall, blonde-haired vision of loveliness walked into the room and draped languidly over the couch. She then proceeded to peer over Graham's shoulder with a look of exquisite boredom on her face.

Carol-Ann Clancy, Monica's daughter by her first marriage, was sixteen now, and had a yen to become a supermodel.

Fortunately for the peace of mind of her mother however, Carol-Ann was also doing very well at school, and her second choice of career was that of a computer-games designer. Needless to say, Monica and Graham were still crossing their fingers that the lure of endless days spent in front of the computer and having a great time would beat the reality that would be the slog of trailing around the modelling agencies. They'd done their homework and knew, thankfully, that the odds against any young woman making a successful career in that competitive field were astronomical.

'Ahh, the information pack for the conference,' Graham said, leafing through the pile of professional-looking papers that had been in the envelope and handing a brochure over to Monica to peruse.

Heyford Bassett, like so many traditional English villages, had had to adapt to survive the fast-changing pace set by the outside world, which was why the local shop now stayed open till eleven at night, and several farms had diversified by converting barns and outbuildings into holiday lets. One of its inhabitants had adapted far faster and more successfully than most, though.

Sir Andrew Courtenay had refurbished and refitted his large, sprawling manor house, turning it into an increasingly popular hotel and conference centre. As Sir Andrew had pointed out to his bank manager, the village had its own railway station, and London was only an hour or so away. There was a motorway within half an hour's driving, and having

Oxford and Birmingham so close made for a particular selling point, attracting both American and Japanese clientele.

Within five years, Sir Andrew had recouped his original investment, paid off the bank, and now ran a very successful business indeed. So well known was the conference centre that it had been Graham's own bishop, Dr David Carew, who had recommended the place for the upcoming ecclesiastical conference that was to be held in ten days' time.

As well as doing himself a lot of good, it had to be acknowledged that Sir Andrew had done the village proud, too. Many housewives and teenagers found part-time jobs 'up at the big house,' doing everything from the laundry to assorted cleaning jobs and building maintenance. The large gardens — so necessary to sell the place as a luxury package — also provided full-time employment for several village men and one woman. Even the chef had taken on apprentices from within the surrounding area, although rumour had it that he'd only let them prepare vegetables.

There were also many peripheral benefits. Phyllis Cox, owner of the shop-cum-post office, was well aware that she would have been forced to close down by now, like so many of her less fortunate colleagues, had it not been for the conference trade. Many of the conference-goers liked to go for a walk down to the village shop in the morning and buy newspapers, cigarettes or stamps, and have a leisurely browse — usually whilst congratulating themselves on finding this example of rural life. Phyllis, as shrewd a businesswoman as ever owned a shop, had quickly catered to their sense of nostalgia even more by very cunningly buying huge glass jars and packing them with all the old-fashioned sweets that she could find. These she then solemnly weighed out on an ancient set of brass scales, before sliding them into small white paper bags and selling them at exorbitant prices by the bucket load.

'Hmm, looks like we've got a full contingent,' Graham said, glancing briefly at the enclosed list of guests. 'That'll please Sir Andrew. He hates it when the house is left half-empty.'

'And not only because of the loss of revenue, I imagine,' Monica said, distracted from her thoughts of having babies. 'I suppose he's glad when it's busy just because it helps to keep him occupied,' she added, with a sad and rather troubled sigh. 'How is he now? Is he getting over it, do you think?' she asked softly.

Graham sighed heavily and shook his head. 'I don't know. He keeps it all bottled up inside, though I wish he wouldn't. Tragedies like his need to be talked about, but it's no good pushing it. I'll just have to keep on giving him the opportunity to talk to me and hope that he'll eventually take it.'

Monica didn't pursue it further. She knew that Graham was far better at grief counselling than she would ever be, and she trusted his judgement implicitly when it came to pastoral care.

But whilst she knew that Sir Andrew had always been friendly with Graham, without ever regarding himself as a parishioner, per se, to her mind there had always been something intensely private about the man, making the likelihood that he'd ever offer up confidences rather remote. So she could only hope that, should he need to, he'd find the courage to go to Graham if he ever felt that he needed help.

Monica never resented the odd hours her husband sometimes kept or the constant demands on his time. He was never 'off-duty' and she'd known that before marrying him. She was even becoming more and more used to her own vaguely defined role of vicar's wife. At least, she hoped that the village was slowly coming to accept her.

As if sensing her pensive mood, Graham turned back to the conference papers and was determinedly upbeat. 'Well, it looks as if we've got some good lectures lined up at any rate.'

'Including yours,' Monica couldn't resist jibing, and she looked at him with twinkling eyes. She knew he was nervous about public speaking, which was odd, considering he always did it so well.

'Don't worry,' Carol-Ann said, entering into the conversation for the first time. 'You'll slay 'em. Won't you, Pops?' she drawled. Somewhat inappropriately, it had to be said.

Graham paled slightly. 'Don't remind me,' he groaned. 'I still don't know how I let the bishop talk me into giving a paper.'

'Well, you're the village's resident vicar,' Monica chimed in. 'They could hardly hold a big clerical conference right on your doorstep without inviting you, now could they? You'll be very good,' she said loyally. She was well aware that he was especially nervous about speaking in front of so many of his fellow clerics. And she could see his point. Parishioners, she supposed, were always far less likely to have high expectations!

'Let's have a look,' Monica said encouragingly, holding out her hand.

Wordlessly, Graham complied, and Monica ran her eye over the agenda.

THE SECOND MILLENNIUM CLERIC

A Four-Day Conference
To be held at Heyford Bassett Conference Centre
Friday 17 May 4:00p.m. to Monday 20 May 3:30p.m.

Facilities include an enclosed and heated swimming pool, gym, theatre/lecture room, and a fully licensed bar — all situated in extensive and attractive gardens. Every room is en-suite, with satellite television, telephone and tea/coffee-making facilities. This conference is full board and lodging.

Breakfast: 7:30–9:00a.m.
Lunch: 1:00–2:00p.m.
Dinner (Friday and Saturday): 8:00p.m. (Sunday)
5:30–6:00p.m.

GUEST SPEAKERS:
Friday night's after-dinner speech:
Bishop Arthur Roland Bryce (St Andrew's Church, Barnsley)
Preaching on the Internet

Saturday, 2:00–3:00p.m. in the Lecture Hall:
Reverend Graham Noble (St Bede's Church, Heyford Bassett)
A Role For the Young in a Christian Community

Sunday, 7:00p.m. in the Lecture Hall:
Archdeacon Sir Matthew Pierrepont (retired)
Satellite Television — The New Pulpit

Monday, 9:00–10:00a.m. in the Lecture Hall:
Reverend Jessica Taylor (St Stephen's Church, Birmingham)
Working Mums and Christ

SUNDAY MORNING SERVICES TO BE HELD AT ST BEDE'S,
10:00a.m. Reverend Graham Noble presiding.

Workshop information to be displayed in Main Hall.

LECTURES: (with slides)
Saturday, 10:00am–12:00 noon.
Dr John R. Burns (Missionary to Chad)
Aid After an Act of God

Sunday, 2:30–3:30p.m.
Reverend Martin Clarke (Belfast):
Crossing The Gulf In Northern Ireland via Ecumenical Bridges

A book fair will be held all day Saturday. Also that afternoon there will be on display a copy of a six-teenth-century manuscript of the Venerable Bede's *Historia ecclesiastica gentis Anglorum*. This rare glimpse of an ancient document comes courtesy of the Black Friar's Museum, Woodstock.

'My, my,' responded Monica. 'Talk about the great and the good, hmm?' she teased, her eye lighting on the illustrious names of Archdeacon Sir Matthew Pierrepont and Bishop Arthur Bryce in particular. 'You will be hobnobbing with the bigwigs. Think you'll get a promotion out of it?' she added, knowing full well that such a thought wouldn't even have entered her husband's head. She handed him back the literature with a wink, to show that she was only kidding.

Carol-Ann, quickly reading her stepfather's papers over his shoulder, began to grin. 'Uh-oh, which pea-brain thought of the title?' she asked mockingly. 'Not exactly on the ball, was he?'

Carol-Ann, as a then thirteen-year-old, had been shell-shocked to find her mother serious about leaving London for the sticks of darkest, dimmest Oxfordshire, but now had to admit that it hadn't been all that bad. And Graham was such a good-looking guy that all her friends drooled over him. And he wasn't bad as a stepdad, either. In fact, Carol-Ann quite liked him, but wild horses wouldn't have dragged the acknowledgement from her.

'What's wrong with the title?' Graham asked her, scanning the top page.

'Oh please,' Carol-Ann whined, with all the annoying superiority only a teenager can effect. '"The Second Millennium Cleric,"' she quoted disgustedly.

Monica and Graham exchanged puzzled glances. 'What's wrong with that?' her mother finally asked. Carol-Ann wasn't easy on anyone's nerves — let alone those of a mild-mannered vicar such as her husband.

'Well, this conference is supposed to be about how modern you all need to be — the Church, I mean — in order to cope with the changes in this new millennium, right? Even though we've already been in it for nearly two decades . . .' Carol-Ann rolled her eyes, leaning over and pointing to the lecture about using the internet.

'Right,' Graham agreed warily.

'So why have they titled it "The *Second* Millennium Cleric"? The second millennium has been and gone. We're in the third millennium now. Duh!'

And with that devastating statement, she sauntered off to find some low-fat yoghurt in the fridge.

Graham stared at the title page, with its glossy paper and state-of-the-art graphic design, and felt his lips begin to twitch. Monica already had a hand over her mouth and was trying not to laugh outright.

'Oh, Graham,' she finally gasped, eyes sparkling. 'I wonder why nobody else spotted it?' she whispered, half appalled, half highly amused. 'You'd think somebody in the bishop's office — or even at the printers — would have realized.'

'Why? We didn't,' Graham pointed out reasonably enough. 'It takes someone like our daughter to spot such a blooper,' he went on, unaware that Monica had shot him a startled, then loving look.

But the truth was, that 'our daughter' that he'd so casually come out with had made her heart swell and ache with loving pride. Not many men, she well knew, would have been willing to take on a woman past her first flush of youth, who also had a rebellious teenage daughter in tow. Let alone be willing to look upon that child as their own.

Even now, she could still hardly believe that she'd been lucky enough to find a husband like Graham.

'Dr Carew wouldn't thank me for pointing it out now anyway,' Graham continued firmly, and with the wisdom of Solomon, thrust the hilariously mistitled conference papers to one side, and took a long, healthy sip of his ice-cold drink.

'What do you mean?' Monica asked, checking her watch. The casserole would be done in another ten minutes or so and she didn't want it to burn. She still didn't feel herself to be much of a cook and she found herself hoping that it would turn out all right.

'Well, you know what he's like. He'd insist on getting them all redone, no matter what the cost or inconvenience,' her husband pointed out. 'You know what a bee he's got in his bonnet about things being done properly. And if he did that, the committee would have a fit about the added expense — and they're still reeling about his purchase of the St Bede manuscript, even now.'

'But that was years ago,' Monica said in disbelief. 'I hadn't even met you then.'

'I know. But it was a very expensive purchase and, some said, totally unnecessary. Of course, the academics on the committee loved it. And I see the crafty old fox has arranged for it to be displayed at the conference. That's a shot across the bows for his detractors, and no mistake.'

'Where is it being exhibited now? Still at that little place in Woodstock?' Monica asked.

'Yes. It'll do it good to get a proper airing for once. Works of art like that should be seen,' Graham said firmly. Then catching the lecturing note in his voice, he looked a shade abashed. 'Sorry, I'm preaching to the converted, aren't I? Is that dinner I can smell?' he changed the subject abruptly with a rather angelic smile.

Whenever he smiled at her like that, Monica still felt her heart do a little flip.

'It is. A humble chicken casserole only, alas. I dare say the dinners at this fancy conference of yours will offer something much more haute cuisine,' she lamented.

'Oh, I should think so,' Graham teased, aware that his wife still wasn't too confident of her culinary skills. Not that he'd care if she couldn't whip up baked beans on toast. 'That chef of Sir Andrew's gets paid a fortune, or so I've heard,' he continued blithely. 'Still, you'll find that out for yourself. You're invited to Saturday night's big dinner.'

Monica smiled wryly. 'Oh goody! Just the Saturday? Oh well, at least you won't have to sleep over at the manor. I don't mind you sneaking off to eat five-star courses without me, so long as you come back to bed at night.'

'There is nothing that would keep me away,' Graham said, looking at her levelly, and making Monica blush.

'Come on then, let's eat,' she growled, fighting the urge to leap on him then and there before dragging him down onto the floor to ravish him.

And what, she wondered, would the village ladies and the churchgoing faithful have to say about that?

CHAPTER 2

Heyford Bassett Manor was a big, square, solid-looking Georgian house, the main part of which had been rebuilt in the eighteen hundreds. A huge Victorian fern glasshouse now housed a full-length swimming pool, as well as vines and a variety of more colourful hothouse flowers. The stables had been converted into a cinema and leisure complex which included snooker tables, and a portion of the lawns had become a tennis court and croquet lawn.

In his ground-floor office opposite a rather spectacular library, Sir Andrew Courtenay sat reading the same bumper pack of information that had been delivered to the Noble household. Being the manager as well as the owner of the conference centre, he was very conscious that the success of his business rested squarely on his own shoulders. So whereas Graham Noble had barely glanced at the list of guest names, Sir Andrew was staring at it with all the concentration of a cat eying a mouse hole.

He'd been doing so for quite some time.

At first, when he'd opened the pack, his mind had been strictly on his work. Once, a conference on archaeology had consisted almost solely of Jewish academics (something to do with the Dead Sea Scrolls) and the chef had proposed several pork dishes. If it hadn't been for Sir Andrew's eagle eye, he dreaded to think what might have happened. Now he always checked out his client lists carefully. And on this occasion, one name on the list of soon-to-be-arriving clerics had stood out as if written in neon.

When he'd first seen the name, he hadn't been able to believe it. *Surely, surely not!* his brain had screamed. *She wouldn't dare show her face here. Not now. Not after what happened in February.*

But the longer Sir Andrew stared at the list, the larger her name seemed to be written.

With a sudden snarl of fury, he stood up and crumpled the paper in his hand. Any of his staff would have been stunned to see this unusual display of temper. Unlike some people's idea of a landed English baronet, Sir Andrew was neither a 'silly old duffer' nor a 'horse-faced, upper-class twit.' At fifty-five, he was a thickset man, dressed not in tweeds but casual slacks and a sports shirt. He was of medium height, with reddish hair and a florid complexion, and had big brown eyes. He was universally liked, both by his guests and his staff, possessing as he did a naturally friendly manner and a carefully cultivated sense of tact. His employees had never known him to be anything but an unflappable, even-tempered, humorous man, well aware of his good fortune in being born into such a property as the manor house, and the way of life that it afforded him. And so, from the humblest chambermaid to his right-hand man and undermanager, everyone would have been surprised by the fury now visible on his face.

Not that he'd been himself lately, of course, and nobody expected him to be his old cheerful self just yet. It would take time to heal. Everyone knew that, so concessions would have been made.

Sir Andrew, now oblivious to the darkening night outside and the need to go over next week's staff rosters, walked heavily to the mantelpiece and stood staring down into the fireplace. It was unlit, of course, on so warm a May night. Unshed tears made his big brown eyes glitter. He couldn't believe that fate would be so unfair as to bring her here. Not now.

The heart-wrenching cruelty of it was almost too much to bear. He began to chew on his knuckles and unnoticed, a single trickle of blood trailed down his hand and dripped tiny droplets onto the brown tiles surrounding the hearth.

Sir Andrew closed his eyes and took a deep, shuddering breath.

* * *

It was raining in Woodstock the following Monday morning, but the owners of that pretty little market town's many antique shops looked skywards and were cheered by the breaks of blue peeping through. Although the town's biggest attraction, Blenheim Palace, regularly brought in coaches loaded with tourists, rain tended to keep them from the streets. Of course, the pubs and coffee shops did a roaring trade during such downpours.

Dr Simon Grade drove impatiently through the morning traffic and turned into the tiny car park in front of the Black Friar's Woodstock Museum with a distinct sense of pride.

This was his baby, the result of years of hard work, hard study and even harder toadying.

A short man, Simon had smooth silver hair and always wore a well-cut suit. Large grey eyes looked out from a face that was almost good-looking, and the aftershave that was currently wafting from him had been a present from a well-to-do aunt who always bought only the best.

It constantly annoyed Dr Simon Grade that he could never quite afford to buy the best for himself, but he was happy to make the most of his aunt's largess, as well as any other advantages he might happen to stumble upon.

A few years ago, for instance, he'd had the foresight to take singing lessons so that he could join an important local choir. The choirmaster had then very obligingly introduced him to Dr David Carew, the bishop. This had in turn led to the Black

Friar's museum getting the scoop of the decade, when the bishop had bequeathed it a rare sixteenth-century illuminated copy of St Bede's masterpiece on English history. And, touched by Dr Simon Grade's brave but financially challenged crusade to give Woodstock a museum to be proud of, the bishop had offered him more or less permanent guardianship of the document.

It now stood in pride of place in the exact centre of the big exhibition room and was the biggest draw of the museum for theologians and other visiting scholars.

Yes, Dr Simon Grade was doing all right for himself, even managing to accrue a nice little nest egg for his retirement. Not that he intended to spend any of it — at least not yet. It would look far too suspicious if he suddenly became flush.

Now he leaned against the glass casing surrounding the St Bede manuscript and stared at it intently. Finally, he was satisfied. It looked perfect, the superb calligraphy glowing with colour and reeking of antiquity. It was due to be transported to Heyford Bassett at the end of next week for a forthcoming ecclesiastical conference, and he was anxious that the move should go well. He had nightmares about the security van crashing into a ditch, and the manuscript being damaged.

He forced back such pessimistic thoughts and concentrated on something much more pleasing instead. Would he be able to wangle a personal meeting with Sir Andrew Courtenay himself? It would be a real coup if he could. Maybe he could even approach him about lending his name as a 'Friend of the Museum'?

Whatever else happened, he felt reasonably confident that he would be invited to attend the big Saturday night dinner, which would afford him the chance to cultivate some of the other big names that were sure to be in attendance.

* * *

As Dr Grade was anticipating making new friends and influencing people, many miles away, in the lovely Roman city of

Bath, Reverend Celia Gordon leaned back in a large leather chair and sighed deeply.

Her unpaid secretary, Felicity, had always been somewhat in awe of Celia — a female cleric who always looked and dressed more like a powerful businesswoman than a humble person of the cloth. And nor was Felicity the only one to have had their breath taken away. When she'd first swept into the diocese, Celia Gordon's new broom had been more like a rocket-powered vacuum cleaner.

'Right, I think that's everything,' the reverend said, and Felicity felt herself slumping with relief. They'd been going through the church accounts, where Celia had worked her usual magic with the numbers, which would certainly please the bishop. It was no wonder that she had just been awarded the deaconship, in spite of Reverend Goulder thinking that it was in the bag for himself.

At forty-eight, Celia contrived to look a good few years younger, and succeeded. Her blonde hair seemed as natural as ever and she was always well groomed and wore make-up discreetly but well. She wasn't married either, and Felicity knew a lot of men in the Church didn't approve of that. If they had to have a woman vicar, they reasoned, then she should at least be safely and decently married.

But all in all, Felicity mused, she didn't think she actually liked the new vicar all that much. Was that very wicked of her? Oh, she certainly admired her — in a way. Felicity recognized in Reverend Celia Gordon someone who would always succeed in whatever she set out to do.

And Celia made no secret of the fact that her role model was Barbara Harris, the first woman bishop ever appointed. Of course that had been in America, and it was still proving far harder to breach the bastions here in the Church of England, but Celia was determined to do it. Even if it meant easing out old fossils like Archdeacon Sir Matthew Pierrepont.

And no doubt she'd have to cross swords with him next week. She sighed now as she reached once more for the information pack sent to conference-goers, which, this time, was being held somewhere in the Cotswolds. She ran her eyes over the guest list again, lingering on the name of Bishop Arthur Roland Bryce, her main rival for the chair of the United Ecclesiastical Conference to be held in London next year.

Now there was a really important conference.

She leafed absently through the brochure about the hotel, and something about the name of Heyford Bassett sounded vaguely familiar. But then, as she began studying the agenda properly, a specific name immediately caught her eye.

And made her heart leap.

Graham Noble! She smiled, her big blue eyes softening. Could it be *her* Graham Noble?

She remembered being a young and eager theology student, and meeting a young graduate just out of the seminary on a bleak winter's day in a bleak northern city. She'd never seen a more handsome man in her life, either before or since. But he'd been both dedicated and (as she'd discovered both to her chagrin and masochistic delight) determined to stick to his vow of celibacy whilst unmarried.

Could it really be the same man?

She hoped so. Oh she really, really hoped so.

* * *

In a large but not particularly picturesque house nestled comfortably in an acre of landscaped grounds on the outskirts of Barnsley in Yorkshire, the lady of the house was busy cooking in the kitchen. Across the marble-topped work surfaces, she glanced with genuine fondness at the long-haired youth seated at the kitchen table reading a textbook on Oliver Cromwell.

'Not still worrying about prelims, I hope?' she asked gently. Robin Bryce, the only son of Bishop Arthur Roland Bryce and his wife Chloe, glanced up at his mother and shrugged. He was nearing the end of his first year at Cambridge, studying modern history, and exams loomed large.

'Any tea left in the pot?' a surprisingly rich baritone voice cut across the kitchen, preceding a somewhat short but very good-looking man with blond hair and striking green eyes. As he neared the central island where his wife was busy with a pile of raw meat, he took in the domestic situation in a flash.

Chloe shot her husband a swift, vicious look.

There was a deceptive aura of sophistication about Chloe Bryce. At forty-one, she'd managed to keep her figure ferociously trim. It was currently shown off to perfection by fashionable, tight-fitting cream slacks, matched with a dark chocolate-brown cashmere sweater of exactly the same colour as her big impressive eyes. Add to that a chic bell-shaped cap of near-black hair, an impressive array of jewelled rings on each hand, and expertly applied make-up, and she looked as if she could have owned and managed a Parisian fashion empire.

But the expression in her eyes as she watched her husband walk to the teapot and gingerly cup his hand against the side of the ceramic belied her image totally. There was scorn in those eyes where there should have been only amused aloofness. There was pain there too, where there should have been nothing but haughty defiance. And anger. Far too much anger.

For all her outward appearances, Chloe had a very unsophisticated personality.

'No, Robin and I always have coffee. Remember?' Her voice, as ever, brimmed with sarcasm.

Robin looked from his father to his mother and sighed. There'd been another family row, obviously, or rather just a continuation of the old usual one. But whatever had caused the present crisis, Robin was on his mother's side. He always was. No one knew better than he did just what his mother had had to put up with for all these years.

His father sat down opposite him with a big envelope full of printed information, whilst his son eyed him with distinct disapproval. Whatever had caused the latest row was bound to be about another woman — either imagined or otherwise. Nothing else upset his mother to quite this extent.

When the silence finally became too oppressive, Robin got up and took his book into the living room, shutting the door carefully behind him.

'What's that?' Chloe asked shortly, nodding at the information pack Arthur had spread out around him.

'Oh, just the paperwork for this church conference. Are you sure you want to come, Chloe?' he murmured blandly, vaguely scanning the agenda. 'It sounds like it's being held in the back of beyond this year, and I know you've got that AIDS benefit charity ball still to organize.'

Chloe literally snorted. 'Oh no you don't,' she hissed. 'I'm coming to . . . to . . .' she snatched one of the papers from his hand and scanned the address, 'Heyford Bassett, and don't even try to talk me out of it.'

Arthur Bryce sighed wearily. 'All right, all right, I just thought—'

'I know what you just thought,' Chloe interrupted bitterly. 'But you can think again. I'm not about to let you out of my sight for five minutes let alone for a whole weekend. There's no knowing what you might get up to. And then bang goes our shot at the minster.'

Arthur's handsome face darkened perceptibly at this jibe, but whether in anger or guilt Chloe wasn't sure. His next words quickly clarified the matter.

'For pity's sake, Chloe, get a grip! I'm not about to do anything to rock the boat. But if you carry on like this, people will start to talk.'

'Hah! When do people ever talk about me?' Chloe's voice vibrated with anger. 'Don't you dare lecture me about how people can talk. Do I ever do anything to shame us? No. Only you do that, Arthur. Only you — you and your affairs.'

Arthur thrust aside the brochure he'd been pretending to read and rose slowly to his feet. A slinky Siamese cat that had been asleep on the windowsill lifted his creamy head and regarded his mistress with wide, interested blue eyes.

Arthur sighed and walked to the nearest window. There he stared abstractedly outside, where a chaffinch sang heartily on a full bird table. 'One affair, Chloe. Just the one,' he said quietly. 'And that's all over and done with now,' he added listlessly. 'Please, can't we just forget about it?'

He looked at her, noting the turned back and hunched shoulders, and the angry jerking of her hands as she dealt with the vegetables. 'You know that I'm really glad that you're coming to the Cotswolds with me, don't you?' he tried again. 'I just thought that it's so far to go, and it'll be so dry and boring. Have you read the titles of some of the lectures?'

Chloe shrugged, unwilling to be appeased. 'I needn't have to sit through them anyway. I can always spend Saturday in Oxford or Cheltenham, shopping.'

'That'll be nice,' Arthur said, correctly anticipating that the worst was over.

'Any news from the archbishop yet?' she asked dully.

'About chairing the committee? No, not yet, but I was talking to the archdeacon yesterday and he, very discreetly mind you, indicated that I was going to get it. But be sure to keep that to yourself.'

Chloe sniffed. 'Don't I always? Do you really think you'd be where you are now if it wasn't for me?' She turned to glare at him.

Arthur smiled. 'No, Chloe,' he said, just a little sadly. 'I don't suppose I would be.'

And he meant it. Nobody knew better than Arthur just how much a wife could make or break a man in his sort of profession. Which was exactly why he'd married the only daughter of a well-to-do entrepreneur in the first place. The people Chloe knew had come in very handy right from the start. As had her skills as a hostess, her behind-the-scenes management ability, and her good looks and style. Not to mention everything else that she'd brought to this fifty-fifty marriage of theirs.

Chloe nodded, apparently satisfied by his acceptance of her true worth. And as she did so her eyes ran, with some satisfaction, along the far wall, where she kept all her trophies. These included her medals in swimming and hockey from when she'd been a teenager at school, and there was also a first prize for an economics essay from university, and later still, proof that she had completed a rather prestigious gourmet cookery course in France.

She had even designed and helped to make her own wedding dress, which all had agreed was a raging success. Everyone said that she was the kind of person who could turn her hand to anything and do it well. So it was no wonder that her husband's career had blossomed, with her standing behind him.

'So long as you remember,' she muttered. Then her eyes began to glitter. 'And the minster will be ours, too,' she added. 'Right?'

'That's right,' Arthur concurred quickly, his own eyes beginning to gleam. Whatever their troubles, they had always shared the same goals. And to see him ensconced in one of the most beautiful and iconic of minsters in the land had always been their principal one.

Chloe nodded. 'Be sure to butter up Archdeacon Pierrepont at this do next week,' she reminded him sharply. 'He's great friends with Humphrey Crowe,' she added.

Arthur's face went blank. He had no idea who this Crowe person was, or why he might be important to get on their side, but he knew that Chloe must have a good reason for advising him to do so. 'I'll do that,' he said meekly.

Chloe gave a sudden rich chuckle. Startled, her husband looked up at her.

'That'll put Celia Gordon's nose out of joint,' she laughed. Again Arthur looked at her a shade blankly and his wife sighed wearily. 'Celia Gordon — that upstart woman from Bath. I saw her name was on the guest list as well.'

So she'd already read the information pack, Arthur thought, with no real sense of surprise. 'Celia Gordon,' he repeated. 'I don't think we know her, do we?' he asked warily. Was she a good-looking woman?

'No. But she's been seriously canvassing for the chairmanship of the London conference lately. Or so I've heard on the grapevine.'

Arthur shook his head. 'Surely not? A woman wouldn't have a hope of getting it.'

'In the current climate,' Chloe said witheringly, 'don't be so sure. Besides, the Gordon woman's already been awarded that deaconship that's come up in Bath. Oh, don't worry,' she added softly, seeing her husband's concerned frown. 'She won't stand a chance against you. And anyway, as you said, the chairmanship is yours already.'

And with that she gave him a final contemptuous look and left him alone in the kitchen.

It was only then that Arthur Bryce really began to worry.

CHAPTER 3

First Day of the Conference

The cars arrived steadily in Heyford Bassett throughout that warm Friday afternoon. Quite a few of the clerics travelling from farther afield had opted to go by rail, and these walked down into the village from the station carrying either lightweight bags or noisy suitcases on wheels, gazing about them with pleasure.

A family of dippers industriously feeding their chicks on the riverbank held the rapt attention of one young cleric, who stared at this avian marvel in wonder. It was a rare sight to see dippers nowadays, he told anyone willing to listen.

The staff at the manor were busy preparing tea, coffee, cold drinks, white wine and canapés, in order to welcome their latest paying guests. Bags were carried to rooms, keys bearing absurdly long tabs were handed out, and the register checklist ticked off. The lawns, surrounded by rose beds and mixed borders, quickly became clogged with clerical personages all sipping and nibbling, and marvelling at the lovely day, the pleasant house, and their charming host who was still stationed in the foyer, greeting everyone personally with a smile and a handshake.

Bishop Dr David Carew arrived promptly at four o'clock. All around the slim, dark-haired man there was a low hub-bub of voices as people either queued at the reception desk or picked up information sheets in the cool marble foyer. As Sir Andrew spotted the local bishop and moved forward with a welcoming smile to greet him, a woman stepped into the hall from the bright sunlight outside.

'Ah, Dr Carew, how . . . nice . . . to see you again,' Sir Andrew began, faltering in mid-sentence as his attention moved beyond the bishop's shoulder and focussed on the woman making her way towards the desk.

David Carew felt himself shiver. Although his hand was still clasped in that of his host, he was instantly aware that Sir Andrew seemed to have totally forgotten his existence. The smile that had been on his face simply dropped from his features, and into his narrowed brown eyes there appeared something infinitely dark. The bishop swivelled around quickly to see what could have caused such an instant and catastrophic change in the man.

But he saw only a blonde woman dressed in a smart navy-blue suit. And, as she turned, the familiar and inevitable dog collar. David Carew didn't recognize her, but as she moved away from the desk with a key in her hand, she happened to look across their way and her confident step faltered. Her bright-blue eyes flickered as Sir Andrew pulled free of the bishop and walked towards her.

'Reverend Gordon,' Sir Andrew said, somehow managing to give the first word a very ugly edge indeed. It made several of the clerics around them pause and look at him strangely. The blonde woman flushed painfully as David, watching with a curious feeling of helplessness, tried to place her. He was sure he'd never met her before, but he felt as if he should know who she was.

He felt, briefly, a moment of intense pity for her.

'Sir Andrew,' Celia Gordon managed to say stiffly, whilst forcing a polite smile onto her face. 'I'm surprised to see you here,' she added, looking clearly puzzled.

Sir Andrew smiled, or at any rate showed his teeth. 'Rather hard for me to be anywhere else, seeing as I own this place,' he responded in a hard, tight voice.

Celia flushed again. Of course! Heyford Bassett. Now she knew why it had sounded so familiar. A spark of very definite anger appeared in her eyes now. If only she'd known, she'd never have come here! Damn, why had they decided to hold the conference here of all places?

Archdeacon Sir Matthew Pierrepont, one of the earlier arrivals, now walked stiffly down the sweeping set of wide stairs and looked around. And his eyes were also drawn immediately to the two antagonists in the centre of the room. He recognized Celia Gordon at once, of course, and a malicious smile leapt to his lips. So she was already causing trouble, eh?

'It's a very nice house,' Celia said, obviously struggling to make conversation.

'Thank you,' Sir Andrew said sardonically.

Then somebody whispered something to someone else and the little sound served to break everything up. Celia gave a brief nod and continued on her way to the stairs. There, Archdeacon Pierrepont stepped mockingly aside for her, giving a courtly bow as he did so. Celia pointedly ignored his clowning, but her colour was high. As she walked up the stairs she was aware of the many eyes on her back, and cursed her memory for letting her down.

Sir Andrew never took his eyes off her until she was quite out of sight. A small tic beat at the centre of his temple. Then he caught the bishop looking at him and visibly pulled himself together. 'It's a pity you're not spending the nights here with us as well, David,' he said easily, smiling and once more the perfect host. 'But I suppose, living only a couple of miles away, it would be rather pointless.'

And instantly, everyone else broke out into embarrassed conversation.

He rejoined the bishop and asked if he'd seen the menus scheduled for the weekend, and if not, would he like to run his eye over them now? And David Carew, as willing as his host to gloss over the contretemps, agreed that it wasn't necessary as he was sure that it would all be delicious.

Archdeacon Pierrepont stared rudely at Sir Andrew for a long few moments, as if puzzling over something. He knew there was something he'd heard about Sir Andrew Courtenay recently . . . something not quite nice . . . Suddenly, his puzzled look cleared. And as it did, his eyes widened. He looked back to the stairs, where Celia had so recently disappeared, and a curious expression flickered across his face. It was part glee, part pity, and part spiteful speculation.

And part something else far less easy to define.

* * *

An impromptu garden party was in full swing out on the lawns and as the church clock struck five, many of the guests were already sipping drinks and socializing, their unpacking completed. Some of the younger and more carefree clerics were actually lying on the grass, bare arms predominating. A group of ladies sat more decorously on chairs on the lawn that the well-trained staff had begun assembling and bringing out, whilst others were taking advantage of the shade provided by a pair of mature horse chestnut trees. The canapé trays were constantly being replenished. Dinner wasn't for hours yet, after all.

Reverend Jessica Taylor was one of those who'd chosen to sit on the grass itself, although she was sat with her legs tucked ladylike beneath her. A married vicar from Birmingham with two young children, she was an advocate for mother-and-baby groups, which had won her friends in some quarters and enemies in others. In her mid-thirties, slim and pale-complexioned, she regarded herself as neither plain nor pretty, and was not particularly ambitious when it came to climbing the ecclesiastical ladder. She was sipping orange juice, and every now and then she rattled the ice in her glass, enjoying the cold sound on such a hot day. She was talking to a vicar's wife from Bangor, who was herself a lay preacher.

As the other woman finished her tale about a young lad who'd asked her who the 'Holy Toast' was, they both laughed and Jessica leaned forward absently to brush a dried grass stem from her shin. As she did so a shadow fell across her, moving rapidly away to the left. She gave a small start and then a long heavy sigh as she recognized instantly the backs of the man and woman walking towards a tightly knit group chattering away beneath the shade of a far, mighty cedar.

'Isn't that Bishop Bryce?' her companion asked, looking at Jessica with a very definite question in her eyes.

Jessica forced a brief smile. 'Yes.'

'And the woman with him is his wife, I suppose?'

'Chloe. Yes. Wherever Arthur is, his wife is sure to follow,' she added, then glanced at the Welsh woman quickly. 'Or so I've heard,' she added hastily.

The woman, a plump, matronly-looking soul with quicksilver eyes, darted another curious glance at the couple. 'She's very . . . scary-looking, isn't she?' came the Welsh voice, the delightful lilt of which seemed to turn every sentence into the line of a song.

'Yes, she is that,' Jessica agreed wryly.

Today, Chloe Bryce was wearing a long white summery dress with a broad black trim, and a sun hat to match. She wore huge dark glasses. With a bright red mouth and red shoes and jewellery to match, she looked extremely eye-catching, chic and sophisticated. And thus, very scary indeed.

Trust Arthur to be here, Jessica thought, and promptly wondered what his real agenda was. No doubt it had something to do with furthering his career. And Chloe was like a pet pit bull, trained to help in any way she could.

Suddenly a great wave of shame washed over her, and she hastily gave up a quick prayer of contrition for being so cynical. She caught the other woman's eye and muttered something about it being so hot.

'Ah yes. Being a redhead you feel the sun, I suppose. You'll have to be careful not to burn.'

Indeed I will, Jessica thought, with a sudden grim laugh. Indeed I will.

* * *

In their bedrooms, those due to give lectures reread their notes and nervously practised their opening lines as they dressed for dinner. Downstairs, the bar was open for something more uplifting and fortifying than mere wine, and many clerics were taking the opportunity for a pre-dinner drink. One of these, Archdeacon Pierrepont, was sitting alone in a corner and was obviously deep in thought. Pierrepoint was a tall, thin, severe-looking man in his mid-seventies; had he been dressed in black robes and given a long-handled sickle many would have given him first prize as the Grim Reaper at any Halloween party.

An elderly deacon sitting at the end of the bar nudged his companion, a retired prelate who came to these things to get away from his wife and his dog, both of whom nagged him incessantly. 'Old Pierrepont seems rather quiet. Is something bothering him, do you know?'

'No idea,' the retired bishop turned to glance the arch-deacon's way. 'But now that you mention it, it's not like him to be so unobtrusive.'

'That's what I mean,' the deacon nodded sagely. 'Perhaps it's something to do with that business a few months ago. Very nasty that, from what I've heard. Let's just hope that it's taught him a bit of a lesson.'

The former bishop swivelled on the barstool. 'Really? What was that then?'

The deacon's face promptly fell. He'd been hoping that the bishop would know more of the gossip. After all, it was his successor who'd covered it up — or so it was rumoured. 'Well, I'm not actually sure,' thus wrong-footed, the deacon was forced to retreat hastily. 'Nobody's talking about it. Not openly at least, but there's been a lot of muttering under the breath, if you get my drift. Some nasty bit of scandal, I imagine. But if you ask me, the poor chap's getting past it. I'm not the only one, by a long shot, who thinks it's high time he was properly put out to pasture.'

'Going gaga, eh?' the prelate said, with the marked lack of tact that had been one of the factors in his becoming a former bishop. 'In which case, he shouldn't still be driving.'

* * *

The choices on the menu provided many a happy conversational topic as the diners began to file in and take their seats. The seating arrangement was simplicity itself, since all the tables had been formed into a single straight line down the centre of the capacious dining hall. There was, however, plenty of elbow room for everyone, and since there were no name cards, nobody was forced to sit with anyone they'd rather avoid.

The waiters hovered, taking down choices as and when the guests dictated them; many a chocoholic eye had already pegged the profiteroles.

As usual, various cliques had already formed. There was a large older male contingent taking up one area in the centre. Wives tended to be interspersed throughout the party, though.

Chloe Bryce, her hair swept up into an elegant chignon and dressed in a long coffee-coloured evening dress, held court at the far left-hand corner where her husband was due to give the after-dinner speech.

Eventually the last empty places were filled and plates began arriving. Dr Carew had invited Sir Andrew to join them for this first meal, and the squire sat at the head of the table, with Dr Carew at the other end. Tomorrow, no doubt, it would all change.

And if Arthur doesn't manage to sit at the head of one end of the table or the other tomorrow night, I'll eat my hat, Jessica Taylor thought sourly as the soup was served. She'd opted for the asparagus.

Fate had been against her, though, for she'd taken a seat at the bottom end of the table before the Bryces had entered and had then found them only a few seats down from her when she'd looked around a few minutes later. But her Welsh companion of earlier was seated on her right, and to her left was a young and rather lively cleric who was enthusiastically telling her what a thrill it had been to see some dippers earlier on.

Celia Gordon had taken a seat almost in the exact centre of the table, and thus found herself facing a phalanx of male cronies. To her left was a missionary from Chad; to her right, a vicar who seemed to know no one.

'So I said to him, young man, you can't possibly eat rat.' The voice of the missionary from Chad stopped all the surrounding conversations immediately, not because of its level, but — not surprisingly — because of its content. 'And he turned to me and said, "Why not? If I were dead, the rat would most certainly eat me!"'

Someone across the table from Celia laughed. 'So what did you say?'

'I said that wasn't the point — rats are vermin.'

'Did that convince him?' another asked.

'Oh no. He said in that case, he'd stop off at the village and tell the farmer who was growing some maize that he'd done him a big favour in eating the rat, and would he give him a bowl of corn for his trouble.'

Everyone laughed.

'Nobody likes to see a rat in a cornfield, eh?' The voice, cracked with age and malice, and raised to a booming level, belonged to Sir Matthew Pierrepont. His rheumy grey eyes were glittering directly across the table at Celia Gordon.

Several men stiffened, sensing trouble. A few academically minded clerics looked interested. Sir Matthew was a former don and noted scholar, after all, and several within earshot had expectations of an interesting and well-reasoned debate in the making — these people didn't know him very well.

Celia, of course, knew exactly what was coming.

'You're quite right about what you say concerning rats in cornfields, Archdeacon,' she said, interrupting him before he could get started, her voice cool and slightly sardonic. 'Nobody welcomes them. Take our own cornfield as an example,' she carried on smoothly, giving him no chance to get in a word. 'Why, I heard only the other day that some cleric out east somewhere,' she waved a hand vaguely, 'actually attacked a parishioner. And a woman at that, I believe,' she added.

She leaned back to let a waiter with a studiously deadpan face remove her soup plate. 'And can you believe that his bishop actually made sure that it was all hushed up?' she added, smiling across the table at Sir Matthew, who'd suddenly gone pale with rage. 'Now I'm sure we'd all agree that that cleric should have been . . . well . . . at the very least pensioned off quietly. Given the current media attention over cases of abuse committed within the Church, nobody wants to create yet more scandal. And the cleric involved was very old, or so I heard, and going . . . well . . . senile, I expect,' Celia continued brightly. She turned to the hapless vicar next to her. 'Don't you agree that such behaviour shames us all, Mr McReady?'

'Huh? Oh yes. Of course. It's shocking. I don't know what the world's coming to,' that worthy gentleman mumbled uneasily.

Celia glanced across the table, not at Sir Matthew, who was now looking apoplectic, but at his companions. Nearly all of whom had heard the same rumour — or variation thereof — but hadn't necessarily connected it with Sir Matthew.

Until now.

'Of course, a man lacking such self-control will eventually be caught out again,' Celia continued unrelentingly, as the waiters began to distribute silver tureens of mixed steaming vegetables along the length of the tables, 'but until then, who knows what trouble he might cause?'

'I think you'd better . . .' Sir Matthew roared, at the same time as everyone else around him also began to speak — very loudly.

'Did you see that news spot last week about falling Church attendance?' the missionary from Chad all but bellowed, whilst several others turned to their neighbours and began to discuss such unlikely topics as the benefits of having Sir Cliff Richard as a spokesman for something or other.

Celia smiled levelly across the table at Sir Matthew, a flicker of disgust crossing her face as she realised a trickle of drool was actually running down his chin. The man's mad, she thought calmly, meeting his glower head on. Quite mad.

Down at the other end of the table, and not wishing to get embroiled in the fracas, the other guests were also busily conversing between themselves.

'And so, you see, because they're so prone to the effects of pollution, you almost never see dippers,' the young cleric was saying to Jessica.

'What a shame,' Jessica murmured. 'I don't get to see many birds at all, coming from Birmingham.'

'There're some nice birds in Ecuador,' a Welsh voice popped up beside her, and all heads turned, in some surprise, to the woman from Bangor. She flushed. 'Wilbur and I went there for our twenty-fifth wedding anniversary.'

Chloe Bryce laid her hand lightly over that of her husband and turned to the man on her right to ask him what he thought about the current modern thinking on the Gospel of St Luke.

'Lovely holiday that was,' the lay preacher from Bangor concluded. 'You ever been anywhere special, dear?'

With a start, Jessica realized that her companion was talking to her. She'd been trying so hard to keep her eyes from Chloe's manicured, red-painted nails resting atop her husband's hand that she almost missed the question.

'What? Oh no. Actually, it's funny you should ask though, because I was just thinking of a great friend of mine. She moved to Portugal only a few months ago. She said the prices over there were so much cheaper and that she'd be mad to stay in wet and rainy England.'

'I dare say she's right. You ought to go out there and join her for a week or two,' the Bangor lady advised. 'Take my advice — a visit to a foreign country really broadens the mind.'

'Yes, I'm sure,' Jessica agreed abstractedly. 'But I haven't got her address. In fact, I'm getting a little worried about her — I'd have expected her to write to me long before this, telling me all about things, and giving me her contact details.'

Arthur Bryce reached for a glass of wine and smiled and nodded at a waiter who enquired loftily if he might be the beef Wellington.

'Ah, I expect she's having too much of a good time to bother,' the lay preacher prophesied. 'It can't be easy, emigrating.'

Jessica frowned. 'No. Even so . . . I'm really starting to worry that something might have happened to her. You do hear such horror stories sometimes, don't you? There must be authorities I can approach to advise me on that sort of thing,' Jessica mused. 'Is it the Foreign Office, do you think? Or do I need to get in touch with the Portuguese ambassador's office? One way or another, I must track her down.'

At the other end of the table, Sir Andrew Courtenay observed his waiters and waitresses professionally dishing out plates of Dover sole, baked salmon and vegetarian curries with a vague but pleased eye. Luckily, Celia Gordon was seated a long way down towards the middle of the table. But he mustn't think about her. Not now. Not yet. He watched the beautiful bishop's wife in the fetching coffee-coloured dress reach for a glass of wine and wondered how such a woman had ended up married to a clergyman of all people.

Down on his left, an inoffensive curate from Edinburgh was telling him how much he was looking forward to seeing the St Bede's manuscript tomorrow. He even went so far as to confess, a little timidly, that the manuscript was the main reason for his attendance. 'I think history is so important, don't you, Sir Andrew?' he concluded.

'Yes, I do. Yes indeed. My own family has lived here for nearly twenty generations,' he agreed absently.

Don't think about her, he told himself. Ignore her. Pretend she's not here. No, that was impossible. Damn her, why hadn't she left? When she knew who he was and where she had fetched up, why hadn't she had the decency to just turn around and go? And then he laughed at himself. Decency? What would Celia bloody Gordon know about such a thing?

'How wonderful for you. You must almost be able to trace your ancestry back to . . .' the Edinburgh academic went through a swift mental calculation, 'well, very nearly the Restoration?'

'Yes, quite.'

'And your son. Is he keen to keep the house going?'

Sir Andrew blinked. Once, twice, then again. He turned very slowly to look at the curate, and found him to be a pink-faced individual with round cheeks and a pair of rather startling dark blue eyes.

There came upon some members of the party a sudden silence, one of the kind that seems to transmit itself, by some curious sort of ESP, to others. Down the table, Celia Gordon, who'd clearly heard the cleric's question, drew in her breath sharply. Her lips formed into a tight, grim line. Several local people, who also knew Sir Andrew's circumstances, looked at each other quickly, then even more quickly looked away.

The man from Edinburgh went pinker still, embarrassingly aware that he'd made some sort of gaffe, but distressingly unsure how to rectify it.

Sir Andrew forced himself to smile. And to take a long, slow, calming breath. 'I'm afraid not,' he said, his voice steady and affable. 'I have no children any longer.'

From the head of the table he then turned to the cleric sitting down on his right. 'And you, Reverend . . . er . . . ?'

'Fisher, Sir Andrew.'

'Reverend Fisher. Are you much of a history buff?' The table quickly became awash with voices once again. Across from Celia Gordon, Sir Matthew Pierrepont was getting steadily drunk. And as a consequence, was becoming even louder and more obstreperous.

The waiters began to remove plates, and a little while later circulated with the dessert trolleys, which were overflowing with elaborately decorated gateaux and tarts.

And seated somewhere at the table, someone who had only a few short months ago forged a letter and fiddled with a gas cooker, was now feeling as cold as ice, and thinking furiously.

Danger. Totally unexpected, striking from out of the blue, and utterly sick-making.

But who'd have thought to come across such danger here? Here of all places! There must be a way out. There had to be a way out . . .

* * *

It was perhaps not totally surprising that after Arthur Bryce's amusing and informative after-dinner speech, things broke up early. Everyone agreed this was because they'd had such a long day and needed to recuperate — certainly, nobody spoke openly of the uneasy, tense atmosphere pervading the house.

The bar did a surprisingly poor trade that night, as people made their way almost straight to bed.

Just off the foyer was a narrow corridor that led to a door marked 'Private.' This door, which led to the private downstairs apartments of the hotel owner, was usually kept locked. It was nearly midnight when that door opened and Sir Matthew Pierrepont came out and made his slow, stiff-legged way back across the foyer and towards the lift.

His face was thoughtful. Could the man be relied upon to go through with things? That was the real question. Once in his room he ignored the bed, although, from the quietness of the house around him, he was sure that most of his fellow conference-goers were well and truly in the land of nod by now. But for himself, he was wide awake and totally alert.

That viper Celia Gordon was not going to get away with this — making him look like a damned fool in front of everybody.

He sat gingerly down at a small Queen Anne writing bureau and pulled forward a sheet of hotel paper. Sir Matthew knew just the man they needed. Old 'Smuthers' Bodington at *The Times* had no time for troublemaking women any more than he did — ever since that female from *The Telegraph* had pipped him for that journo award. Yes, he'd be interested in a story about scandal and women vicars all right.

As he began to write, a flicker of doubt crossed his mind. Perhaps *The Times* was not quite the right paper for this, but old Smuthers was bound to know of somebody in the ranks of the more trashy tabloids who'd be in the market for a woman-vicar scandal.

* * *

Contrary to Sir Matthew's belief that everyone in the manor was tucked up in bed, several people were, in fact, still very much awake.

In his study, Sir Andrew sat staring blankly at his desktop. The archdeacon had given him much to think about.

In her bedroom, Celia Gordon was unconcernedly going over some paperwork.

And, in another wing, footsteps moved silently across the carpeted floorboards. Bishop Arthur Bryce looked back down a dimly lit corridor and stood pensively for a few moments, resting lightly on the balls of his feet. He could hear nothing except, coming from the door to his right, a faint snoring.

He'd already seen from the register what room number she was in.

He found it a few moments later and looked furtively back down the corridor again. And told himself not to be such a rabbit. All the doors were shut fast. Nobody was watching him, or would be likely to hear him.

He turned and knocked very softly on the door in front of him.

Inside, Jessica Taylor was sitting on the edge of the bed and just about to slip under the covers. She froze and picked up her small portable alarm clock, checking the dial. It was after midnight. Who on earth . . . ?

Again, there came a discreet tap, a bare brush of knuckles. She walked to the door and found herself holding her breath as she stood up on tiptoe to peer through the tiny spyhole set in the door.

Further down the corridor, a door handle turned very slowly and a door opened an inch or two. Chloe Bryce pressed one dark eye to the gap and stared down the corridor at her husband knocking on the pretty redheaded vicar's door.

Jessica let out her breath in a small hiss as she recognized her visitor — Arthur. He's got to be kidding, she thought crossly to herself. No way was she letting him in! Oh, she knew what he wanted to talk about all right, but there was just no way she was going to indulge him. Besides, she'd promised her husband before coming here that she wouldn't do anything that she might regret. And she'd regret having anything to do with Arthur Bryce and his wife, all right.

She turned and walked resolutely away from the door, got into bed and determinedly turned off the nightlight.

Arthur Bryce knocked just once more, waited for a long moment, and then turned away, his shoulders slumped in defeat.

Chloe quietly shut the door and got quickly back into bed. She was still pretending to be asleep when her husband slipped into bed beside her a minute or two later.

Eventually, the manor fell silent.

CHAPTER 4

Saturday morning dawned with a thick layer of picturesque summer mist. Early risers took to the village in search of a paper, or were content to walk through the dew-wet meadows, whilst trying to avoid the cowpats. The late risers eventually came down the stairs from their comfortable beds and snug bedrooms until eventually all the fifty-two conference-goers were assembled in the dining hall for breakfast.

Luckily the tables were now separated, allowing for more harmonious groupings to arrange themselves, and soon the waiters were busy circulating with tea and coffee pots and taking orders from the extensive breakfast menu.

By the big bay windows, Chloe, her husband, Archdeacon Pierrepont and two other clerics were busy giving their choices.

'Do you think you could bring me an extra glass of orange juice please?' Celia Gordon caught the attention of a passing waiter with a smile and a raised voice. She was seated at a table for four with only one other companion, a very deaf verger who'd come in place of his boss, who'd been taken ill at the last minute. 'I do love oranges,' she added loudly to her deaf companion, who smiled disinterestedly. At the table opposite her, Jessica Taylor, her new Welsh friend and two other

44

clerics who didn't seem to know anyone else at the conference, politely pretended not to overhear the rather loud voice.

'I swear I haven't had a cold in years and that's all because I always eat an orange a day. Besides, I love the taste of them.'

'I prefer apples myself,' Jessica said comfortably, breaking ranks to take pity on Celia's rather isolated position.

Celia smiled and looked across at her, shaking her head. 'Give me oranges every time,' she said firmly, catching the eye of a deacon seated at a table on the other side of her, who was glaring at her quite obviously. 'Vitamin C is so very good for you.'

'I'm afraid my weakness isn't for anything so healthy,' Jessica confessed with a light laugh, trying to lighten the mood. 'I'm a bit of a cake fanatic myself. Any kind of cake, I simply can't resist it.'

'I can't understand why anybody has to talk so loudly, can you?' she distinctly heard the deacon say to his dining companions. 'I do think it's rather rude — especially in a roomful of others.'

The deaf cleric, who could lip-read very well, offered him a stiff, disappointed smile.

Chloe Bryce temporarily excused herself, and ignoring the many eyes that followed her progress across the room, she headed towards the ladies' room.

Sir Andrew entered the room at that point, throwing a brief smile at those seated at the nearest table. 'I hope that everything's satisfactory, gentlemen?' he asked, already sure of the answer. His chefs had worked hard to make sure that the breakfast menu was every bit as extensive as the lunch and evening meals. There were murmurs of assent from around the table. 'Did everybody have a peaceful night?' He went on to the next table, ever the circulating and attentive host.

A waiter brought a bowl of cornflakes for Celia and kippers for her deaf companion. 'I hope these aren't those honey-nut ones,' Celia said, the sharp edge to her voice momentarily silencing the room. 'I'm very allergic to nuts, you see,' she added to the flustered waiter, who hastily assured her that the cornflakes were most definitely the 'plain' ones.

'Perhaps I'd better have toast instead,' she said, pushing the dish away from her as the waiter headed obediently back to the kitchens.

Over by the window, Archdeacon Pierrepont snorted loudly. 'Trust her to make a fuss. It's like I've been telling you, Arthur, you can't trust a woman to do even the simplest thing.'

Arthur Bryce smiled wryly. The academic had obviously never met a woman as efficient and single-minded as his Chloe. As if his thoughts had summoned her up from the ether, his wife suddenly appeared in the room again and made her way back to the table. Once again, covert and appreciative eyes followed her progress and Arthur felt a flush of pride, as he always did, whenever Chloe took her seat beside him. Today she was wearing a pale mint-green skirt and matching jacket with a jade, white and black-patterned blouse underneath. Dangling green earrings and green eyeshadow complemented her dark colouring. Her shoes and handbag were black leather. Once again, she could have stepped off the cover of *Vogue*.

Her muesli had arrived in her absence and as she lifted her spoon and glanced across at the archdeacon, she smiled briefly. 'And how is Cambridge, Sir Matthew?' she asked sweetly.

Somewhat grudgingly, Sir Matthew told her how Cambridge was, unbending just a little when she told him that she had a son there.

Jessica Taylor ate with her head down and kept her gaze firmly averted from the window table. Sir Andrew finished his rounds, having spoken a few words at every table, except, very noticeably, the table where Celia Gordon was seated. As he passed through the room, he overheard several whispered and unhappy comments about Celia's loud and pushy ways.

Sir Andrew walked steadfastly on, heading towards the kitchens.

* * *

Dr Simon Grade climbed up awkwardly into the passenger seat of the big security van that had pulled up in front of his museum. It was one which belonged to the fleet of a very discreet firm he used whenever he needed to transport his more valuable items, although alas, he hadn't had much use for them thus far. Today the St Bede manuscript, still in its locked and now well-padded glass museum case, had been carefully secured in the back.

As the driver climbed in beside him, started the van, and gingerly backed out into the road, Simon straightened his tie a shade nervously. It was important that nothing go wrong.

He was wearing a well-cut but relatively inexpensive black suit with a deep-red tie and black onyx cufflinks to go with it. His suit could, with the addition of a colourful silk cummerbund and the black bow tie currently stowed in his briefcase, be transformed into a passable dinner suit.

Dr Grade was feeling particularly happy with his lot this morning. He was confident of being able to give informative and interesting impromptu lectures to any number of conference-goers who wanted to inspect the manuscript. And the thought of rubbing elbows with the landed gentry and a plethora of bishops and noted academics was making him rub his hands together in glee.

Yes, all was right with his world. He didn't know, then, that he should have been making the most of it whilst he was still able to — for things were just about to change.

* * *

Those conference-goers not attending workshops or other activities had gravitated naturally towards the small village shop-cum-post office, where many emerged, guiltily bearing bags of sweets.

'Want a gobstopper, Hubert?' one old man asked of an even older one.

'Not my thing, old boy. Sherbet?' The other offered back his own bag in response. 'Or would you prefer a liquorice stick? I haven't seen a liquorice stick in years!'

Inside the shop, Graham Noble, walking on ahead of his wife, bought their usual newspaper and cast an eye over a packet of custard creams. He was due to give his lecture that afternoon, and already his nerves were beginning to tap dance. No, perhaps it wouldn't be a good idea to indulge in anything sweet. On the other hand, an empty stomach might make him feel nauseous. Then he spied a small bag of peanuts hanging on the wall and, on impulse, bought a packet.

If he ate the tiny nuts one at a time, they might just last him until two o'clock, but not sit too heavily on his stomach.

As he stepped outside he nodded and smiled at the milling clerics, introducing himself to some as the local vicar, and being assured, somewhat alarmingly, that they were all looking forward to his lecture. He glanced behind him to see where Monica had got to, and saw her inside the shop talking to the owner, Phyllis. They seemed to be discussing the merits, or otherwise, of tinned rhubarb.

Jessica Taylor came upon the scene and felt her heart sink a little at the sight of all her fellow clerics clogging the square. Nevertheless, she straightened her shoulders and walked through them into the quaintest little shop that she'd seen in many years. As she browsed, several village women joined her. She listened half-heartedly to talk about the price of beef and someone's mother's varicose veins. She finally selected a middle-of-the-road newspaper for herself and walked to the till. There, a pretty dark-haired woman with striking blue eyes moved aside to make room for her.

'Say what you like, Phyllis,' she was saying, 'I still think home-grown and straight from the garden is the best.'

'Ugh! Too strong and tart,' Phyllis shivered, but put away the tin of rhubarb in defeat. 'I'll bet Vera Ainsley uses tinned rhubarb,' she couldn't resist getting in the last word.

Jessica's ears pricked up at the mention of the famous cook. 'And I can assure you she doesn't,' Monica shot back with a smile. Vera Ainsley had an apartment at the converted vicarage where she and Graham lived. 'John has a rhubarb patch that everybody raids. Including Vera.'

Phyllis took Jessica's money for the paper and then glanced behind her. 'Hello, Deirdre. More baby food?' she asked, and Jessica in her turn moved away to allow a young mother with a basket full of small jars to get to the till.

'You said it.' Deirdre, a short, harassed-looking woman with pretty brown curly hair and a freckled nose, reached for her purse. 'You'd never think such a small thing could eat so much.'

'I know,' Phyllis, who was happily childless, answered sagely.

'Well, as of Monday, it's my poor mum who'll have to keep the ever-empty tummy fed,' Deirdre sighed. She looked far from happy about this development, however.

'Oh yes? Oh right, you start that part-time job at the canal boatyard, don't you?' Phyllis asked, busily punching away at the till.

'Right. It's only housework really, doing the narrowboats over before the visitors take them out. But they're tiny, aren't they, so I'm hoping there won't be much to it. I mean, how much vacuuming can they need?'

'And how's Jack taking it? You having to work, I mean?' Phyllis asked with thoughtless nosiness as she packed away the jars.

And Deirdre, equally seeing nothing wrong with this shameless probing, shrugged. But even as she did so, Jessica Taylor couldn't stop herself from shooting the women a quick and disbelieving look.

Monica, noticing it, smiled to herself. She has to be a city slicker, just like I used to be, she found herself musing. She'd also found the village a bit of an eye-opener when she'd first arrived. Here, everybody knew everybody else's business, and this was just accepted as the norm. It took some getting used to.

'Well, he's not happy still,' Deirdre muttered. 'He doesn't like my working when the baby's so young, but what else can I do? The rent comes due every month, dunnit?'

'True,' Phyllis said, blithely adding to her customer's money worries by telling her the total of the baby food.

Deirdre sighed and handed over some notes. 'I think Jack's worried me and the baby won't bond.' She looked up at Phyllis. 'I blame Oprah Winfrey,' she added darkly, and somewhat obscurely.

'Oh, but that's nonsense,' Jessica felt obliged to say, then stopped, appalled. But all three women looked at her with interest, rather than censure, and she felt herself relax. 'There's no evidence that says mothers and infants don't bond, even if the mother works full time. And so long as your baby is looked after by, did you say her grandmother?'

Deirdre nodded her brown curly head emphatically.

'Well then, obviously she'll get all the love and attention that she needs. I dare say your mother loves having her and adores her,' Jessica said firmly.

'Oh she does,' Deirdre agreed as she, Monica and Jessica all began to head for the door, aware of the queue that was growing somewhat impatient behind them.

'There you are then,' Jessica said as they all piled outside. 'Don't let anyone make you feel guilty for being a working mum,' she said forthrightly. 'The time when women were tied to the kitchen sink is long over.'

It wasn't until she looked around at so many disapproving male faces that she realized they were suddenly the centre of attention. She flushed, then lifted her chin defiantly. 'Back in Birmingham, we formed a working mums' club,' she said firmly. 'Just to give each other mutual support, trade the names of good and reliable babysitters, that sort of thing. It's remarkable how helpful that kind of information can be.'

'What a splendid idea,' Monica said mildly, feeling obliged to come to the other woman's defence. 'Deirdre, why don't you have a chat with all the other mums with young toddlers that you know. I'm sure . . .' here she glanced questioningly at the other woman.

'Jessica Taylor,' Jessica said, throwing Monica a grateful look.

50

'I'm sure that Reverend Taylor would be only too glad to send you some material on how to get your own club started,' Monica finished.

'Of course I would,' Jessica agreed warmly.

Deirdre, not entirely convinced but happy to feel that someone was on her side, nodded her curly head, and before she knew it, Monica found herself agreeing to forward on material and act as a liaison.

'I'm Monica Noble, by the way,' she added to Jessica as Deirdre, in a much more upbeat frame of mind, trudged off with her heavy bags. 'My husband,' Monica looked around and spotted Graham, who was smiling somewhat wryly at her and quickly stepped forward, 'is the vicar here. Graham, meet Jessica.' The two shook hands. 'Jessica, do you want to come back to the vicarage with me? I'll give you our email address and perhaps we can have a chat over a cup of coffee?'

'Thanks, that sounds great,' Jessica agreed, and together, still running the gauntlet of largely disapproving male eyes, they slowly headed across the square towards the church.

'Just what we need,' someone in the crowd muttered anonymously. 'More women's libbers.'

Coming around the opposite corner, Arthur and Chloe Bryce were just close enough for Chloe, who had better hearing than her husband, to catch this somewhat uncharitable comment.

'Hello, Arthur, come for a paper?' the former bishop, who was busy chewing old-fashioned humbugs, asked somewhat unintelligibly.

'If there're any left,' Arthur said, indicating the clerics all standing about with various papers under their arms. Everyone smiled.

'At least you'll be able to buy your paper in peace,' a familiar cracked voice piped up from one side, as Archdeacon Pierrepont turned to stride away in disgust. 'Without having the joys of feminism rammed down your throat. Working mothers with babies, indeed. That's what's wrong with society today,' he continued, unaware that as he walked further away, he was talking to nobody but himself.

There was a rather embarrassed silence for a while and then Arthur smiled. 'Frank, what on earth have you got in your mouth? A boulder?'

'Hmmm, naaa, a goooobbsmokcher,' came the somewhat slurped reply.

'It's like a treasure trove in there, Arthur,' someone else said. 'You ought to see it. I found some of those rhubarb-and-custard sweets you used to get. Delicious.'

Obligingly, Arthur and Chloe entered the shop whilst the others began to drift off, in a half-hearted way, back towards the conference centre. And Archdeacon Pierrepont, still mumbling away to himself, disappeared around the corner.

'He's right,' Arthur said, looking around the small but attractive shop with a smile. 'This place is a real throwback. Look there, a kit for a model aeroplane. I haven't seen one of those in years. What is it — a Spitfire?'

Chloe sighed heavily. 'No. And don't get maudlin. I wonder what all that fuss was about outside?'

'What, old Sir Matthew? You know how he feels about women. No doubt Celia has said something to upset him,' Arthur said vaguely.

Phyllis, who'd overheard the conversation through the open door, sniffed loudly. It was her opinion that it was men, and not women, who ought to know their places. 'If you ask me,' Phyllis said, startling the Bryces, neither of whom had asked her a thing, 'that woman vicar had it right. Why shouldn't Deirdre work part-time?'

Chloe and Arthur, not surprisingly, looked at one another blankly.

'Well, well,' Arthur said, rather helplessly.

Chloe, who'd seen from the itinerary that Jessica Taylor was down to lecture about working mothers in a Christian environment, shrugged. 'Personally, I'm glad that I never had to work when my son was growing up but no doubt she knows what she's talking about.'

Arthur, sensing friction, made a grab for a paper. 'We'll take this please,' he said hastily, reaching into his pocket for some change. 'All the same,' he said, thinking of all the trouble that Celia Gordon had caused so far, 'I do wish she would be more discreet. If she wants to go far, she really should learn to be more . . . well . . . accommodating. Only this morning she was making a fuss about her breakfast, changing her order around because she's allergic to nuts. Even though there was nothing wrong with the cereal she'd ordered.'

Chloe's head shot up, and she gave him a strange look. 'Well, that sounds reasonable to me, Arthur,' she pointed out crisply. 'People with allergies have to be careful.'

Arthur drew in a quick, angry breath. 'Oh, of course I agree. But it was the way she did it. With so little grace.'

'Perhaps we'll have some of those dried apricots,' Chloe interrupted him firmly.

Arthur promptly shut up. He'd become very good at knowing when to do so.

Phyllis nodded her head and smiled approvingly at Chloe. Now that was a well-trained man if ever she saw one.

* * *

'What a charming place,' Jessica said, stepping into the living room at the Nobles' flat. 'I envy you living all on one floor. A house is all right, but vacuuming the staircase is a nightmare.'

'Yes, I prefer it too,' Monica agreed. 'I hope instant coffee's all right? It's all we have, I'm afraid.'

'Oh that's fine,' Jessica said, trailing her hostess into the kitchen, where she sat comfortably at the table.

Monica opened a tin of biscuits. 'So, how's the conference going?' she asked. Jessica screwed her face up expressively and Monica laughed. 'Ah. Like that, hmm?'

'Well . . .' Jessica sighed. 'It's all right, I suppose. I just wish . . . Oh never mind,' she said. 'Have you booked a holiday yet?' she rather abruptly changed the subject.

Monica put the mugs of coffee on the table along with the creamer and sugar bowl. 'No, but it'll probably be somewhere modest and affordable again,' she admitted with a smile.

'I know what you mean,' Jessica sympathised. 'But I'm determined to go to Portugal this year,' she added. 'I've a friend there I need to track down.'

'Oh that'll be nice,' Monica said. 'Here, let me give you my postal and email addresses before I forget. And don't let all those narrow-minded men get you down,' she warned as she reached across for the notepad she kept handy for grocery lists. Quickly, she jotted down her details and handed them over.

'Oh, I try not to. It's just — you know what it's like. Out of fifty or so of us, there are about four or five women clerics, all told.'

Monica shook her head in sympathy. 'Still, most people are on your side surely? They're the ones who voted women vicars and now women bishops into the Church, after all.'

'Yes. I suppose so,' Jessica agreed, but didn't sound all that convinced.

'I noticed Bishop Bryce was on the guest list,' Monica said. 'He's a very firm ally for women clerics, surely?' Monica found it prudent to keep up with Church politics. Not that Graham ever intended to dip a toe into those particular waters. He was quite happy where he was.

Jessica gave a surprisingly harsh bark of laughter. 'Oh yes. Arthur's a fan of women all right,' she agreed tightly.

Monica, catching the undertone, decided that it might be wise to change the subject again. 'You know, this working-mother group sounds like a good idea. What does it entail exactly?'

The next half hour passed pleasantly as Jessica talked about her favourite topic.

* * *

Lunch once again brought all the conference-goers together. Graham, invited to Saturday lunch since he was due to lecture right afterwards, walked into the lobby and looked around with real pleasure. He'd always thought the manor house a very fine example of its type and Sir Andrew hadn't butchered it at all (well hardly at all) in its makeover into a working enterprise.

As he passed through the spacious entrance hall he watched two men carrying in a large wood-and-glass showcase, and realized with a quickening of interest that this must be the controversial St Bede's manuscript.

A dapper man in a smart black suit darted about like a distressed jackdaw, giving instructions in a slightly high-pitched and nervous voice and admonishing one of the men to lift his end a fraction higher. Correctly supposing that they could do without any bystanders to jinx the operation, Graham walked on quickly into the dining room, and straight into a dim and unpretentious corner.

There he found an empty spot beside a young cleric and a very old one, who were animatedly discussing the mating habits of grey wagtails. Across from him, a Welsh couple were talking about Ecuador, their lilting voices delightful on his ear. In his working life, Graham hadn't attended all that many conferences, so this was quite a new and interesting experience for him.

Halfway through his choice of a very light meal indeed, Graham thought he recognized Archdeacon Sir Matthew Pierrepont, who left the table after his soup and was gone for quite a long time. The waiter, he noticed, came to the table and then retreated without depositing his main course.

Graham's own lunch was superb and he silently admitted that Sir Andrew's fancy chef really deserved his accolades. He'd opted for the carrot and coriander soup, which was exquisitely flavoured, and the whitebait with aioli. During this course he noticed, with gentle amusement, how everyone watched the progress of a very chic, dark-haired lady, who left her table presumably to go to the powder room. A few minutes later, the man that she'd been seated next to — a handsome, rather short man with striking blond hair — also rose and left. Within a few minutes, however, they'd both returned, and Graham wondered if the man realized how admired his wife was.

Probably, Graham thought with sympathy. As the husband of a very lovely woman himself, he knew only too well how sensitive he was to the looks other men gave her.

He wasn't going to have a dessert until the waiter pointed out the oriental fruit kebabs with mango sauce. As he ate and learned a lot about the mating habits of various British birds from his two companions, he thought guiltily about Monica at home making do with ham sandwiches.

That he could eat at all was a tribute to the chef, for his stomach was still fluttering with butterflies.

Jessica Taylor finished early and left early. As she crossed the hall, she noticed Celia Gordon bent almost double as she scrutinized something in a glass case. She seemed to be speaking animatedly to a man dressed in black, who was watching her anxiously.

As the lunch hour drew to a close, Graham wandered into the hall and noticed that several people were now gathered around the case, and Dr Simon Grade's voice, now low and commanding, was expounding knowledgeably. Intrigued, Graham moved closer.

'As you know, St Bede, or Baeda, is better known as the Venerable Bede,' the museum curator was saying, his eyes flicking over his audience and effortlessly picking out the most important members. 'He was born circa 673, and died in 735. His feast day, actually, is not far away, being on the 25 May.'

There was a small appreciative murmur. The services of Dr Grade had not been accredited on the agenda, but nobody doubted his expertise, such was the man's confident and erudite manner.

'As you probably also know, the entire world relies on his manuscript, the *Historia ecclesiastica gentis Anglorum*, or the *Ecclesiastical History of the English People*, as the source of almost *all* our information on the history of England before the year 731.'

This piece of information was indeed impressive, and many eyes returned to the ancient, illuminated manuscript. It was, of course, almost impossible for anyone but an expert to read or understand it.

'Of course, the Venerable Bede wrote other works, mainly homilies, hymns, epigrams and works on chronology and grammar, as well as the lives of certain saints, but this is by far his greatest work.' As he spoke, voice ringing with pride, Dr Grade patted the top of the wooden and glass showcase affectionately.

Graham, perhaps more sensitive than most, was almost sure that he detected a certain amount of concealed distress in the museum owner's manner. And yes, wasn't he sweating? Yet the hall was remarkably cool.

'This, of course, is not the original,' Dr Grade glossed this piece of information over very quickly, 'but a superb sixteenth-century copy, done by Benedictine monks before Henry the Eighth caused so much trouble.'

There were a few polite laughs.

'This is most appropriate since, of course, St Bede himself studied at a Benedictine monastery. He was born near Monkwearmouth, Durham, and later transferred to Jarrow, where he was later buried. However, sometime in the eleventh century his bones were removed to Durham.'

Graham glanced at his watch, and in spite of his nearly full stomach, he nervously opened his bag of peanuts and began to nibble. Fascinating though Dr Grade's impromptu lecture was, Graham found it almost impossible to concentrate. He knew in his own mind that his lecture was sufficiently insightful, helpful and well written, but he wasn't sure of his ability to deliver it with any real panache.

Graham offered the bag of nuts to several of the people immediately around him; most refused, but some smiled and took a few.

'What's going on?' a soft voice asked in his ear and Graham turned with relief to smile down at his wife.

'A lecture on the manuscript,' he whispered back. 'What are you doing here?'

'Offering you some moral support. I thought I'd say hello before your lecture. Have your knees gone all wibbly wobbly?' she teased.

'Yes. Have a peanut.' He offered her the bag and she took one, chewing thoughtfully.

The lecture over, the clerics began to separate, with rather a lot of them, Graham noticed with alarm, heading for the small theatre/lecture room off to the right.

'Well, good luck,' Monica said, squeezing his arm encouragingly.

As she spoke, a blonde woman dressed in a very well tailored and severe suit came down the main stairs and turned as if towards the lecture hall. Monica observed that the dapper little man who'd been giving the lecture had also noticed the new arrival and had quickly turned away. He then bent down, as if to tie his shoelaces, his face carefully averted. It took Monica only a second to realize that the museum director was actually wearing slip-ons. Obviously the man was trying to avoid catching the newcomer's attention.

As she glanced around the hall, Celia Gordon's head did a swift double take as it took in the tall, elegant, very handsome figure of Graham Noble. And instantly, a huge smile spread across her face. Several conference-goers, who'd become accustomed to her rather aloof and opinionated manner, stared at her in open amazement.

'Graham!' she said loudly and with obvious delight, and turned towards them.

Graham started and looked up.

Then he saw Reverend Celia Gordon and went pale. Very pale.

CHAPTER 5

'Graham, how lovely to see you again,' Celia said, smiling widely and reaching out to take his free hand in both of hers. Instead of shaking it, however, Monica noticed that the other woman simply kept hold of it. 'I did see your name on the list, but I wasn't sure that it would be you. How marvellous that it is.'

'Celia,' Graham said blankly. 'I didn't know that you were coming here,' he admitted, and wished wholeheartedly that he'd paid more attention to the guest list.

Celia laughed, her eyes sweeping over him, taking in the still-flat stomach, the dark hair and the undeniably handsome face. 'You haven't changed a bit,' she said, and there was a definite throaty suggestive quality in her voice that set Graham blushing. Around them the hall began to fill up, but people seemed oddly reluctant to file into the lecture hall. Several were watching the byplay and looking fascinated.

'Celia, this is Monica, my wife,' Graham said loudly — rather too loudly — and took an instinctive step closer to Monica.

Monica saw the sparkle falter in the other woman's eyes and felt her spine stiffening as the middle-aged blonde woman turned her way. As well as the striking suit she had on, her face was very artfully made up. She met Celia's eyes with a smile and was pleased to note that the other woman's blue eyes weren't nearly as blue as her own. She held out her hand. 'How do you do, Reverend . . . ?'

'Gordon,' Graham supplied hastily.

'How do you do,' Celia said with a smile. Her eyes swept over Monica, assessing her age, looks and clothes and narrowing slightly after the inventory. Then she turned back to Graham. 'Well, you sly old thing, you've finally tied the knot. And I thought you said you were unlikely ever to get married . . .' she trailed off, perhaps realizing that she'd been rather less than tactful. 'But then, we were both so young. What did we know?' she laughed, a shade harshly.

Her eyes became slightly glazed as the years fell away. She'd been fresh out of college when she'd first met this man, her BA just behind her and a post-graduate course stretching ahead.

'I did volunteer work for Graham's first church, oh . . . too many years ago now to count, isn't that so, Graham?' she said, turning back to give Monica a more searching assessment. Monica had no doubt that she was wondering what it was about her that had tempted Graham to give up his single lifestyle, when he'd evidently been so determined to hang on to it back then. Because one thing was for certain — Monica would have bet her severance cheque that Reverend Celia Gordon had tried, and failed, to persuade him to give it up all those years ago.

Instantly, Monica found herself wishing that she had chosen to wear something more prepossessing than the lightweight floral summer dress and sandals that she had on, and she found herself taking a closer step towards Graham. Instinctively their hands touched, and they clasped fingers, each seeking and offering trust and unity.

Celia, for her part, caught the gesture and turned back to Graham, her eyes harder now, her smile becoming more fixed in place. 'Well, well, well,' she drawled. 'And have you any children?'

'One daughter,' Graham said promptly, and made no effort to explain Carol-Ann's status as his stepdaughter. And Monica could have kissed him for that. It was around then that she began to notice the amount of covert speculation they were attracting, and decided it was time to set the record straight. Let them see there was nothing to gossip about here, and no mileage to be gained. She was not, after all, some jealous teenager bristling over being introduced to the ex.

'So, Reverend Gordon, you knew my husband long ago,' she said firmly. 'That must have been when he was up north, yes?'

'Yes, a depressing place,' Celia confirmed, barely flicking her a glance. Her attention was fixed solely on her husband, a fact that was making Graham shift in a slightly uncomfortable way from foot to foot. 'But Graham was determined to bring some light to the place. Did you ever manage it?' she added, her question as barbed now as a thorn bush. She was clearly beginning to feel angry and Monica felt herself becoming correspondingly antagonistic. She tried to damp it down. No good could come of raking over old coals and stirring up trouble.

Graham, looking distinctly unhappy, smiled bleakly. 'No. I don't think I did,' he admitted humbly.

Celia started. She'd forgotten his disconcerting and heart-tugging habit of being so simple and honest. It was only one of many things that had attracted her to him so long ago. And was still attracting her now. In her rise to her current position, she'd become used to two-faced, so-called friends, both male and female, willing to stab her in the back. She'd forgotten that there were still men like this around.

Her eyes softened.

'Celia was an eager volunteer in those days and fresh out of college with a degree,' Graham said, shooting his wife a look full of hidden messages. 'Medieval history, wasn't it?'

'And comparative theology,' she acknowledged. 'I then did a degree in medieval languages. Of course, as soon as the ordination of women was permitted, I joined up,' she put in smoothly. 'I now run St Jude's in Bath.'

Monica blinked. Very swanky! No doubt about it, Reverend Gordon was doing well, and she couldn't help but wonder, with a nasty little twinge of resentment, just how she'd managed it. She couldn't see poor Jessica Taylor ever being transferred to such a powerful position. Then she told herself not to let her own feathers get too ruffled. After all, it would have been foolish to believe that Graham hadn't had some kind of a relationship with women in his past. The thing to remember was that it was past. And that she had no reason at all to feel threatened now.

In fact, it was absurd to feel even mildly put out. Her fingers in his hand squeezed gently. She trusted him and the strength of their marriage implicitly.

'That's nice for you,' Graham was responding to her news without a hint of envy. 'This is my parish.' He waved a hand in the general direction of the village. 'Has been for over twenty years and I wouldn't want to leave it now.' As he spoke, he looked her long and levelly in the eye.

'So you found your niche,' Celia said, somehow managing to make it sound like a crime. 'I always thought that you were going to be a lone crusader. If I'd known you craved domesticity quite so much . . . well.' She smiled teasingly, becoming definitely provocative now. In spite of her good intentions, Monica felt her face flame. Around her she could fairly hear all the speculative wheels turning as people pretended not to eavesdrop.

Of all the damned cheek! she fumed silently. Why didn't the woman just come right out and say out loud that she'd have been after him like a shot?

'Ah but Graham hadn't met me then,' she pointed out sweetly, and slipped her hand further up and around his elbow, tugging his arm to her side. He turned to look down at her, his gaze slightly troubled and a little bit pleading. 'Had you, sweetheart?' she asked, looking up at him with a soft, tender expression.

Graham looked back at her gratefully. 'No,' he said simply. Then he glanced at his watch. 'Good grief! Celia, I simply must go, I'm giving a lecture. It's been really nice to see you again,' he added hurriedly and rather mendaciously.

'Oh yes, your lecture. I'm looking forward to it,' Celia said, shooting Monica a triumphant look. 'Shall we go in?' she said to Graham who, of course, had no option but to allow her to monopolize him. Somewhat reluctantly, he allowed Celia to lead him away towards the lecture hall where many of the others, who had been prodded into sudden action, quickly preceded him. He shot a last, quick glance at Monica over his shoulder as he left, but couldn't read from her face what she was thinking.

As he walked into the hall, he reflected that at least all his nervousness about giving his talk had now faded!

He walked to the podium and only then realized, with some embarrassment, that he was still holding on to the open bag of peanuts. Flustered, he walked to the blackboard behind him, which had been left there mostly for decorative purposes since the room was equipped with a large white screen that could be accessed by a laptop. He put the offending packet on the rim, along with the unused old-fashioned chalk and wooden-backed duster, whilst members of his audience politely pretended not to notice his consternation. When he turned back to the room, it was disconcertingly full. And there, sitting right in the middle of the front row, was Celia.

Graham almost smiled. He simply couldn't help it. Of all the silly, unwanted things that could possibly have happened.

His memories of Celia were mostly vague — he'd been a young, newly ordained vicar and Celia had been a very young, ambitious, forceful woman. He'd known, of course, that she'd had something of a crush on him and had tried gently to discourage her, although, if his memory served him right, she had been very persistent. She'd found it very hard to believe that anyone would reject what she was offering. Eventually though, Celia had left to attend graduate college, and they'd parted, if not on the best of terms exactly, in some form of mutual understanding. And from that day to this, he had quite literally never given her another thought.

Nevertheless, it had been an awful shock to see her bearing down on him just now — especially with Monica right by his side. And who knows what she had made of that little contretemps. He suspected that he and his wife would be having a long, long chat come teatime.

Quickly, he pulled himself together. 'Ladies and gentlemen, thank you for coming,' he began, his voice, he was relieved to note, coming out clear and even. 'I hope I won't bore you too much with the subject of my lecture . . .' And he was off. With his notes in front of him, and his excellent memory coming to his aid, he launched into his lecture with renewed confidence.

And if he noticed a certain amount of unwelcome speculation in some of the faces in front of him, he ignored it. It had been a little embarrassing just now, true, but that wouldn't kill him — besides, he reminded himself comfortingly, he'd probably never meet any of these people again. And come Tuesday, Celia would be back in Bath, where he heartily hoped she would stay.

* * *

'Want to come into Oxford with me?' Monica called outside her daughter's bedroom as she passed it, picking up the car keys from the hall table as she did so. As expected, Carol-Ann's bedroom door opened rapidly.

'You bet,' Carol-Ann rushed out, long blonde hair flying. 'I didn't know you were going into town today. Can we go to the cinema? There's a Brad Pitt film on.'

'No,' Monica said firmly. 'You know I've got to get back. We're having dinner at the manor tonight.'

'Oh yeah,' Carol-Ann yawned hugely. 'How fascinating for you.'

Monica grinned at her wryly and together they headed for the car.

'So what are you after? Lampshades?' Carol-Ann drawled as they headed south towards the famous university city. 'Some material for new curtains? A collar for the cat?'

'We haven't got a cat,' Monica said, playing the game. 'And I'm looking for a new dress, if you must know.'

Carol-Ann shot her mother a quick look. 'I thought you were going to wear that long velvet thing tonight,' she said airily. 'It's what you usually wear to all the fancy dos.'

'Well tonight I'm going to wear something different,' Monica said grimly, an image of Celia Gordon's fair-haired elegance uppermost in her mind.

Carol-Ann frowned at her, something in her mother's tone alerting her to trouble. 'What's up, Mum?' she demanded instantly.

Surprised by her perspicacity — teenagers were more known for their introspection than intuition — Monica glanced across at her. 'Nothing,' she denied automatically. And then after a moment, because she and Carol-Ann were always honest with each other, added, 'There was an old friend of your father's at the conference.'

'Oh? Old female friend?' Carol-Ann probed ruthlessly.

'Yes.'

'Pretty?'

'A lot older than me.'

'But pretty?' Carol-Ann insisted, beginning to enjoy herself hugely.

'Yes,' Monica admitted very reluctantly.

Carol-Ann chuckled. 'Who'd have thought the old dog had it in him.'

'Less of the old dog,' Monica snapped. 'And I'm sure that they were just friends.'

'Hah!' Carol-Ann snorted. Then, seeing the look on her mother's face she quickly dropped the teasing. 'Don't worry. Everyone knows that Graham's crazy about you, Mum. You've got nothing to worry about.'

Which Monica was sure of too, deep down. But she was only human, and a woman, and she wasn't about to let herself be outdone at that evening's dinner.

Her first stop, much to Carol-Ann's disgust, was Debenhams. There, to Carol-Ann's immense surprise, she found two dresses that suited her, looked designer-label, wouldn't break the budget and would be perfect for a dinner at the manor.

'I still like the blue one better,' Carol-Ann said half an hour later, crammed into a changing cubicle and eyeing her mother with a knowledgeable, fashion-conscious eye. 'It showed more skin.'

'That it did,' Monica agreed wryly. 'That's why I'm going for this.'

The dress she was wearing and admiring in the full-length mirror was a very deep, rich apricot in shade and provided a sharp and alluring contrast to her blue eyes, whilst remaining a perfect complement for her dark, nut-brown hair. It was of a vaguely satiny material and had a simple boat-shaped neckline and half-length, tight-fitting sleeves. It also had a very clever waist that made her slender figure look even more so, and a very romantic full skirt, with a net underskirt to give it a bit of a flounce. It came to mid-calf length, thus showing off her (even if she did say so herself) nicely shaped calves and ankles, and would be perfect with some strappy heels. And buying those, she supposed with a sigh, would be next on the agenda. Thus blowing her budget. Oh well. They'd just have to go without meat next week.

'Besides, I've got just the jewellery to go with this,' she added, suddenly remembering. 'Nana's silver and tiger's eye set.'

Carol-Ann pursed her lips as she contemplated the ensemble. 'Ye-esss,' she agreed reluctantly. 'But I still think the blue is better. If you want to show up this rival . . .'

Monica glowered at her daughter. 'She is not a rival and I have no intention of making a fool of either Graham or myself by showing up in something inappropriate. I'll be jiggered if I'll let her goad me into doing something foolish.'

'Way to go, Mum!' Carol-Ann yelled, making a woman in the next changing cubicle grin.

* * *

In his private lounge, Sir Andrew Courtenay opened the French windows leading out onto the back lawns and glanced around. As he'd suspected, there was not a soul in sight. He'd noticed before that the hours between two and four were usually very dead at conferences, mainly because nobody had an excuse not to be hard at work taking notes at lectures or in workshops.

He slipped quickly across the lawns and dodged through a thicket of rhododendrons to the back gate, silently passing out of the manor grounds and into a narrow leafy lane. It was a no through road that ended in a barred gate a hundred yards or so further on, which in turn led to a local farmer's field.

He glanced at his watch nervously. It was nearly three o'clock already. He hoped his contact hadn't been and gone, but Sir Andrew didn't really think so. These types of people always wanted money and would do anything to get it. He should know.

Hell, he hated doing this. Hated it. He wasn't going to back out now, though.

The sound of an engine had him looking away towards the village, but it was only someone heading out of Heyford Bassett, a red car flashing past the entrance to Church Lane. He paced back and forth at the side of the road, looking haggard. And as he paced, he wondered about Archdeacon Pierrepont and his unexpected proposal.

The man made a certain amount of sense. And his idea of poetic justice appealed to him greatly. Also, he was a powerful ally to have. Between the two of them, surely they could pull this thing off? For his daughter's sake, Sir Andrew was willing to try. Was willing, in fact, to take any kind of risk necessary. But there was something about the man, something unstable that worried him and . . .

He heard another car and glanced towards the entrance to the lane, his heart suddenly pounding as he noticed a sports car with darkened windows coming slowly towards him. Sir Andrew stood stock-still as the car cruised past. For a moment he wondered what he was supposed to do. Was he supposed to make a gesture? Follow on after the car? But before he could move, the car quickly reversed into a turning, and came back towards him again. As it drew level, the driver's side window slid down automatically.

No doubt the driver had just been checking to make certain that there was no one else around, Sir Andrew supposed with a bitter smile. A surprisingly young face looked back at him from the driver's seat.

'You the geezer Davie told me about then?' The voice was pure cockney.

Sir Andrew, leaning in a little, nodded. 'Yes.'

'You don't look the type,' the youngster said suspiciously. Sir Andrew noticed he had an angry-looking pimple on his chin. The boy was barely out of puberty.

'Well I am,' Sir Andrew growled, and reached into his rear trouser pocket, withdrawing a leather wallet. The boy's eyes sharpened as the older man began to extract and count out a wad of twenty-pound notes. The young man's eyes flickered everywhere, but saw only cows in meadows, the tree-lined lane and a big house in the near distance. His eyes narrowed on it nervously.

'Here, this is the amount Davie mentioned. Right?' Sir Andrew said, thrusting his hand inside the car. He wanted this over with quickly. Already he was feeling soiled and dirty.

The youngster snatched the money from his hand and for a bare instant Sir Andrew thought he was simply going to drive away and rip him off. Then he felt something small and soft being pushed into his hand and leapt back just in time as the sports car shot away.

He glanced down at the small object lying so innocuously in the palm of his hand and a look of disgust and fury crossed his face. Quickly he thrust it venomously into his back pocket. He then turned and headed back towards the manor. But for all his anger, his strides were long and confident. His back was straight, and for the first time since February, he had a purpose in his life.

And things to do.

* * *

Not everyone at the manor was attending Graham's lecture or the other two small workshops that had been scheduled for that afternoon.

In the main hall, sitting beside the St Bede's manuscript, Dr Simon Grade stared miserably down at his feet. That damned woman and her comments about the ink colouration and some of the lettering. What could she possibly know about it? And yet, he suspected glumly, she knew an awful lot. She was just the kind that would. Simon had known a lot of women like her in his life. Besides, hadn't that poor vicar she'd attached herself to like a leech said something about her having a BA? The trouble was he'd been too far away and there'd been too many people crowding around him to be able to hear properly. What had the BA been in exactly?

Simon took a handkerchief from his pocket and wiped it across his perspiring forehead. He felt quite nauseous. He tried to comfort himself with the thought that things could have been worse.

A lot worse.

He'd been quite within his rights to refuse to remove the manuscript from the glass case in order to give her a better look, and he'd done so vehemently. Besides, there'd been no gloves available for her to wear, and you couldn't handle an artefact like that with bare skin. The gall of the woman! But she obviously didn't lack that. Even from where he'd been standing, he could see that she'd been all over that poor woman's husband. And her, in her dog collar! And didn't it make all the others goggle! Why, Bishop Bryce's charming wife had been staring at them positively wide-eyed. But then, she was a real lady, Simon thought with a sniff, and not used to such outrageous behaviour.

No, common sense assured him, he had nothing to fear from Reverend Celia Gordon. Nobody else liked her either, that much was clear. Surely no one would listen to her or take her seriously. Would they? If she even said anything, of course. He didn't know her well enough to call that either way.

Dr Simon Grade continued to sit in the deserted hall and sweat. For him, it was to be a long, long, afternoon.

* * *

Back in his study Sir Andrew sat at his desk staring down at a photograph of a smiling girl holding the reins of a magnificent chestnut hunter. She'd loved that horse. Sir Andrew wished he hadn't got rid of it. But he couldn't bear to see it in the paddock, not after . . . And now she'd never ride him again.

With a start he realized that he was crying. And that would never do. He couldn't break down. Not now. He pulled open a desk drawer and with one last, lingering look, he put the photograph away.

* * *

It was nearly seven o'clock and a glorious summer evening. In their rooms, best bib and tucker was being donned by all the conference-goers in preparation for the grand dinner. Dr Simon Grade had got his wish, for Dr Carew had indeed invited him to join them in the dining hall, and the museum curator was currently in the gents, transforming his suit.

Arthur Bryce stood still as his wife adjusted his dog collar.

In her bedroom, Jessica Taylor stood in front of the mirror and sighed over the dark red, nearly black crushed velvet frock that she'd had for over ten years. It was very plain, and it still suited her to perfection. But was it becoming just a shade shabby now?

Celia Gordon donned a long pencil skirt in jet black, and added a cream jacket with black piping to match, over a black lace blouse. She added just a touch more lipstick to her already dark red lips.

Sir Andrew went to the kitchens to offer his usual moral support to the staff.

In his room, Archdeacon Sir Matthew Pierrepont drank his third whisky of the day and cackled in delighted anticipation of things to come as he negligently brushed down his old suit, so ancient it was almost greening with mould.

At the converted vicarage, Graham rose from the edge of the bed and slipped into a pair of dark polished shoes. He was wearing a basic black suit, crisp white shirt and pale blue tie, and looked devastatingly handsome. He turned at the sound of whispering material and his eyes opened wide as his wife walked through from the bathroom.

'Monica, you look . . . ravishing,' he said. He smiled and held out his hand. 'I love you,' he said again. He'd said it twice that evening already, but he wanted to make sure she understood.

Monica did. 'I love you too,' she said, reaching up on tiptoe to kiss him. Even in high heels, she was shorter than Graham by quite a few inches.

It was a lovely night as they walked towards the manor. The sun was still a long way from setting, and blackbirds, thrushes, robins, chaffinches, greenfinches and sparrows serenaded them all the way down the lane towards the big house. The air was perfumed with honeysuckle and roses and wild flowers.

It didn't seem like the sort of night for murder at all.

CHAPTER 6

In the dining room the tables had once more been set out to make one long length, and the whole arrangement sparkled with glass and silverware. In porcelain bowls abundant flowers gave the scene a fairytale prettiness whilst silver napkin rings enclosed fine white linen napkins, and in big silver candelabras white candles flickered and flamed.

'Wow,' Monica said softly to Graham as they walked arm in arm into the room.

'Sir Andrew certainly likes to push the boat out,' Graham agreed. Then, more uncertainly, 'Do you see any name plates?'

'No. I think we just sit wherever we want to.'

'I notice that Bishop Bryce is seated at the head of the table down at the bottom,' Graham said, then laughed. 'If you see what I mean. I wonder who's supposed to sit at the head of the table at this end?'

'Your boss, I expect,' Monica said somewhat irreverently, spying Bishop David Carew. 'Here he is now. Do you suppose anyone here has told him that we're all in the third millennium yet?' she whispered teasingly.

Graham's lips twitched. 'I certainly hope not.'

'Let's not sit too near the middle,' Monica said nervously. 'How about somewhere discreet, down at the bottom end?'

'And what if I want to show you off more?' Graham said promptly. 'You're easily the most beautiful woman in the room.'

Monica smiled and fidgeted with her silver and tiger's eye pendant, making sure that it was still showing the right way around in the tender hollow above her discreet cleavage. 'Flatterer,' she said, but she was pleased and her eyes sparkled.

They chose their seats as Monica had wanted, and soon the entire table was full. The wine waiters began filling glasses with various tipples of distinguished vintage; perhaps not surprisingly, given their profession, quite a number of guests opted for non-alcoholic beverages.

'Starter, sir?' a discreet voice asked in their ears, and Monica and Graham quickly perused the menu, giving their choices for the main course at the same time. Monica opted for the lobster, Graham for the rack of lamb.

Chloe Bryce, looking dramatic in black, drained her glass of exquisite French red wine and absently played with the carved silver medallion hanging around her neck. The intaglio scene it depicted had a nubile female form swimming elegantly through the waves, and was complemented by her slim silver wristwatch and a pair of silver and jet earrings. 'I see that Sir Matthew has tried to make something of an effort at last,' she pointed out to her husband wearily. In spite of her make-up, she was looking tired and had distinct dark circles under her eyes.

Arthur glanced across at the archdeacon and frowned. 'He's still wearing that mouldy old black-green thing,' he said, puzzled.

'Yes, but he's brushed it,' Chloe drawled. 'Which is something of a sartorial statement from him, don't you think?'

Arthur, feeling more puzzled than ever, merely smiled and nodded. He'd learned that when his wife was in this sort of odd, vindictive yet fey mood, he should merely nod and say as little as possible so as to avoid provoking her.

Celia Gordon, having waited in the wings until she'd seen where Graham was seated, moved quickly forward and took a chair almost opposite him across the table where she couldn't fail to be in his eye-line. She smiled across at both Monica and Graham as, with a deft flick, she opened her folded napkin and draped it across her lap. 'Monica, Graham, hello again,' she said pleasantly, her eyes running over Monica's outfit then quickly away again.

Seeing that the woman cleric was dressed smartly, but not so smartly that it appeared that she cared overmuch about fashion, Monica had to wryly admit a point to her. But a little while later, the flattering attentions of two male canons, one on her right and one diagonally across from her, was surely a point for Monica's side.

A little while later Dr Carew rose, and a slow but amiable silence spread around the room. His opening speech was very brief, and he hoped that all the guests were pleased with the choice of conference centre that year, to which there were genuine murmurs of approval. He then wished them all a good dinner, said a brief grace, and sat down.

In the kitchens, the waiters and waitresses began to come and go in a steady stream. Sir Andrew watched over them in a desultory fashion. He badly wanted a stiff drink.

'So tell me,' Celia, with an untouched melon boat in front of her, looked across the table at Graham, 'how do you think your lecture went this afternoon?'

Graham shrugged a shade ruefully. 'You'd be in a far better position to say than I would,' he pointed out.

Celia laughed. 'Modest as ever, but I'm sure you know how well it was received. You spoke with a real affinity for the young.'

Monica sighed heavily. Did the woman never quit? Flattering Graham so flagrantly was almost embarrassing! If she kept it up, people would really start to talk.

Graham mumbled something and attacked his prawns magenta starter with determination. Taking the hint, Celia turned to the man beside her and struck up a lively and interesting (if rather hard-to-follow) discussion about the dissolution of the monasteries.

In the hall a grandfather clock chimed with mellow, self-important chimes. The noise level began to rise steadily, as did the heat. Waiters began opening windows, allowing in a cooling breeze and the beginnings of an early moonlight. And at last Monica began to relax and to truly enjoy the occasion.

Sometime later, after the main courses had been enjoyed, a low murmur of approval greeted the arrival of the dessert trolleys, which were overflowing with delicious goodies. Monica eyed the wonderful towering gateau, the bowls of exotic fruit cocktails, the sorbets and roulades, the tortes and chocolate and coconut trifles with a small sigh of surrender.

Graham opted for cheese and biscuits, as she'd suspected he would. She herself was seduced by the trifle. She noticed Celia went immediately for the orange gateau, but only after thoroughly checking the cream layer on the top for something. Apparently satisfied, she tucked in with the first signs of genuine pleasure that Monica had been able to detect in the older woman.

She noticed the after-dinner speaker glance ever so casually at his watch and, somewhere to her left, someone was talking about the bad press magpies were being given. Then a slight sound, a sort of choking cough, suddenly impinged on Monica's consciousness, not because it was loud so much as because it sounded so out of place amid the cheerful, inconsequential chatter. She began to turn her head to try and locate its source when a second, louder and much more choked sound drifted across the table.

Monica's eyes widened as she looked across at Celia Gordon, discovering that the lady's own blue eyes were beginning to bulge alarmingly. The expression in them was unmistakable horror. Blank, fierce, hopeless horror.

Monica went cold as, instantly, she began to notice other things as well. Celia's colour was not good, and her hand was to her throat, scrabbling at it compulsively. Worse, and most incongruous of all, her mouth was hanging inelegantly open. Monica was so astonished by this, of all things, that for a moment she couldn't even react. Her heart lurched in her breast, though. Celia was staring straight at her.

The man to Celia's right gave her a quick, embarrassed look. Celia began to gasp. And this time there was a rasping, awful quality to it that had their end of the table falling completely silent. At the other end, though, the chatter went on as people failed to realize that something was seriously amiss.

'Reverend Gordon,' Monica said sharply, half rising to her feet at last. Out of her peripheral vision, she saw Graham's head swing around. By now Celia's face was turning reddish-purple and she was holding onto the edge of the table and pulling the tablecloth towards her with white-knuckled fists. A wine glass toppled and fell, its contents staining the tablecloth. Celia's pale blue eyes protruded quite hideously now, the look of terror in them escalating wildly, and with a heart-dropping sensation of fear, Monica realized that the other woman couldn't breathe.

'Graham!' she cried urgently, her cry silencing the entire room now. Those at the top end looked at her in surprise and then at Graham, who was already on his feet.

The man beside Celia, suddenly realizing that this wasn't a time for embarrassment but for action, also sprang up. 'Is there a doctor here?' he called.

This, of course, caused outright consternation, but although the room held a number of academics with doctorates, it seemed that none of them were in medicine.

'Ring for an ambulance,' Graham looked straight up the table towards David Carew, who rose quickly to his feet and reached for his mobile phone.

By now Celia was toppling over onto her side, her hands making distressing grasping movements at the tablecloth, at her throat, at anything that she could grab hold of in her frantic state.

Monica found herself unable to tear her eyes away from the wretched spectacle. She was aware of Graham moving behind her, racing around to the bottom end of the table, where he passed Arthur and Chloe Bryce, who were staring, like everyone else, at the stricken woman. On both of their faces a kind of blankness seemed to have wiped out their features, making them look like people in a bad painting.

Celia fell fully off her chair and onto the floor, even as her immediate neighbours got to their feet and bent over her.

'I know CPR,' someone eventually spoke up, since there obviously wasn't a doctor to be had.

Dr Carew's voice could be heard as he called calmly but urgently for an ambulance. Standing just outside the kitchen entrance, Sir Andrew Courtenay heard his end of the conversation and quickly came into the dining room. There he found the room in utter chaos.

'I can't seem to get her airway open,' a slightly panic-tinged voice came from somewhere in the middle of a small group towards the end of the table.

Monica alone still stood at her place, staring white-faced across to where someone was kneeling over Celia. But even as she watched, Celia's black stocking-clad legs began to thrash about. Monica's mouth went bone dry. There was something so . . . inhuman, so ghastly, about that sudden, primitive movement.

'Hold her down!' someone yelped. 'Is she having a fit? Is she epileptic?'

Monica hoped so, she even prayed so, but she couldn't quite bring herself to believe so. Although she knew little about epilepsy, some atavistic sense was already telling her that the woman she so disliked was fighting for her very life.

'What's going on?' Sir Andrew whispered to Dr Carew.

'I'm not sure,' the bishop replied. 'Someone's been taken ill,' he added, rather unnecessarily.

With nobody speaking, the harsh, distorted breathing of the stricken woman was now clearly audible. Monica winced with every blood-curdling, choking effort Celia made to breathe. She felt tears spurt to her eyes as the poor woman's neat black-shod feet began drumming against the carpet.

'She's turning blue!' one of those around her whispered, his voice appalled.

'Is that a siren?' one of the diners asked hopefully, but everyone knew that it was far too soon for that. Minutes seemed to pass like hours. The brave man doing CPR huffed and worked with growing desperation. Celia's breathing became even more laboured, and then, suddenly, the unmistakable sound of a siren was heard, its eerie, ululating wail releasing a collective sigh of relief.

Sir Andrew turned and headed for the front doors and was back in moments, leading in two paramedics with a stretcher. With relief, the man doing CPR rose and everyone backed away, giving the professionals room. The paramedics began issuing sharp orders to one another, the stress in their voices indicating, if any indication had been needed, the seriousness of the situation.

Within moments they had Celia strapped onto the stretcher, where she writhed and choked, and moved her rapidly towards the door. Sir Andrew and another quick-minded guest held the doors open for them, and then ran through the hall to the front door, to open the big outside doors as well, allowing easy and quick egress.

No one left in the dining hall spoke. It was as if they were all listening for something, some signal maybe, giving them permission to move. Although nobody could have said quite what that might be.

The ambulance left, the sound of the siren dashing away into the night.

And in the silent room, Dr Simon Grade suddenly squeaked something incomprehensible, and dramatically toppled over. The small circle around him made gasping, hopeless noises, and scattered like startled sheep, but it was quickly established that he'd merely fainted. The CPR man slapped his wrists and face and called for brandy. Coming to, and staring up at all the faces around him, he felt tears spring to his eyes.

'Sorry,' he muttered. 'I'm so sorry. I've just never seen or heard anything so . . . ghastly . . . in my life. Sorry to be so feeble. Thank you,' this last to the CPR man, who pressed the brandy glass against his lips.

'Don't worry,' he assured the museum owner kindly. 'I feel a bit weak about the knees myself. I imagine we all do. Here, drink it all up. It'll do you good.'

Several women then began to cry — due in part to the sudden release of unbearable tension, but mostly from shock. Husbands began to lead their wives from the room, as the CPR man helped Simon to his feet.

Chloe Bryce did not cry, but stared blankly at a painting on the wall. Beside her, Arthur wondered if he too could ask for a brandy. Jessica Taylor, sitting on a chair with her back to the wall, was staring down at her feet. She was as white as a sheet. Sir Andrew came slowly back into the room. He'd been watching the ambulance disappear into the night, a tight, hard, frozen look on his face. Now he returned to the room and looked around at his silent, shocked guests. Belatedly, the astute businessman in him took over.

'Ladies and gentlemen,' he said, his pleasant, cultured voice affecting everyone in the room. Backs slumped and nerves began to settle. 'The bar is open. I think it would be best if . . . well, the room were cleared.' He glanced across at a few of his waiters and waitresses who, like everyone else, had stopped what they'd been doing and were now waiting, unsure of what to do next. 'I'll get my staff to er . . . clear away.'

'Yes,' it was David Carew who spoke up next, taking up the rallying cry to return to normal. 'I think we'd all like to leave here. And I, for one, need a stiff drink,' he added, thus cunningly giving everyone else the excuse to have one too.

Eagerly now, they all began to troop out. About a third of the guests, wanting only to be alone, drifted to the stairs and elevator to make their way to their rooms. Without doubt, many prayers for their stricken colleague would soon be winging their way heavenward. Most, however, went straight into the bar, where the bar staff, taken by surprise by the sudden surge of business, began quickly setting up drinks.

At the back of the now goggling throng, Graham and Monica lingered by the open doorway. 'Are you all right?' Graham asked her, his voice shaken. 'Do you want a drink?'

Mutely Monica shook her head. 'No. I think I just want to go home,' she said in a small voice.

Graham nodded, squeezing her arm and instantly instilling her with some of his strength. 'Just let me have a word with my bishop and then we'll go,' he promised. Monica nodded and watched him start to weave his way through the crowd in search of David Carew.

'Waiter, champagne for me,' a cracked old voice spoke up from the corner of the crowded bar room. There was another moment of absolute silence before someone blasphemed loudly and with feeling. Sir Matthew Pierrepont stared defiantly at a waiter. 'Make it a bottle of your best.'

Around him, a small space cleared as people anxiously put some distance between themselves and the aged cleric.

Monica shuddered. Surely she was mistaken in thinking that she saw a look of intense satisfaction on the old man's face? He was probably just having a strange reaction to shock.

'Ready,' Graham said a few minutes later, his voice carrying easily over the now more subdued conversation going on around them. 'David is going to drive over to the hospital and see what's happening.'

Monica nodded and together, feeling utterly miserable, they left the manor.

'Poor Sir Andrew,' Monica said sadly, once they were outside in the cool silver-and-dark world of the lovely evening.

Her husband glanced across at her quickly. 'What made you say that?' he asked her curiously, as they walked hand in hand down the lane and towards the sanctuary of their home.

'I don't really know,' Monica said at last, frowning in puzzlement. For some reason, it had simply been the first thing that had popped into her head.

* * *

In his study, Sir Andrew listened to the sounds of the house falling silent around him. It was now late — very late. His guests had finally retired for the night, worn out by the drama of recent events, and the house was silent. Sir Andrew had already given the staff a quiet pep talk. The general consensus of opinion seemed to be that a guest had had a heart attack. It was sad, of course, and it had inevitably ruined the evening, but the younger generation of workers had quickly shrugged it off. These things happened.

Tomorrow was Sunday and another day. They were young and knew no better.

Sir Andrew, who did, sat at his desk and simply waited.

* * *

In her room, Jessica Taylor was on her knees, praying. She was praying hard.

A few doors down the corridor, Arthur Bryce was brushing his teeth, a deep frown pitted between his fair brows. He looked worried. Very worried. In their bed, Chloe lay on her side with her make-up carefully removed, and stared at the small night-light that was burning. Occasionally, she blinked.

Sir Matthew Pierrepont had taken the bottle of champagne to bed with him, and was quite happily drinking it.

On a life-support machine in the John Radcliffe Hospital in Oxford, Celia Gordon knew nothing.

* * *

Graham jumped, blinked, and looked around in confusion. It was the bedroom, his bedroom, and it was pitch black. The clock showed it was nearly three o'clock in the morning. Beside him, the warm, comforting length of his wife was pressed against his back. What . . . ? In the half-second since waking he remembered the events of the previous evening, and then his telephone buzzed again. That was what had brought him so sharply awake.

Beside him, Monica rose silently onto one elbow and sensed, rather than saw, her husband reach out for the lamp. She blinked her eyes in sudden pain as the light dazzled her eyes, then watched his face as he answered his mobile.

'Yes? Oh, Bishop . . . I see. That's such a shame. I know. Any idea yet what caused it? No, of course not. Yes. I think that would be best. Yes, of course I'll . . . rewrite the service. No, I don't mind going back, if you think it best. Yes. Thank you for calling. Goodnight, David,' he finished gruffly.

As he slowly hung up, he felt small, gentle hands on his arm and shoulder. 'She's dead, isn't she?' Monica whispered sadly.

Graham took a deep, shuddering breath and nodded. 'Yes. The bishop wants me to say something at the service tomorrow and then go back to the manor. He wants me to "be available" until the end of the conference. In case anyone wants to talk things over with someone that they're unlikely to have to meet again.'

Monica said nothing but thought that David Carew was wise to offer her husband as an unofficial counsellor. He'd do a good job of it. She leaned forward to kiss his shoulder through the cool silk of his pyjama top. 'Was it a heart attack?'

Graham shook his head. 'The hospital didn't say. They have to contact her next of kin first, and I have no idea who that would be.'

Monica sighed, then said forlornly, 'Graham, I feel a bit guilty.' Graham's fingers instantly closed over hers. She didn't have to explain it any further. She hadn't liked Celia Gordon and now regretted that she hadn't been more charitable.

'I know,' he said softly. 'Me too.'

* * *

The following morning, Sunday, dawned bright and warm, as if deliberately thumbing its nose at mere human tragedy. 'What time's the service?' Monica asked Graham as she put the coffee pot down on the table between them. She hadn't bothered with breakfast — she didn't think either of them would be hungry, and Carol-Ann wouldn't stir for hours yet.

'Not till ten,' her husband replied. 'I think I'd better go down to the manor first.'

'I'm coming with you,' she said firmly.

Graham didn't argue. He'd be glad of her presence.

As they walked through the double wrought-iron gates of the impressive house, the first thing they saw were two blue-and-white police cars and, just getting out of a dark blue sedan car, a tall, handsome fair-haired man and a woman with dark hair.

'It's Jason,' Monica blurted in surprise. 'What on earth's he doing here?' Beside her, Graham stiffened slightly, and she suddenly sought for his hand and held on to it tightly. Together, the two of them moved forward, their feet making small scrunching sounds on the gravel lining the driveway. Hearing it, Chief Inspector Jason Dury turned his head, his ice-blue eyes narrowing on the couple walking towards him.

His eyes went straight to Monica, dressed in a black skirt and blouse. Her eyes, when they were close enough for him to see, looked troubled and sad.

'Reverend Noble,' Jason Dury said, greeting Graham first, and beside him his sergeant, Flora Glenn, turned sharply around. Her eyes too went straight to Monica Noble, then back to her superior. She didn't look best pleased.

Jason Dury was a local working-class boy made good. He'd been in the Thames Valley Police from the start of his career, rapidly gaining promotion to his current position as chief inspector. Unmarried, at just turned forty he looked much younger, and his well-cut blond hair and classically handsome face made him the obvious target for station-house gossip. And rumour had it that he could have a different girl every night, and probably did. But never a fellow police officer, since he seemed to operate a strict policy about keeping his working life and private life absolutely separate.

Rumour also had it that DS Glenn was trying to change all that.

'Mrs Noble,' Jason said politely, holding out his hand first to Graham and then to Monica. 'We meet again,' he added, with just a touch of bite to his tone.

They'd first crossed paths when a murder had been committed at the converted vicarage where the Nobles lived. Then they'd crossed paths yet again at a neighbouring village fete, when another killing had taken place. In both instances, Monica Noble had proved very helpful in bringing the perpetrator to light. He could only hope that this occasion would be different. He didn't much care for having his cases solved for him by a member of the public.

'Inspector,' Graham said pleasantly. His gaze, as he met that of the policeman, was perfectly affable.

I wonder, Jason found himself thinking uneasily, if he knows just how attractive I find his wife. And how I wish that she wasn't here right now. Already he could feel himself wanting to look at her.

'It's Chief Inspector actually,' Flora corrected him. She didn't think they'd be staying long, and with Monica Noble around that was her main worry dealt with. Because, from the sounds of the brief report they'd been given that morning, Flora was almost sure that this would prove to be a 'death by misadventure' case. They just needed to tie up a few loose ends and they'd be on their way. It was just her bad luck that the powers that be had wanted a senior man on the spot due to the 'delicate' nature of the circumstances. More likely, Flora thought cynically, an ecclesiastical bigwig who played golf with the chief constable had got on the phone and bent his ear.

Monica smiled briefly at Jason. Then, looking him straight in the eye, demanded simply, 'Jason, why are you here?'

CHAPTER 7

Something taut in Monica's tone sent just a faint shiver of warning down Jason Dury's spine and made him look at her a little more closely. His quick glance of surprise must have alerted her to just how abrupt she'd been for he saw her flush faintly in embarrassment.

'Sorry,' Monica apologized contritely. 'I just meant . . . well . . . there isn't anything . . . wrong, is there?' Her voice still sounded strained and tense and her eyes were definitely troubled.

Jason sighed. 'We hope not. Reverend Gordon's death was caused by anaphylactic shock, brought on by her allergy to peanuts.' As the senior officer assigned to the case, he'd been informed of the MO's preliminary findings as a matter of urgency.

'Oh, how awful,' Monica said. But it explained Celia's heart-wrenching symptoms. So it had been an accident, then, not an illness . . . Slowly, she began to frown. 'But surely people who have allergies like that are always very careful,' she began, then gave a mental snap of her fingers. 'So that's what she'd been looking for on top of her gateau,' she added suddenly.

'Gateau?' Jason said sharply. 'What do you mean?'

Briefly Monica described how Celia had checked the cream on the top of her dessert. 'I wondered why she was looking at it so carefully,' she admitted. 'But a lot of restaurants sprinkle chopped nuts on the top of gateaux, so she obviously checked first that they hadn't.'

Jason nodded. 'Sounds reasonable to me,' he said. 'Well, if you'll excuse us,' he added in polite dismissal and nodded at Flora. And together the two of them went into the house.

'Quite some place,' Flora said, looking around the hall, her gaze lingering on the woman seated behind the reception desk who was watching them curiously.

'The kitchens are this way, I expect,' Jason said, pointing to a set of doors off to one side.

The big kitchen, which was accessed down a short corridor, was a curious L-shaped room and a mixture of old and new, with cupboards, tables and workspaces in a small, partially hidden room off to the left. At this time of the day it was busy with breakfast preparations, but even so, they were immediately challenged by one of the waiters.

'Sorry, no guests allowed, sir. If you'd . . .' his voice trailed off as Jason showed him his ID.

'I'd like to know what courses Reverend Celia Gordon had at dinner last night. And, if possible, I want samples of the same. Can you arrange that?' Jason asked succinctly.

The waiter quickly called out, 'Chef! Chef, I think you'd better speak to these officers.' He then grabbed a tray of fruit juices from a kitchen worker who was thrusting them towards him and exited through the swing doors. A medium-built man in traditional chef's hat glanced round part of the dividing wall. He had a spatula in one hand, and his pale brown eyes narrowed on the two strangers ominously. Everyone else looked too busy to pay them any attention.

'Yes? What are you doing in my kitchen?' he barked.

'And you are, sir?' Jason prompted, not in the least offended, or intimidated either. He wondered, though, if all the media tales of tyrannical chefs were true. Certainly, if television performances were to be believed, some of them could be right tartars.

'I'm Rory Blundell, head chef here.' He spoke the name as if Jason should recognize it. Jason didn't, and once again repeated his requests. Somewhat to Jason's surprise, the chef did not send someone to fetch the manager or owner, nor did he demand explanations. Instead he narrowed his eyes for a moment on the chief inspector and then snapped his fingers — presumably at one of the waitresses, who was just that moment passing him by with a tray full of prunes, porridge and kedgeree.

'Tell Marcel I want him, Felicity,' he said brusquely.

'Yes, Mr Blundell,' she murmured meekly in passing. Her eyes swept across Jason, met Flora's and skidded away again.

The chef came forward, wiping his hands on a clean white towel. 'I hope you don't think that there was anything wrong with the food last night,' he said bluntly. 'No one else has complained of any symptoms.' He had a vaguely continental tinge to his accent, and Jason wondered if he'd trained in France.

'No, there's no question of food poisoning. Only of peanuts,' he added, watching the man intently.

The chef stiffened. 'Peanuts?' he echoed, his mouth falling open a little in surprise. 'There were no peanuts in any of my recipes last night,' he stated flatly.

Jason felt Flora stiffen beside him. 'Are you sure?' he asked quietly.

'Sure I'm sure,' the chef snorted. 'Ah, Marcel. He looked behind Jason's shoulder, his face set and tight. 'What did the woman who had the heart attack last night order for dinner?'

Jason didn't bother to correct the 'heart attack' theory as they all turned to look at the young man who'd just come in. Under the chef's hard stare, he swallowed noisily and quickly thought back. But he was a good waiter, with a good memory. 'The blonde vicar had the asparagus soup, followed by the duck à l'orange and the orange gateau, sir.'

The chef nodded, and without consulting Jason waved him away. Flora bridled a bit at this bit of alpha male behaviour, but Jason let it pass. He could always talk to the catering staff later, if it proved necessary. He was still hoping that this was going to turn out to be a case of misadventure. Right now he was anxious to get the samples off to the lab as soon as possible. Until that was done, it was impossible to know where they stood.

'This is Sergeant Flora Glenn,' Jason introduced Flora, who glared at the chef. 'I want you to give her samples of all those dishes — the soup, duck, the vegetables that would have been served with it, and the dessert.'

'But . . . if there were any leftovers, they're probably in the bins by now.' The chef was quite pale. 'I'm not sure . . .'

'There's still some soup left in the pan, Chef,' an anonymous voice spoke up from around the dogleg corner. 'I saw it on the rear right stove this morning.'

The chef flushed. 'It should have been disposed of, and the pans washed up long ago!' he yelled, outraged. 'Why wasn't it?'

The kitchen went momentarily deathly silent. Nobody spoke. Jason, who was very glad indeed that it hadn't been, smiled gently. 'I'm sure your staff were . . . distracted last night, Mr Blundell.' The cacophony of noise started up again as the crisis passed. 'And, I'm sorry to say, Reverend Gordon died last night,' he added quickly.

The chef slowly reached up to scratch his chin. His brown eyes looked more thoughtful than shocked.

'There's still some plates of duck and vegetables, Chef,' some other brave voice piped up from further back in the kitchen. 'You said we could have it for lunch, if we preferred. Remember?'

The chef sighed. Eating the leftovers not served to guests was a main kitchen perk, and the duck had been a popular choice. 'Marianne, check the fridge, see if there's any orange gateau left as well. Bring it all out here. You, Phillip, take the sergeant here and get her some samples of the savouries,' Rory Blundell ordered calmly.

Jason nodded to his sergeant, who promptly set off, and then looked up in interest as a waitress brought the remains of a delicious-looking orange gateau towards them and put it on the worktop nearest to them. It was huge, and even with half of it gone it still looked impressive. 'Is this the only gateau you made?' he asked.

'Of this type, yes. Would you like a piece?' the chef asked, with just a touch of humour in his voice. Jason smiled right back at him.

'Not for breakfast, sir, thank you,' he said mildly. 'But if you could cut a slice for my sergeant to bag up, I'd be grateful.'

Rory Blundell obliged, reaching into a drawer and wielding a sharp wedge-shaped knife with skill. He set aside a slice and then, to Jason's surprise, cut another. 'I don't know why you're bothering,' the chef said, taking a bite out of the cake. 'There's no . . .' Suddenly, his pale brown eyes widened. For a moment he looked as if he was going to be sick, but then he chewed and quickly swallowed. He stared at the cake between his fingers, a frown tugging at his dark brows.

'What's wrong?' Jason asked sharply.

The chef tore his eyes from the cake and back up to the policeman. He was pale. 'I don't believe it,' he mumbled. 'I can taste peanuts in here. But . . . there shouldn't be any.'

Jason took a slow breath. 'Is it possible you simply think you can taste peanuts, sir? The mind plays some funny tricks sometimes, and now that you know that the reverend . . .'

The chef didn't let him finish the psychological analysis. 'Chief Inspector, my palate is my life,' he declared somewhat dramatically. 'I tell you, there are peanuts in here. But the recipe doesn't call for any.'

And as Jason watched, the chef pulled the layers of cake apart. First he tried the orange cream topping, licking delicately, then decisively shook his head. Next the top layer of sponge. He seemed to roll the mouthful against the roof his mouth before swallowing. Again he shook his head. Next he tried the citrus cream layered between the two, and made a small sound. 'There's a tiny bit . . . look. There . . .' he pointed to the bottom layer of sponge, and a slightly shining glaze that had been spread on top of it. He ran the tip of his finger across the glaze, sucked on it, and nodded emphatically. 'That is peanut,' he said flatly. 'Not peanut butter, but a peanut glaze.'

He then made Jason jump as he suddenly yelled at the top of his considerable voice, 'Maurice! Maurice, come over here!'

Flora Glenn, sensing trouble and clutching a bag of small plastic sterile containers, each holding either a sample of soup, vegetables or duck and orange sauce, watched the almost-running figure of the manor's pastry chef.

'Maurice, did you put a peanut glaze on the orange gateau?' Rory Blundell demanded.

Maurice, a very tall, thin man with grey hair and green eyes, stared at his boss in some amazement. 'Peanut doesn't go with orange, Chef,' he said blankly.

'I know that,' the head chef shot back angrily. 'And that wasn't what I asked you. Did you make a peanut glaze and put it on the bottom layer of sponge in the orange gateau?'

'No, Chef.'

The chef turned back to Jason. 'And neither,' he said flatly, 'did I.'

The pale brown eyes met Jason's unflinchingly, challenging him to call him a liar.

'See if anyone else in here yesterday did so, if you please,' Jason said firmly.

'They wouldn't dare,' the chef said arrogantly, then nodded at Maurice, who hastily began doing the rounds of kitchen staff. It didn't take him long to come back with his answer.

'No, sir. No one touched the gateau,' he reported, half to the chef, half to Jason.

'I told you,' Rory snorted. 'The waiters and waitresses have nothing to do with the food except to serve it, and apart from myself, Maurice and two sous chefs, nobody prepares the food. What's more, any nuts and nut products used in my recipes are kept in a locked cupboard in the pantry over there, separate from other food.'

Jason sighed heavily. This was not looking good. Not good at all. He looked around the kitchen helplessly. How many people had mucked around in here since last night? He could count twelve at this moment. And that didn't even take into account the forensic evidence that might have been obliterated whilst breakfast was being made. Hell, what hope could forensics have in here now? But there was no use crying over spilt milk. 'I want you to take me through the preparations of the gateau yesterday. Exactly what you did, when and where,' he said to Rory.

The chef sighed hugely. 'Can't this wait? We're still serving breakfast out there.' He waved a hand around the kitchen, where the staff had carried on working throughout their talk, albeit with ears straining.

'No, it can't wait,' Jason snapped. 'When did you make the mix for the sponges?'

And so the chef gave Jason his recipe for orange gateau and a complex and full cooking lesson in the process. When he had finished, Jason was convinced that no peanut glaze could have been made and added by mistake. The chef was clearly both well organized and meticulous in his work. And, apart from anything else, he was sure that Rory Blundell was the kind of man who was always aware of every little thing that went on in his kitchen, so the chances of a mistake being made seemed minimal. He also seemed to treat the serving staff as a lower form of life, and if one of them had been seen tampering with his creation, all hell would undoubtedly have been let loose.

Which meant . . . what? That someone from outside must have done it. But how? And, more importantly, who knew about Celia Gordon's allergy? And how did they know she would choose to eat from that cake, given the vast array of desserts that had apparently been on offer?

'Did you let the sponges cool before adding the fillings?' It was Flora who interrupted the thoughtful silence that followed this demonstration.

92

Rory shot her a caustic look. 'Of course.'

'So where did you put them to cool?' she asked, unfazed.

'On the cooling trays in the workspace room.' He indicated the room around the other side of the dogleg. Quickly, they all trooped back there.

And Jason saw at once how easily it might have been done. He glanced at Flora, who nodded.

The big kitchen itself was a hive of activity, with people coming and going through the double doors as waiters and waitresses served breakfast in the dining hall. But here, in the smaller room, somebody could easily have slipped in and worked unseen. The dogleg made it a distinct blind spot from the main kitchen itself, and there were plenty of cupboards to duck into or hide behind if necessary.

'And the sponges were left to cool in here . . . when?' Jason asked, checking his notes.

The chef shrugged. 'I baked them late yesterday morning — sponges need to be fresh. I left them in here around eleven-thirty, I guess, and I didn't start to construct the gateau itself until nearly . . .' he gave it some thought, 'three-thirty? I like the finished articles to be refrigerated for a few hours. It helps things set, and it improves the flavour of the Cointreau liqueur I use to make the cream.'

Jason ignored all the culinary tips. 'So, between eleven-thirty and three-thirty, anyone could have come in,' he looked around and located a second entrance to the room, 'that door there, and added a peanut glaze to one of the sponges? And no one working in the kitchens need necessarily have known about it?'

Flora walked to the door in question and looked out. 'There's a small corridor that must lead back to the main hall, sir,' she said. 'I can hear the woman on reception talking on the phone.'

Jason nodded. OK. So how hard would it be for a guest to explore and learn the layout of the kitchen? Not hard, surely? 'Would the Cointreau cream disguise the taste of the peanuts?' he asked, then added wryly, 'from anyone, that is, who didn't have your superbly well-trained palate?'

The chef considered, then nodded. 'Yes. Probably.'

It's looking more and more like murder, Jason thought grimly. And once again he remembered the hard, sharp, almost fearful voice of Monica Noble as she'd asked him what he was doing here. He was beginning not to like this setup. Not like it at all.

He nodded at the chef and left the kitchens, walking slowly down the corridor and out into the hall. There he paused, thinking hard.

'Sir,' Flora said urgently. Jason knew that she wanted action, and understood her keenness. Murder investigations were always more exciting than death by misadventure.

'Call in the team,' Jason said heavily. 'Get those samples off to the lab, and tell the chief we're going to need help. There's something upwards of fifty-odd people at this conference, and we're going to have to interview them all.'

'Sir,' Flora said, and sprinted back to the car to use the radio.

Aware of the noise level coming from the long set of French windows to his right, he glanced briefly into the crowded dining hall, feeling his spirits sag. So many people! And one of them must have wanted Celia Gordon dead.

He withdrew, trying to get a handle on how best to tackle the logistics of the thing. He saw that the lounge door was partly open, and through it, glimpsed a pair of lovely legs that he instantly recognized. He walked quickly forward and pushed on through. Monica and Graham Noble looked up from their armchairs, arranged around a low coffee table. Graham rose to his feet. 'Chief Inspector,' he said amiably.

'Reverend Noble,' Jason said.

'Graham, please.'

'Graham,' Jason repeated, not at all sure that he wanted to call the man Graham. He had a nasty feeling that he was going to need to keep himself as aloof as possible from the

Nobles whilst investigating this particular case. 'Are you a guest here?' he asked, trying to get a picture of the setup. Surely the Nobles hadn't moved out of their flat in the village?

Quickly, Graham filled him in on what he was doing there. 'So you were here all day yesterday?' Jason asked promptly.

Remembering how useful an eyewitness the vicar had proved to be in the past, he was aware of a certain amount of relief. If he could get a solid grasp of the background before the main thrust of the investigation began, he'd at least have some sort of a starting point.

Because this was a very curious case of murder — if murder it was. A peanut for a murder weapon! A cake as a means of death. And a killing that took place under the noses of fifty-odd Church people. The media were going to have a field day. He could almost picture his chief superintendent holding his head in his hands and groaning.

'Everyone's on their way, sir,' Flora had returned from the car just in time to see her boss disappearing into the lounge. The samples were locked in the car awaiting collection, and she was not best pleased to note the room's only other occupants.

She smiled briefly at Graham Noble. 'Reverend,' she acknowledged, and, her tone dropping several degrees, added, 'Mrs Noble.'

'Hello, Sergeant Glenn,' Monica mumbled. 'Jason, what's going on?' she blurted the same question again.

Jason, of course, had no intention of telling her. 'Perhaps, Reverend Noble, you can go through yesterday's timetable with me. Just to give me a general idea of what's what?'

Graham took a moment to arrange his thoughts and did his best. 'Well, I arrived here in time for lunch,' he began, and went on to describe the lunch, the impromptu lecture Dr Grade had given some of them about the manuscript afterwards, and then about his meeting Celia again. At this point, Jason interrupted him.

'You knew Reverend Gordon personally, Reverend Noble?' he asked, something sharp and surprised in his voice making Monica, who'd been watching her husband fondly, glance sharply up at the policeman.

'A long time ago, Chief Inspector,' Graham said calmly. 'It must have been . . . a good twenty-five years I should think, since I last saw her. That was when I'd been sent to a parish up north. Yesterday was the first time I'd seen her since.'

Jason felt, for some strange reason, relieved. 'I see,' he said. 'Carry on. What then?'

'Then it was time for my lecture. I was nervous.' Graham briefly described it. 'It seemed to go well. Then I went home. Monica and I changed for dinner at about seven, and then walked back here.'

Monica had sat very still throughout this recital with her eyes cast down. Obviously, he'd forgotten that he had had a bag of peanuts with him just before the lecture, and wondered, suddenly, what had become of it. Graham, oblivious to her worried thoughts, was now describing the dinner to Jason, trying to remember anything of importance, but failing. 'Really, it was just the usual dinner chit-chat,' he apologized. 'And then, during dessert, Celia just suddenly . . . collapsed. Without any warning.'

Jason nodded. 'I know this isn't going to be pleasant, but can you describe exactly what happened?'

Graham took a deep breath and did so, tight-lipped, his eyes looking haunted. 'Then the party broke up — well, naturally it would,' he concluded grimly. 'A lot of the others went to the bar, no doubt in need of a stiff drink, but Monica wanted to go home, so we did. My bishop called me in the early hours to tell me that Celia was dead,' he finished.

'And do you know of anyone with a grudge against Reverend Gordon?'

'Really, I couldn't say, Chief Inspector. Her parish was in Bath, I believe. You'd be better off speaking to the people down there about that.'

Jason nodded. 'We'll certainly be doing that,' he agreed. 'But was there anybody here at the conference that she spoke of in particular? Did she mention anybody that she was having trouble with?'

'Not to me, no,' Graham said cautiously. 'But then, apart from the short conversation just before the lecture and one or two words over dinner, I never really spoke to her,' Graham said firmly.

Flora lifted her head at that. There seemed to be something more in the vicar's voice than the words themselves called for. And, she noticed with a quickening of interest, Graham Noble was looking not at Jason as he spoke, but at his wife.

Jason, too, picked up on the hidden tension, but couldn't quite place it.

Monica, distracted, was still thinking nervously about peanuts. About Celia being allergic to them. And about her husband eating peanuts and offering them around during the impromptu talk about the manuscript. She opened her mouth to tell Jason about this, then caught Flora Glenn's eagle eye on her and for some reason the words died in her throat. Later, she thought guiltily. When he's alone. I'll tell him about it then.

'I see. And what can you tell me about any of the others at the conference?' Jason probed relentlessly.

'I don't know anyone here, really, apart from my own bishop — Dr Carew. I know Bishop Arthur Bryce by reputation. But that's really all,' Graham answered, and shrugged helplessly.

No help there then, Jason thought sourly. And with so many important personages about, they were going to have to tread carefully. He himself would take all the 'notables' and leave the others to the uniformed teams. At least for the preliminary interviews. But damn it, why did a vicar get murdered at a conference of other vicars? It didn't make sense. He wouldn't have thought that clerics were the murdering sort. Well, not in this century, anyway.

'Did you know that Celia Gordon was allergic to peanuts, sir?' Flora asked abruptly.

Graham blinked and looked at her guilelessly. 'No. I'd no idea,' he said truthfully.

Jason smiled, a mere tug of the lips, but Flora saw it and looked away mutinously.

'Sir Andrew Courtenay owns this place, doesn't he?' Jason judged it wise to try another tack.

'Yes,' Graham said. 'He's done a splendid job of it too. When he inherited the manor from his father, it was going downhill fast. But he's managed to make it pay for itself in a remarkably short time.'

'And did the village a big favour in doing so,' Monica put in, a note of warning in her voice. 'He's the biggest employer around here and he subsidizes the shop.'

Jason nodded. He understood the warning all right, but he had no intention of stepping on the squire's toes unless it became necessary. 'I see. I'll need to speak to him at some point.'

'Please be careful,' Monica said quickly, then catching his curious look, sighed heavily.

'He lost his only child, a daughter, just this February,' she said sadly. 'In rather . . . tragic . . . circumstances. He's still very fragile at the moment.'

Jason nodded with sudden comprehension. So that's why the chef had dealt with everything himself this morning, and didn't pass the buck. Obviously his staff were still trying to shield Sir Andrew as much as possible. It spoke well of the man. Obviously he was well liked.

'In that case, we'll see him first and get it over with,' he said. 'And don't worry,' he added, catching Monica's anxious eye. 'I'll keep it brief and to the point.'

CHAPTER 8

It was, in fact, over an hour later before Jason eventually met the hotel owner. During that time, reinforcements had arrived, together with technicians, and he'd been busy deploying his people. With the permission of the undermanager, a harassed individual answering to the name of Geoff Banks, the lounge had been set up as the resident 'incident' room. The food samples had been sent off to the labs, and he'd explained to forensics about the problem with the kitchen.

With breakfast now served to all the guests, the chef had reluctantly cleared the room to make way for the scientific men in white overalls, and several of the conference-goers were wondering why the waiters and kitchen staff were now grouped together on the lawns. Jason was relieved when they all trooped off to the local church for the Sunday morning service. As far as he knew, no formal announcement had yet been made about the police presence or Celia Gordon's death, although he wouldn't be surprised if both circumstances weren't already common knowledge.

Bad news had a way of travelling fast, even in such saintly circles.

So it was well after ten when, with the desks and equipment set up in the lounge, Sir Andrew Courtenay was shown in. Jason glanced at Flora, who'd gone to fetch him, and saw her frowning slightly. He wondered briefly what had bothered her.

Jason rose. 'Sir Andrew, I'm Chief Inspector Jason Dury. I'm sorry to have to commandeer your lounge like this, but your undermanager assured me that it would be all right.'

Sir Andrew waved a hand in a vague conciliatory gesture. Jason had been half expecting this man to come blustering in and demanding explanations all morning. After all, no businessman liked the police on their premises. But now that he was face to face with the man, Jason wasn't quite as surprised any more. Although the thickset squire was dressed in well-cut slacks, a polo shirt and expensive-looking sports jacket, his face was haggard and pale. The big brown eyes looked flat and dull, and as he took a seat Jason noticed that his hands were trembling visibly. He looked exhausted, and as tense as piano wire.

Flora took a seat at a right angle to her boss and took out a notebook and pen.

'I just need to ask a few questions, Sir Andrew,' Jason began gently. 'I'm sure you've heard by now of Reverend Gordon's death?'

Sir Andrew stiffened and his face tightened. He nodded once, briefly. So far he had yet to utter a single syllable, and Jason wondered if Monica Noble hadn't underestimated the man's condition. Even to someone like himself, with only a layman's limited understanding of psychology, the squire looked like a man on the verge of a breakdown.

'I've been told you have suffered a family loss recently,' Jason began delicately. 'I don't want to add to your burdens, Sir Andrew, so I won't keep you long.'

Sir Andrew shrugged. He was staring at a point midway on the oriental carpet and his hands, which were resting on his lap, twitched spasmodically.

'My daughter,' Sir Andrew suddenly spoke. 'She married a bastard. A drug dealer.'

Flora shifted in her seat and shot her boss a quick, excited look, clearly urging him to follow up on this interesting titbit, but seeing his warning look in response, she bit her lip and subsided.

'Bastard got her hooked on drugs,' Sir Andrew carried on, in a curious, emotionless monotone. 'Then he got hold of what they call a "bad batch." They both died. The neighbours alerted the police and they found them dead in bed.'

Jason sighed heavily. Even here, in this pleasant corner of rural England, the blight of drugs had reached in and wrought its usual havoc. It made him feel helpless and angry.

'I told her not to marry him. I even disinherited her, but it wasn't any good. His family had money too, you see.' Sir Andrew raised his eyes from the carpet long enough to look at the blond chief inspector, then dropped them again. 'They kept giving him money, so of course, he kept buying the stuff. Bastard.'

Flora turned a page in her notebook.

'I'm sorry to hear that,' Jason said gently. 'Now, about the conference, Sir Andrew,' he said more firmly, getting back to the matter in hand. 'Do you have a list of those attending?'

Sir Andrew nodded. 'Office,' he said briefly. 'Geoff will give you a copy.'

Jason nodded. 'Thank you. That'll be most helpful. Your business here is a successful one, Sir Andrew?' he asked, more to ease the man into the questioning rather than anything else. Already a full background check was being run on the conference centre as a matter of routine.

'Yes,' he replied simply.

'And this particular conference was booked when exactly? And by whom?'

The next ten minutes were taken up with details about how the conference came about, who the organizer was, and how the conference centre was run day to day.

'Thank you, that's all very clear. I don't suppose you know how the guest list was arrived at?' Jason asked, but Sir Andrew shook his head.

'No idea. You'd better ask David that — David Carew, the local bishop.'

Jason nodded. 'Now, sir, can you tell me anything about Reverend Gordon?'

Sir Andrew blinked. Once, then twice. Then he said heavily, 'No. I didn't know her.'

It struck Jason, for some unknown reason, as a strange kind of answer. It seemed oddly evasive. And yet why he should have thought so, he couldn't say. It was a simple enough statement.

'I see. Did you notice her arguing with anyone whilst she was here?' he prodded.

For a second, the big brown eyes flickered and his wide shoulders tensed. Flora, as alert to body language as her boss, leaned forward expectantly, her pencil poised, obviously anticipating an affirmative answer. So it surprised them both when Sir Andrew shook his large, brownish-red head and said, 'No,' rather flatly.

And Jason was certain this time that the man was lying. But he was experienced enough to know that there could be several explanations for this, ranging from the fact that he might feel too tired and ill to want to get involved, to a businessman's reluctance to start telling tales on his guests. He decided, for the moment, to let it pass. He could always come back to it later, if need be.

'I see. And you weren't present at the dinner when the reverend collapsed?'

'No, not at that one, although I was in the building. The dinner I actually attended was on the first day of the conference. On Friday.'

Jason frowned, unsure how to continue. Sir Andrew seemed to be willing enough to answer questions, but he was also being singularly unhelpful. As if determined to say the bare minimum. Also he looked so damned fragile. Jason could almost smell the pain and grief emanating from the man, and he had the feeling that Sir Andrew's loss, even now, was like a fresh wound for him, rather than a healing one.

'Were you aware if any of the other guests knew that Celia Gordon was coming to this conference, Sir Andrew?' he tried another tack.

The squire shook his head. 'I wouldn't know. I table-hop from time to time, pass the time of day with guests and talk about the gardens and that sort of thing, but I don't get chatty with them. They're usually attending workshops or lectures anyway.'

It was the longest speech he'd made so far, and it seemed to exhaust him. He gave the odd impression of shrinking right in front of their eyes. And Jason was only human. He didn't like feeling as if he were badgering someone who so obviously had no reserves of strength or energy left with which to fight back. He was also aware of what a nightmare it could become if a suspect or a witness were to fall ill, or even worse, die, whilst in police custody or under police questioning. Common sense told him now wasn't the time to push things.

'Well, you've been very helpful,' he said, standing up and watching the other man rise wearily to his feet. 'Just one thing before you go, Sir Andrew, if you don't mind,' he added, before the squire could start for the door. 'Did you know that Reverend Gordon had a fatal allergy to peanuts?'

Sir Andrew looked at him blankly. 'No,' he said dully. Jason nodded and watched him go. At the door, he passed through without looking back.

Flora let loose a long, tremulous sigh. 'Poor sod,' she said succinctly.

Jason nodded and slowly sat down again. 'Where was he when you found him?'

'In his study, sir. He'd been there since about eight this morning, according to the undermanager. Funny, you'd have thought he'd have come to see what all the fuss was about,' she echoed his thoughts of earlier.

'Perhaps he didn't know,' Jason mused. 'Perhaps Geoff Banks didn't even tell him that the police were here. The chef didn't. I think his staff have been shielding him from unpleasantness for some time now.'

'Hmm,' Flora mused. 'You can see why they want to protect him though, can't you?' she agreed grimly. 'That chap needs a good grief counsellor if you ask me.'

A knock came at the door and a constable stuck his head around it. 'Forensics are finished in the kitchen, sir. They said it was more or less hopeless. Too much stuff, too many staff.'

Jason nodded. He hadn't expected anything else really. 'OK, get a list of the conference-goers from Geoff Banks, and then get Harrington to set up a roster of interviews.'

'Sir,' the man said smartly. 'Oh, and Dr Carew is outside, wonders if he could have a quick word.'

Jason nodded. 'He's just the man I want next anyway,' he said, and to Flora he added, 'Perhaps he can shed some light on how the guest list was set up. We need to try and find out if this crime was properly premeditated, or if someone was just winging it.'

Dr David Carew, Graham Noble's boss, entered just then. A lean man with dark hair and eyes, he looked a bit like you'd expect a country solicitor to look. He was dressed in a simple black suit and dog collar. And in the following ten minutes he told Jason all that he would ever want to know about how an ecclesiastical conference was arranged.

'So, apart from a couple of specific invitations, mostly the guest speakers, it was more or less a free-for-all,' Jason concluded when the cleric had finished speaking.

'Yes,' the bishop acknowledged, 'Otherwise, the conference was simply advertised through all the usual channels, and anybody wanting to come came.'

'And is fifty-two a high number of attendees?'

'About average, I'd say.'

Jason sighed. 'So there was nothing significantly different about this year's conference in any way?'

'Nothing,' Dr Carew said firmly.

'You didn't get any strange requests or letters from candidates that mentioned Reverend Gordon specifically? Say, wanting to know if she'd be here?'

'No. Nothing of that kind.'

'And Graham Noble is here because it's in his back yard, so to speak?' Jason persisted.

The bishop smiled and nodded. 'As you say.'

'Did you know he and Celia Gordon were old friends?' Jason asked sharply, hoping to catch him out, and indeed a look of astonishment crossed the bishop's face.

'No. No, I didn't know that,' Dr Carew said quietly. 'I'll have to talk to him after he's finished giving the Sunday service.'

But what he had to talk to him about, the bishop didn't say. Jason nodded and looked at his watch. The other guests should be back soon. As clerics, every single one of the conference-goers would have gone to the church service, and he'd bet Graham Noble had never had his church so full before.

'Now, Dr Carew, if you can just tell me your own impressions of dinner last night.'

It took about twenty minutes for Dr Carew to go through his own eyewitness account, by which time the conference-goers were back and wondering why they'd been banned from the lounge. The bar was open, however, although not serving alcoholic drinks yet, and several large groups had taken to the grounds. Jason wasn't worried. His next task was to get the rounds of interviews started. As Flora showed the bishop out, he could only hope that *someone* would be able to give them a lead. So far, they had spectacularly little to go on.

'We'd better take all the bigwigs ourselves, I suppose,' Jason said, knowing his chief constable would expect him to proceed with tact with a capital 'T'.

Flora smiled in sympathy.

'Dr Carew seemed to pick out several names as "worthies,"' he noted, marking them out on the list. 'Find Harrington and tell him we'll take those I've ticked.' He handed the list to his sergeant. 'And let's start with Bishop Arthur Bryce.'

* * *

Never had Jason met a man who could talk so much and say so little.

Arthur Bryce came in, conservatively dressed in grey slacks, white shirt and maroon cardigan. His hair was neatly combed and Jason didn't need Flora's gaze of open admiration to realise that here was a man who was very attractive to the opposite sex and one who possessed more than his fair share of charm. But, a quarter of an hour later, the chief inspector had come to the conclusion that, for all his smooth and expansive talk, Bishop Arthur Bryce was doing a remarkably good impression of the three wise monkeys.

'So you don't remember any incident involving Reverend Gordon that struck you as at all unusual?' Jason persisted, going over the same ground again and again in a bid to get the man to say something, *anything* useful. He simply couldn't believe that things had been as normal and nondescript as this man would have him believe. After all, a woman was dead.

'No, Chief Inspector, I'm afraid not.'

Jason looked the man in the eye — a pair of very level green eyes — and sighed. He consulted the floor plan that Geoff Banks had given him, with all the delegates' names clearly marked. 'And you were staying in the east wing, and Dr Gordon . . .' he sighed, 'was in the opposite wing?'

For some strange reason, the man's confident smile seemed to waver for just an instant. 'I can't quite see what that has to do with anything, Chief Inspector,' Arthur murmured, his voice still pleasant and amiable, but at last sounding something other than well rehearsed.

Jason's eyes narrowed. He hadn't, in fact, meant anything by it at all, but had merely consulted the room allocations for another angle to try. But he'd obviously hit some kind of nerve in the man — at last — but what? Celia Gordon hadn't died in her room, but at dinner (well, in the hospital, to be strictly accurate). But she'd taken the fatal bite of gateau in full view of everyone. So why had Jason's interest in room allocations given Arthur Bryce sudden cause for concern?

'Did you know Reverend Gordon before coming here, sir?' Jason had a vague idea that a bishop, according to the rules of protocol, should be referred to as 'Your Grace' or some such nonsense, but he was damned if he was going to do that. Especially with this man.

Arthur spread his hands in a fulsome gesture. 'I knew of her, a little,' he admitted. 'I understood that she'd just been offered a deacon's position, which would have been a considerable step up the ladder for her.'

Jason's eyes glittered. Something at last? 'I see. And was anybody else in line for this promotion?'

Was it his imagination, or were Arthur's cat-green eyes suddenly laughing at him? 'Well, no one who's here now at the conference, Chief Inspector, at any rate. Her diocese is . . . was, in Bath. I don't think there's anyone here from there. Though Reverend Fortescue is from Bristol, I believe,' he added. 'Which is quite close.'

And there it was again. He was saying a lot, but telling him nothing. 'I see,' Jason gritted, determined to keep his temper. 'Was there any ill feeling surrounding Reverend Gordon at all?' he asked.

Arthur hesitated for the first time since entering the room. He saw the two police officers fasten their gaze on him, and smiled reluctantly.

'Well, I don't think it's any secret that Sir Matthew Pierrepont was not a Celia Gordon fan,' he said dryly. 'But really, is all this . . . fuss quite necessary? Surely Celia's death was an accident?'

Jason's eyes sharpened. 'Accident?' he repeated coolly. 'Why do you say that? I was under the impression everyone here thought that she'd died of a heart attack.'

Arthur flushed in obvious chagrin at having made such a basic mistake, then smiled ruefully. 'But there are two things against that, aren't there?' the bishop from Yorkshire said softly, and again spread his hands in a we're-all-friends-together gesture. 'I've seen someone suffer a heart attack before, Chief Inspector, and it was nothing like . . . what Celia endured. A heart attack means chest pains, mainly. But Celia was having fits. And her breathing . . .' Arthur shuddered. 'No, I was always sure that it wasn't a heart attack.'

'And the other thing, sir?' Jason asked silkily. And seeing the bishop frown in puzzlement, prompted, 'You said there were two things against it being a heart attack.'

Arthur shrugged. 'Well, obviously, Chief Inspector, your presence here and the presence of all the other officers would indicate . . .' he trailed off and shrugged eloquently.

It was like trying to pin down a snake, Jason thought, with a real sense of distaste.

'And what, exactly, had the archdeacon against Celia Gordon?' he asked crisply.

But Arthur shook his head. 'Oh, I wouldn't know specifically,' he demurred. 'You'd have to ask Matthew that.'

Jason sighed. This was getting him nowhere. 'Well, thank you for all your help,' he lied, smiling like a crocodile. It didn't improve his temper to see Flora leap eagerly to her feet to see him out. When she looked back at her superior from the door, her face became instantly serious.

'Remember he's a bishop,' Jason said laconically. 'And married, I believe.'

Flora flushed, then smiled reluctantly. 'Well, he is very attractive, sir,' she pointed out.

Jason smiled back. Then frowned. 'Did you notice how he reacted when I mentioned the sleeping arrangements?'

Flora nodded, a shade reluctantly, Jason thought. 'The archdeacon next, sir?' she hazarded, and Jason nodded.

'Oh yes. I think we want to see the archdeacon next. So far he's the only person we know of who seems to have had any kind of feeling for our departed reverend one way or another.'

* * *

And that feeling was one of intense hatred, as they soon found out.

The man Flora returned with was so nearly a perfect caricature of an aged cleric that for a moment as he watched the old, incredibly thin and stooped figure shuffle in, Jason wondered if some cosmic force wasn't taking the mickey out of him.

Sir Matthew was wearing an extremely old black suit that was also wrinkled and stained. He had a mass of messy white hair and vast white caterpillars for eyebrows. As he sat down, he withdrew a pipe from one pocket, and without asking lit it up. Flora silently got up and opened a window. The archdeacon shot her a dirty look. It was surprisingly malevolent, and took both Jason and Flora by surprise. Apart from really hardened criminals, hardly anyone ever looked at a police officer like that.

'You're Sir Matthew Pierrepont?' Jason snapped, bringing the old man's head swivelling his way. Her boss's obvious anger on her behalf made Flora glow, just a little.

'That's right,' Sir Matthew assented, puffing on the pipe, which gave out a rather nice, mellow scent of tobacco. To Flora's intense annoyance, she found she rather liked the smell.

'What can you tell me about Reverend Celia Gordon's death?' Jason shot out, deciding that tact was going to be lost on this man.

'Apart from the fact that it couldn't have happened to a better wench, nothing,' Sir Matthew shot back.

Flora's pencil flew abruptly across the page. For a long moment, Jason stared at the man in disbelief, then slowly relaxed. Well, they were going to get something at last, although quite what, he had no idea.

'Oh? How so?' he asked mildly.

Sir Matthew smiled, a singularly nasty smile. 'Celia Gordon was a menace,' Sir Matthew said succinctly. 'Like all females in the Church.'

Flora bit her lip. Hard. She kept her eyes on the notepad, but Jason noticed her knuckles turning white. She knew better than to interrupt, of course, but he knew what the effort was costing her.

'Is that all?' Jason drawled, sounding so bored that it goaded the old man perfectly.

Beautifully, like a trout to the fly, Sir Matthew rose to the bait. 'No, sir, damn it, it isn't. She was *ambitious*.' He said the word as if it were a dirty one. 'How she got that position in Bath I'll never know.'

'It was a good appointment, was it?' Jason kept his voice mildly polite and barely interested, knowing that it would only serve to egg the old man on. Not that it would need much, Jason understood. Never had he met someone so keen to vent their spleen as this man.

'A plum!' Sir Matthew snorted. 'There were at least five good men who'd been in the calling far longer than that upstart in skirts, and any one of them would have been more worthy of the position. I wouldn't be surprised if she didn't—' Sir Matthew suddenly broke off, and then snorted. 'Oh well.' He took a long drag on his pipe.

Flora almost laughed. She had no difficulty in guessing what Sir Matthew had been about to say. It was the same thing that most men of his type said about women who got on in life — that they must have slept their way to the top. Except in this case he hadn't been able to say so in so many words, because it would have meant that Reverend Gordon had seduced members of the Church of England's synod!

Jason also let it pass. 'I understand from Bishop Bryce that she was about to get a deaconship,' he said instead.

Sir Matthew went alarmingly white. He shot upright in his chair. 'The devil she was!' he all but roared. It was a strange sound, since his voice was an old man's voice, cracked and raspy. Rage didn't suit it.

'You didn't know?' Jason smiled charmingly.

Matthew subsided, his mind working so furiously they could almost hear the wheels turning in his brain. Jason shot his sergeant an amused look. 'No,' Sir Matthew finally admitted, grudgingly. 'I hadn't heard that yet.'

In other words, nobody had told him, Jason correctly interpreted. And with a man like this, he could understand how that would rankle.

'Do you know of anyone else with a grudge against Reverend Gordon?' Jason asked, and saw a crafty, knowing look creep plainly across the old man's face. It couldn't have been more obvious if he'd written his knowledge on his forehead in felt-tip pen.

'No, I don't,' Sir Matthew said quickly.

'You're lying,' Jason shot back.

Sir Matthew's eyes flared. 'Don't you dare call me a liar, young man,' he roared, again in that cracked voice. His old face flushed with humiliated anger. He wasn't used to being spoken to like this, and it showed.

Jason, not impressed, slowly scratched his chin. And Sir Matthew was about to learn what many other people had already learned, and much to their cost — namely that Jason Dury was a man of infinite craft.

'Don't they call the devil the father of all lies, Archdeacon?' he asked mildly. 'I've always wondered why that was. After all, there are such bigger sins, aren't there? Murder, theft, adultery. Why don't they call him the father of all murderers, or thieves? Why does your church single out lies as the worst of all things to call Satan?' he asked mildly.

Sir Matthew's eyes were bulging by now, and Jason, in a sudden flash of understanding, realised what had been niggling away at him about the old man for some minutes now.

He was going senile.

'You want to talk about sins?' he hissed, leaning forward, the parchment-dry skin of his face and hands giving him an eerie, reptilian look. 'You ought to find out about her,' he spat. His eyes were glittering now, and a fine trail of saliva slid from one corner of his mouth. Flora looked hastily away, a grimace of distaste contorting her pretty features.

'You mean Reverend Gordon?' Jason prompted.

Sir Matthew laughed. It was a hate-filled cackle that sent the hackles on Flora's back standing to attention. 'Who else? You found out what she died of yet?' he suddenly barked.

Jason instantly became cautious. 'And what if we had?'

'Whatever you found out, you're wrong,' he said, confusing them utterly. 'She died because she deserved to,' he stated, nodding his head vigorously. 'It was retribution for her sins. You see if I'm not right.' And with that the old man stood up and marched to the door.

'Sir Matthew, I've not finished with you yet,' Jason said sharply, getting to his feet.

'No, young man, but I've finished with you,' Sir Matthew tossed magnificently over his shoulder. 'Anything else you want to say to me from now on, you can say with my solicitor present.'

On that note, he yanked open the door and strode through. He'd probably not moved so fast, or so fluidly, for years.

'Bloody hell!' Flora said, on a half-whispered, awestruck breath as the door slammed shut behind him. Jason burst out laughing. He couldn't help it. And Flora also, after a surprised moment, began to chuckle. 'But seriously, sir, the old man's as nutty as a Toblerone,' she finally said.

'I rather think it's more a case of senility,' Jason corrected her mildly.

'You think he did it?' she asked him, watching him closely. She had a great deal of respect for Jason's opinions.

'Oh I think he was capable of doing it, certainly,' Jason said slowly. In his own mind, he was sure that the old man was capable of almost anything. The question was, had he done it?

'Did you notice the look on his face when I asked him if he knew of anyone else who had something against her?' he asked thoughtfully.

Flora nodded. 'He had someone in mind all right,' she agreed.

'So we know that he's not the only one who wasn't a fan of the victim, don't we?' Jason pointed out. 'But we're never going to get him to say who.'

Flora sighed in agreement. 'Who next?'

Jason rubbed his chin thoughtfully. 'Flora, get someone down to the shop and pub. I want to know if any strangers bought any packets of peanuts since, say, Thursday.'

'You don't think we're looking for a local then?' Flora asked, already nodding her head. It made sense — Celia was a long way from home. She'd hardly have had time to make any enemies in Heyford Bassett. 'I'll send Carpenter, sir,' she said.

'And when you've done that send in Bishop Bryce's wife.' Jason was rather interested to meet the woman who'd married a man like Arthur Bryce.

CHAPTER 9

Chloe Bryce came as a distinct shock to both of them, which probably said more about their prejudices than about her. Jason, expecting to see a motherly, untidy and kind woman, instead looked up to see a slender, chic lady with a cap of elegant black hair, dressed in a lilac suit with a cream blouse. Long amethyst drop earrings and a diamond-and-amethyst bracelet flashed in the sunlight. She wore smart grey shoes with a definite heel. Her make-up was light, but perfect.

She would have looked at home on a catwalk — either as a designer or a model.

'Mrs Bryce, thank you for coming,' Jason said politely, rising to his feet and rapidly revising his expectations. So this was Arthur Bryce's wife. Somehow they didn't fit. Or fit too precisely. He couldn't say for the moment which it was.

'Not at all, er . . . ?'

Feeling abruptly gauche, Jason deliberately smiled the most charming smile in his repertoire. 'Chief Inspector Dury, ma'am,' he said.

Chloe's eyes flickered briefly over the unexpectedly good-looking policeman, noting both the charm and the confidence with some surprise. A wary look crept into her dark eyes, but she smiled as she took the seat offered. 'I'm not at all sure that I can be of much help, Chief Inspector,' Chloe said deprecatingly. 'I didn't know Reverend Gordon at all well.'

'Perhaps not, but it's surprising the amount of things that you can pick up about people, even if you've only been around them for a short time,' Jason said. 'For instance, when you think of Reverend Gordon what's the first thing that comes into your mind?'

Chloe crossed her slender legs and sighed. 'Well, the fact that she didn't seem to be very popular, I suppose,' she admitted with seemingly genuine reluctance. 'That is, nobody . . . well . . . liked her much. Which is surprising, really, when you think that churchmen usually get on with everyone. It is, after all, their job to do so, isn't it?'

Jason nodded, and glanced at Flora. She was busy scribbling away in shorthand and seemed unaware of any vibes. But Jason was getting them, strong and sure. For all her elegance and charm, he sensed something very brittle about this woman. He felt if he were to press in just the wrong spot, she might shatter into a thousand pieces. And she had the most cautious eyes he'd ever seen. Yes, there was definitely something going on under the surface here.

'I see, yes,' Jason mused. 'Do you think Reverend Gordon was aware of her . . . unpopularity?'

'Oh, I'm sure of it,' Chloe laughed lightly. 'She just didn't mind.'

At that Flora did look up.

'You didn't like her either, Mrs Bryce?' Jason asked delicately.

Chloe met his eyes levelly. 'Not much, no, although as I said, I didn't really know her well,' she admitted. 'But then, I don't suppose that would have worried her either. She was very ambitious you know, and in the grand scheme of things, a bishop's wife from Barnsley would have been neither friend nor foe.'

Jason felt a slight tingling in his spine. Here, he felt at last, was a witness who might shed some unbiased light on their victim. She was obviously very intelligent, had an insight into the ecclesiastical world, and wasn't averse to stating her opinions clearly and concisely. He'd just have to be careful not to let her lead him up the garden path.

'So that's how it was?' Jason mused, none of his astuteness showing on his face. 'I understand Reverend Gordon was shortly to be promoted?'

Chloe raised one dark, plucked eyebrow. 'Really? It doesn't surprise me.' She sounded almost bored. But was that real or just a facade?

'We've just been speaking to Archdeacon Pierrepont,' Jason admitted. 'He's a very odd man, don't you think?'

Chloe smiled. 'Yes. If you were to be kind, you'd call him eccentric. There are, of course, many other words you could use to describe him that definitely aren't so kind. I suppose he told you about the big disagreement he had with her?'

'No,' Jason said quickly. 'When was this?'

'Oh, at the dinner on Friday night. He tried to start up his usual tirade against female clergy, but Reverend Gordon very neatly turned the tables on him. I'm not sure exactly what she said since Arthur and I were seated quite some distance away from her. But whatever it was, he certainly didn't like it.'

'Do you have even a vague idea what it was?' Jason pushed. 'An impression?'

Chloe gently pulled on one earlobe in an abstracted gesture, then sighed. 'She hinted at something . . . well . . . unsavoury in his past, I believe. It was quite awkward really — she made him look very foolish. Everyone at the table was embarrassed,' she said, rather in a rush, her hands refolding themselves genteelly in her lap.

And Jason could quite see why both Chloe Bryce the woman and Chloe Bryce the bishop's wife would find embarrassment to be a particularly horrific concept.

'I see. You're being very candid,' he said, and before she could comment on that, added quickly, 'You can't know how refreshing that is.' And again he smiled charmingly.

Chloe considered this for a moment, and then shrugged elegantly. 'Well, murder is murder,' she murmured humbly.

Flora's pencil jerked on the pad.

'Who said anything about murder, Mrs Bryce?' Jason asked silkily.

Chloe opened her bitter-chocolate eyes wider. 'Well, everyone's talking about it as murder. Isn't it?' she asked, seemingly guilelessly.

Jason smiled. 'Perhaps.'

'Well, in that case, it's our duty to help the police as much as possible, isn't it?' Chloe continued smoothly. 'It's not that I want to gossip or spy or report on my husband's colleagues, but there's also our duty to the truth to be considered. And of course, God sees everything and will judge accordingly.'

This sudden piece of piety took Jason by surprise, until he remembered that he was talking to a bishop's wife, after all. He'd almost begun to forget that the people he was dealing with had jobs like no other.

'I'm glad you see it that way,' Jason said, and meant it. He was beginning, for some reason, to dislike this woman almost as much as her husband, but he knew a good source of gossip when he saw it.

'I only hope . . . well, that you weigh all the evidence carefully,' Chloe again took him by surprise. 'I mean that you don't jump to conclusions,' she clarified, seeing his puzzlement. 'Take Sir Matthew for instance. Just because of what happened earlier this year, I hope you won't immediately assume that because he had one violent episode that he was responsible for another.'

Flora's pencil stopped, then started again.

Jason met the dark level eyes and smiled briefly. If she wanted to play games, he was more than willing to let her.

'I'm not sure I follow you, Mrs Bryce. What was it Sir Matthew did, exactly?'

Chloe immediately began to backpedal. 'Oh, I don't know the specifics, Chief Inspector, I assure you. I only heard

. . . well, one does hear things, of course. I believe there was some kind of incident at the beginning of the year involving a parishioner at his church. A woman, I believe.'

'And he attacked her?' Jason asked, wondering why he didn't have a report of the incident in his hand by now. The computers back at headquarters in Kidlington should have long since spewed out any past criminal records of the conference-goers.

'Oh, as to that I couldn't say,' Chloe said again. 'It was dealt with quietly by his bishop, naturally,' she explained with exquisite delicateness.

Jason felt a flash of anger rise in his gorge, but quickly forced himself to swallow it back down again. 'I see,' he gritted. Having police matters dealt with by anyone other than the police was anathema to him, as it was to all good coppers, and the thought that some bigwig had managed to prevent the course of justice didn't sit very well on his shoulders either. If a criminal assault had taken place then he damned well wanted it dealt with properly. Not covered up by a powerful private citizen pulling strings.

'Do you happen to know the name of the parishioner involved?' he asked calmly instead, no trace of his ire apparent on his face or in his voice.

'No, I'm sorry,' Chloe said sweetly.

And you wouldn't tell me even if you did, Jason thought to himself grimly. He smiled again. 'But the rumour was that it was a woman who was involved, and that Sir Matthew made some kind of violent overture towards her?' he persisted.

'Yes, it was something rather nasty, I believe. But as I said, I don't know the details,' Chloe confirmed, unruffled.

'And at dinner on Friday night, Celia Gordon threw this in his face?'

'Oh no, nothing so crude,' Chloe said quickly. 'I imagine she merely hinted at it. It was enough, at any rate, to stop Sir Matthew's usual bad-tempered tirade before it got started.' And she smiled, this time with obvious amusement.

'I see. Did you happen to see what Reverend Gordon ordered for dinner the night she died?'

'Oh no.'

'So you don't know which dessert she opted for?'

'Of course not. But I imagine if there was an orange choice on the menu that she took that.'

Jason felt himself tense and beside him Flora began to quiver like a pointer spotting a fallen grouse.

'Oh? What makes you say that?' he asked, very nonchalantly.

All along he'd been wondering how a killer could have known what dessert Celia Gordon would choose. It was the main stumbling block, in his own mind at least, of this being a proven case for murder at all, as opposed to some sort of accident, or death by misadventure.

'Oh, it was no secret that she loved oranges,' Chloe said, offhandedly. 'At breakfast yesterday she demanded second helpings of orange juice, then lectured some poor man on the benefits of vitamin C, and generally made a big song and dance about how much she loved the taste of them.'

Chloe, seemingly unaware of the bombshell that she'd just dropped, shrugged delicately. 'She had such a loud voice,' she added sadly. 'You couldn't help but hear all her opinions.'

Jason blinked. 'She said this at breakfast yesterday?'

'That's right.'

'How many people do you think heard her?'

Chloe laughed, a gentle, soothing sound that nevertheless managed to grate on his nerves. 'Oh, everyone in the dining hall I imagine. Like I said, she had a loud voice.'

'I see,' Jason said, and glanced at Flora. So the reverend was a big orange fan, was she? And they all knew it. He suddenly remembered that the waiter who'd served Celia Gordon at dinner last night had said that she'd even had the duck à l'orange for her main course.

Which seemed to confirm it.

So the killer knew of her preference for oranges. But how did he or she know of her fatal allergy to peanuts? Did someone have access to her medical records?

'Did you know Celia Gordon was allergic to peanuts?' he asked her, his voice suddenly sharp.

Chloe shook her head. 'No. I had no idea,' she said quietly.

'What else can you tell me about Reverend Gordon?' Jason asked after looking at her long and hard for a few seconds.

Chloe sighed and shrugged. 'Nothing really. Oh, only that she had made a decided play for the local vicar here. Not surprising, perhaps, since he is a very good-looking man, but then, he is married. And you'd have thought Celia would have more decorum, if not sense.'

'The local vicar?' Jason interrupted her sharply. 'You mean Graham Noble?'

Chloe nodded. 'Yes, I believe that's his name. He gave us a very good sermon this morning — really quite excellent. And of course I've listened to a few in my time.'

'Yes, yes,' Jason said impatiently. 'But are you saying . . . What exactly are you saying? About the reverends Noble and Gordon?'

'Oh, I'm sure it was nothing,' Chloe said hastily, in that relentlessly genteel voice of hers that was really beginning to get on Jason's nerves. 'It was just that yesterday afternoon, most of us were gathering in the hall. That funny little man who fainted gave us a talk about his manuscript — rather interesting, I thought. And then, well . . . again it was rather embarrassing, but Celia Gordon came down the stairs, gave this funny double take and called out a name . . . Graham, I believe it was, and made a beeline for this very good-looking man. He was listening to the lecture and offering around a bag of nuts. He looked, I have to say, rather disconcerted to see Reverend Gordon.'

Jason took a few seconds to let everything simply wash over him. 'A bag of nuts, you say?' he finally picked up on the most obvious prompt. 'Do you happen to know what kind of nuts?'

'Oh, peanuts I think,' Chloe said offhandedly. And very curiously made no comment on the coincidence of the policeman asking her if she knew that Celia was allergic to peanuts, and the fact that Graham Noble had had a packet of that very same nut on him earlier in the day. 'Anyway, she went up to him and all but draped herself around him. The poor man was very embarrassed, especially with his wife standing right there beside him, and looking, not surprisingly, quite put out.'

Jason jerked in his seat, very visibly. Beside him, Flora began to smirk.

'Mrs Noble was present at this time?' he asked, rather pompously.

'Well, yes, I assume it was she — a dark-haired, attractive woman, with rather nice blue eyes. You could tell that she was furious about it — not that I could blame her for that,' Chloe said with a sudden and very real bitterness. 'Celia Gordon was being quite blatant about flirting with her husband. Apparently she and Reverend Noble knew each other a long time ago. In fact, she hinted . . .'

'Yes,' Jason put in. 'What did she hint?'

But for once Chloe seemed reluctant to be drawn. 'Oh, I really couldn't say. I was standing some yards away, and there were a lot of people around, talking among themselves. I probably misheard. Or misunderstood.'

Jason brooded. Why hadn't Monica told him about that little scene? At least Graham Noble had mentioned it, but he'd certainly played it down. Jason wondered whether Chloe Bryce was to be believed anyway. And why had neither of them mentioned the bag of peanuts that Graham had apparently been offering around at the time? *If* it was a bag of peanuts. He wouldn't put it past Chloe Bryce to be lying about that.

But why?

'Which man fainted?' It was Flora who stepped into the sudden silence, her question making both the others look at her in some surprise. 'You said a man fainted,' Flora prompted. 'When was this?'

Chloe's frown abruptly cleared. 'Oh, him. Yes, it was the rather funny little man who brought the St Bede's manuscript. Dr Simon something. Grange? Grand? Something like that.

He runs the museum where the manuscript is usually kept, or so I understand.' Chloe spread her hands helplessly. 'He was invited to attend the dinner yesterday evening by Dr Carew, I imagine, who is such a nice man. Well, anyway, the poor thing fainted. The museum man, I mean, not Bishop Carew. Mind you, I'm not surprised. It was all very ghastly. Reverend Gordon . . .' Chloe went pale herself in remembrance, and shook her head. 'It was . . . hideous. I felt weak at the knees myself and quite sick. But it was Dr Grade, that's it, Dr Grade. He was the one who keeled over and fainted, poor man.'

Jason sighed. 'All right, tell me as much as you can remember about the dinner yesterday. Who sat where, what was said, anything at all that springs to mind.'

'Oh dear!' Chloe laughed. 'Where to start? Well, two of our party were deep into a discussion about birdlife, I know that. The missionary to Chad was telling a gruesome tale . . . Oh, no, wait a moment, that was at Friday night's dinner . . .'

And it was nearly half an hour before she'd finished. When she had, Jason and Flora had a much clearer idea of the social chit-chat that had gone on the previous night, but very little else. Flora gave her cramped hand a tired shake at the end, and looked back in bemusement at all the shorthand squiggling she'd made.

Jason could sympathize with her. If Chloe's husband was like the three wise monkeys, his wife was exactly the opposite. He wondered again whether it wasn't deliberate on her part.

She'd certainly given them a lot to go on, but the question was, again, why? Her own explanation, that it was her Christian duty to do so, he dismissed out of hand. Could it be, as she'd implied earlier, that because she was so totally uninvolved and unimportant to the inquiry, she felt free to give her opinions free rein? Could it be as simple as that? Or was she trying to lay false trails? And why had her husband been so jumpy when he'd mentioned the sleeping arrangements?

'Tell me, Mrs Bryce, have you ever been disturbed during the night?'

'I beg your pardon?' Chloe asked archly.

Jason, to his extreme annoyance, felt himself flushing, and could have kicked himself, or her. 'I mean, did you hear anything on either night that disturbed you. An argument perhaps. Someone creeping about. Anything of that nature?'

Chloe tossed her head. 'Certainly not,' she said primly. 'I'd have told you at once.'

And again, he knew he'd hit a nerve. For the first time since meeting her, she looked distinctly discomfited. He smiled. If nothing else, it made him feel better. 'Well, thank you very much for all your help. If we ever need to speak to you again . . . ?' he said smoothly.

'Oh, please,' Chloe said, and swinging her leg elegantly back onto the floor, she rose without a ripple and walked off, a tall, graceful figure in lilac. As the door closed behind her, a heavy silence fell.

'So,' Jason said at last, rousing himself and looking at his sergeant. 'What do you make of all that?'

Flora heaved a long sigh. 'Not sure, sir. That was a real blinder about Reverend Gordon loving oranges, wasn't it? And she certainly seemed to have it in for Sir Matthew.'

'Hmm, not that I'd read too much into that,' Jason said. 'If I were a woman I wouldn't mind dropping the old misogynist in it either.'

Flora grinned. 'No, sir. Mrs Bryce seemed to go out of her way to implicate Graham Noble, too, didn't she?' Flora knew she was treading on dangerous ground here and spoke carefully. Ever since that last murder where they'd come across the Nobles, Flora was uncomfortably aware that Jason seemed to find Monica Noble an admirable woman.

Jason grunted. 'Yes. Has the report from the local shop and pub come in yet?'

'I'll go and see, sir,' Flora said, glad to get out of the room for a little while. The atmosphere in there was becoming distinctly oppressive, and not for the first time Flora found herself thinking of Monica Noble with something less than fondness.

Jason slowly paced about the room, coming to stand in front of the windows that overlooked a rose garden and a pretty koi-carp-filled pond. Was he really going to have to regard Graham Noble, of all people, as a possible murder suspect? Technically, yes, of course he was. After all, no one was above suspicion. But in reality?

From all he knew of the man from their previous encounters, it was absurd. And would you really kill someone just because they'd embarrassed you in front of your wife? No. But what if Celia had been more determined to cause trouble in the Noble household than either of them had admitted? Would Graham kill to remove the threat to his marriage? Would he kill to keep Monica Noble?

Jason began to feel distinctly uncomfortable, not least because he felt that in Graham's position, he himself would do almost anything to keep her safe.

* * *

Lunch in the dining hall was a distinctly subdued affair. All morning they'd been answering questions put to them by fresh-faced policemen; those not yet interviewed knew that the afternoon would soon bring their turn. Nobody was quite able to meet anyone else's eye. There was a rumour going around that Celia Gordon had died because of her peanut allergy. Someone had heard one of the waiters talking with a waitress about peanuts in the gateau, and by now the story had done the rounds, and people were beginning to accept the theory as fact.

It was a terrible thing of course, but surely it had to have been an accident?

Nevertheless, the waiters reported back to the kitchens that the desserts, which consisted of apple pie, apricot crumble and blackcurrant cheesecake, were singularly unpopular. Most people went straight to the coffee after their main courses.

* * *

Jason's unease was not helped later on when Flora confirmed that the village shopkeeper, one Phyllis Cox, remembered Graham Noble buying a bag of peanuts yesterday morning. Nor, to the best of her memory, had she sold any nuts to anyone else who'd been attending the conference. The landlady at the Bridge and Wagon confirmed that two of her regulars had bought peanuts that week, and although a constable had been dispatched to ask the two bemused villagers what they'd done with them — 'Well eaten 'em of course, sonny, what'dya think?' — Jason wasn't really putting them in the picture.

Damn it, why couldn't the man have made due with a packet of crisps like anyone else, he fumed.

The preliminary forensics reports were not encouraging, nor were the results of the interviews so far. Nobody, it seemed, had particularly liked Reverend Gordon, and some had mentioned the bad feeling between Sir Matthew and the lady. But there was nothing new. Nothing he could really get his teeth into.

'I notice the interviews all focus on the dinner last night,' Jason said, tossing aside the interview reports. 'Put the word out that I want them to ask about Saturday breakfast time as well, and Saturday lunchtime.'

'Yes, sir,' Flora said.

'And see if you can track down this Dr Simon Grade,' Jason added.

'Right, sir,' Flora said, pushing away her plate. There was one good thing to be said for having an incident room on the premises — they weren't going to starve. The chef had insisted on feeding all the unexpected police guests and the food was fabulous, as you might expect from such a well-regarded establishment.

'And get on to pathology. I know it's early, and I don't expect they'll have come across anything startling, but you never know.'

'Yes, sir,' Flora said. Then, a shade more tentatively, 'Do you want to speak to the Nobles again?'

'No,' Jason said shortly. 'Not just yet. Let's get all the interviews over and done with first. Besides, I want to read up on any background material the office has come up with next.'

Flora nodded, her face deadpan. When she came back ten minutes later her arms were full of folders. 'I've found Dr Simon Grade, sir,' she said, putting the papers down with a grunt on the nearest desk. 'He's the proprietor of the Black Friar's museum in Woodstock. I called him up and asked him to be here and available for interview at three-thirty.'

'Fine,' Jason said shortly. 'These the faxes from Bath?'

'Yes, sir. Her bishop, Reverend Gordon's bishop that is, would be glad if you could call him.'

Jason sighed and nodded. No doubt he would. 'Later,' he said succinctly.

And for the next half hour there was silence as the two police officers read up on the life and times of Celia Gordon.

'She was quite a goer in her own way, wasn't she, sir?' Flora said finally, shutting the last folder with a snap and looking across at Jason thoughtfully. 'I can't understand why someone like that, with a university degree and all, would want to join the Church though. With qualifications like she had, she could have become a lecturer or consultant or anything.'

Jason grunted. 'If you ask me, she had her eye on becoming the first female bishop of England,' he said flatly. 'But you know what I really don't like?' he suddenly demanded of his sergeant. 'There's nothing in here,' he indicated the paperwork that made up the victim's history, 'to say why someone wanted her dead. It's been bugging me all along. These are vicars we're talking about,' his voice rose slightly in obvious frustration. 'Vicars don't kill vicars because they're ambitious. Or because they flirt with you. Or because they make you look like a fool at dinner. There's just no motive here.'

Flora nodded. 'I know what you mean. Unless Sir Matthew did it because he's loopy. That might make sense — you don't need a motive if you're nuts,' she pointed out prosaically, and oblivious to her rather poor choice of words, given the circumstances.

Jason sighed. True. A madman didn't need a motive. But it just didn't seem to fit somehow. 'Let's go about this another way. We're agreed that the best time to go into the kitchen to doctor the sponges would have been during the lunch hour, right, when all the staff were busy in the other part of the kitchen?'

'Right,' Flora nodded. 'There'd be far less chance of being seen then.'

'So let's go through the interviews and see what people can remember of the comings and goings during that time.'

And people remembered rather a lot, it seemed. At least thirty or so never left the table from the moment they came in until they left after the meal. Some visited the facilities, but some, unfortunately, came in and then left early, meaning that they could have slipped into the kitchen and done the deed then. Several remembered both Arthur Bryce and his wife leaving their table at some point. And Flora and Jason noted with equal interest that Sir Matthew Pierrepont had been gone for quite some time in the middle of his meal.

Graham Noble, Jason was pleased to note, had been seen in plain view at his table throughout all that lunchtime, and hadn't moved from it.

A knock came at the door and another constable stuck his head around it. 'Sir, there's a Dr Simon Grade outside. Says you called him in for interview?'

Jason closed the folders and nodded. 'Yes, thank you. Send him in.'

CHAPTER 10

Dr Simon Grade walked in, dressed in spotless white tennis slacks and a dark green shirt. Jason smiled. 'Dr Grade, thank you for coming over.'

'Oh, yes. I quite understand. It was terrible. I heard it on the radio this morning. No, I don't mind coming at all. Besides, I'd already put St Bede back to bed, as it were.'

Jason blinked. 'Sorry?'

Dr Grade looked at him somewhat disapprovingly. 'The St Bede's manuscript. That was on loan here yesterday.' He spoke as if the manuscript should have been all that he was thinking about. 'It was removed very early this morning so that none of the guests would be disturbed. I was here to oversee the operations.'

Jason nodded. 'Oh yes. The manuscript.' He wondered why he hadn't been told more about it, then silently wondered what possible bearing a centuries-old piece of paper could have to do with anything.

'Yes, it was as safe as houses here last night, I know. Sir Andrew was kind enough to show me his security arrangements. I'd just got everything back in order when your sergeant called.'

Jason observed the man in silence for a moment. He was babbling, of course, but that in itself meant nothing, especially in a man as self-important as this one. 'The manuscript is valuable, I expect?' he asked mildly.

'Oh I should say,' Dr Grade said quickly. 'It's not the original, of course, but . . .' and before either Jason or Flora could stop him he was off and running. Eventually, even Simon Grade could think of nothing more to say on the subject and sat looking at Jason helplessly.

The chief inspector shifted slowly on his seat. 'That's very interesting. Graham Noble was telling me that you gave very much the same speech yesterday afternoon to a group of people waiting to go into his lecture.'

Simon Grade paled just a little. 'Oh. Oh yes. I suppose I do get carried away,' he admitted, picking an imaginary bit of lint from his trouser leg.

Flora's eyes sharpened. She had at last picked up on something that Jason had begun to suspect almost from the first minute of meeting the museum owner. He was upset about something. Very upset.

'Did you happen to notice if the reverend was eating anything at the time, Dr Grade?' Jason asked casually.

Simon started nervously. 'Sorry? Which reverend are we talking about? There were so many . . .' He spread his hands in a helpless gesture and smiled apologetically.

Jason smiled back. 'I'm sorry. I should have been more explicit. Reverend Noble is the one who . . . well, I've been told that Celia Gordon, the woman who died, made quite a thing about meeting him again,' he clarified delicately.

Simon flushed. 'Oh him! Poor man. Yes. Er . . . sorry, what was the question again?'

Jason nodded. Yes, the good Dr Grade's mind was definitely fixated on something else. 'Was he eating anything, do you know?' he repeated patiently.

Simon looked at the carpet. Then at the windows. Then at an inoffensive computer printer. 'Er . . . I believe he had a bag of something that he offered around,' he acknowledged reluctantly.

'But you don't know what?'

'I wasn't close enough to see, Chief Inspector. Some of the others were still crowding around, asking questions.'

'Yes, I understand that,' Jason said. Then took a shot in the dark. 'Was Reverend Gordon one of those asking questions?'

Bingo!

He watched the little man literally jump in his seat and then give a rather sickly smile. 'Oh I don't think so. As you say,' he suddenly said, a relieved smile taking the place of his rather cheesy grin, 'she was flirting with the local vicar.'

'But earlier on, before the lecture was due to start. Or afterwards even. Did she inspect the manuscript then?' Jason insisted.

The man began to sweat. Jason could quite clearly see his pores oozing just below his hairline.

'I don't believe so,' Simon said, making a show of giving it some thought. 'But then, I might not have remembered,' he hastily covered himself, realizing that the police might find witnesses to prove that she had. 'So many asked about it. It's such an important document you see. To clerics.'

'Did you know that Reverend Gordon was something of an expert on medieval languages, Dr Grade?' he asked quietly. 'And, I imagine, was something of an authority on documents of the same era?'

The sweat turned into a veritable torrent, so much so that the museum curator was forced to reach into his tennis whites for a handkerchief to mop his brow. 'Phew, it's certainly hot again isn't it?' Simon once again offered them his cheesy grin. 'As to your, er . . . question . . . er, no. No, I had no idea Reverend Gordon was . . . er . . . an academic.'

And he didn't like that, Jason thought wryly. Not one little bit. 'I understand that you fainted last night, Dr Grade?' he said, causing an embarrassed flush to take the place of his sickly pallor.

'Yes. It was so awful. I'm afraid I've always been rather sensitive,' Simon babbled. 'It made my life hell at school. I was bullied—' He suddenly broke off, as if aware that he was beginning to make himself seem ridiculous. He stared at the carpet again.

'Did you know Reverend Gordon, Dr Grade?'

'No!' he squeaked. 'Of course not,' he clarified in a more normal tone. 'Why would I?'

'Oh, I don't know,' Jason mused. 'She had a parish in Bath. As a curator and museum owner, I assume you do a lot of travelling, on the trail of artefacts and donations and so forth. Bath, I would have thought, would be just the kind of place that you'd frequent.'

Dr Grade smiled tremulously. 'Well, as a matter of fact, I came across some rather interesting Roman artefacts from Bath . . . but the price was too high. But I assure you, I didn't run across Reverend Gordon,' he added primly.

Jason shrugged. 'Did you know she was allergic to peanuts?'

Simon Grade blinked. 'Good gracious, no.' And then, if he'd been a bird, Jason would clearly have seen all the museum owner's feathers ruffle up. 'How on earth could I have possibly known something like that, Chief Inspector?' he demanded challengingly. It was the first hint of bravado that he'd shown since entering the room, and Jason had to wryly acknowledge a hit.

How indeed could he have known such a thing?

'Well, perhaps you can tell me what you remember of dinner yesterday?' he pressed.

Simon, reassured, launched into his remembrances of the dinner. Unlike Chloe Bryce's recital, his was filled with name-dropping and self-aggrandising, but nothing helpful. When he was finished, Jason nodded. 'Do you recall what Reverend Gordon ate?'

Simon blinked. 'Sorry. I can't say I noticed,' he said stiffly.

Jason nodded. 'Well, I think that's all for the moment. Oh, Dr Grade,' he added quietly, as the man leapt to his feet.

'You will be available for further questioning, should the need arise? I mean, you're not scheduled to go abroad for your summer holidays or anything?'

Simon Grade paled a little, but shook his head. 'No, I'm due to go to Malaysia but not until September.'

Jason smiled. 'I hope you have a good time,' he said blandly.

The museum owner looked at him blankly for a few seconds, then nodded, burbled something, and walked quickly towards the door. When it had shut behind him, Flora sighed heavily.

'How did you get on to him so quickly, sir?' she asked, a shade plaintively. 'It took me ages to catch on. All that guff about St bleeding Bede!'

Jason smiled. 'What do you make of it?'

'He was certainly scared about something,' Flora said promptly. And frowned. 'But . . .'

'Not about the dinner itself,' Jason helped her out.

Flora nodded. 'No.'

'But something certainly happened earlier that day that put the wind up him,' Jason said. 'Of that I'd bet any amount of money you'd care to wager.'

'Not me,' Flora snorted. 'And he didn't like it when you told him Celia Gordon was a bit of an egghead.'

'No, he didn't. I want you to get someone checking up on our Dr Grade. Make it a priority. And check the statements when we've finished to see if anybody recalls Celia Gordon inspecting that manuscript of his. Because something tells me that she did — and in quite some detail.'

'Sir. You think he's a real suspect?'

'I think he's hiding something,' Jason corrected, 'and is most definitely scared about something. I want to know what it is. But whether it has any bearing on the murder . . .' Jason shrugged elegantly.

'And he wasn't really in much of a position to put peanut paste on the sponges was he?' Flora mused. 'According to Mr Banks he arrived during lunchtime, but was in the hall, setting

132

up the manuscript. He had two security men with him most of the time.'

'It isn't likely, I admit,' Jason said. 'But when someone's as nervous as that, it makes me very curious. Oh and, Flora, come back with Graham Noble, will you?' he added flatly.

At the door Flora nodded, her face studiously blank. 'Yes, sir.'

* * *

With her errand run, and an eager-beaver constable despatched to prepare a 'This is Your Life' for Dr Simon Grade, Flora found Graham Noble on the lawn. His wife, she noted, was busy chatting to someone on the far side under some cedar trees. She very neatly and discreetly hooked him out from the impromptu garden party and ushered him into the lounge.

'Hello, Graham,' Jason rose briefly and pointed out a seat. 'Please sit down. I've learned something in the course of the morning that I hope you can help me clear up.'

Graham noted the policeman's cautious voice and tone, and nodded a shade warily. 'Of course. Anything I can do to help.'

Flora took a seat and glanced at the vicar. He really was good-looking in a totally different way from her boss. And, like Jason, she quite liked him. There was something quiet and strong and gentle about the man that touched something in her. She imagined that it would have the same effect on most women, and could well understand why someone like Monica Noble would chuck it all in to marry him.

'When we talked first thing this morning and I told you that Reverend Gordon had died due to a peanut allergy, didn't that . . . mean anything to you?' Jason asked, rather obscurely. In fact, he wanted to give the vicar every chance to volunteer the information, rather than have it prised out of him.

Graham frowned at him. 'Sorry? I'm not sure . . . Oh.' His face suddenly cleared, then darkened again. 'Oh . . . yes,' he said again. 'You mean it's about the bag of peanuts that I bought at the shop yesterday morning?'

Jason nodded. 'Yes. Why didn't you mention it this morning?'

Graham looked at the policeman openly. 'I didn't think to. To be perfectly honest, I'd forgotten all about it.' There was nothing apologetic in his voice. Nothing challenging either. Just a simple statement of fact, and one that both Jason and Flora found themselves instantly believing. Not that either of them would ever indicate it.

'I see. Can you tell me about it, please?' Jason asked.

So Graham obliged. 'I was nervous that morning, you see. That's what it all boils down to. I was due to give a lecture, and I don't know about you, but I think it's always worse when your audience is comprised of members of your own profession. They're apt to know as much about the subject as you do! Anyway, when I get nervous I tend to nibble. There were a lot of conference-goers at the shop when I got there, and they were all buying bags of Phyllis's sweets, but I thought if I did that I'd eat the entire bag within ten minutes or so and make myself feel thoroughly sick. So I chose something savoury instead.'

'The peanuts,' Jason said. 'Can you remember who was there when you bought them?' He wanted to know exactly who might have noted the purchase, and possibly begun formulating a plan.

Graham blinked. 'Oh. Well, Monica, of course. And there were several clerics there I could recognize by sight, but not by name . . .'

'That's fine. When we've finished, I'll have you point them out to one of the constables so that he can take their names. Anyone else? Anyone you recognized?'

'Hmm, let's see. Bishop Bryce was present, as was his wife. And, oh, what's her name . . . Jessica Taylor, she struck up a conversation with my wife. Monica took her back to our place for coffee afterwards. Oh yes . . . and Archdeacon Pierrepont,' Graham said, his voice becoming ultra-expressionless.

'You don't approve of Sir Matthew,' Jason hazarded wryly.

Graham smiled faintly. 'He's very . . . old-fashioned,' he contented himself by saying.

Jason nodded. 'I see. So what did you do next?'

Graham went back over his movements — going in to lunch, watching the men installing the big glass manuscript case and then the impromptu lecture after lunch. 'And then Celia came over to say hello,' Graham said, and paused.

He's expecting it, Jason thought, and felt strangely reluctant to go on. But of course, he had to.

'I've heard from several witnesses, Graham, that Celia was . . . rather obvious about how happy she was to see you again.'

Graham flushed very faintly. Flora tensed. Like Jason, she hated moments like this. When it was somebody she liked.

'Yes, I can imagine it appeared that way. Celia was very . . . self-confident.' He had no wish to speak ill of the dead.

Jason nodded, appreciating the reasons for his careful language, but not willing to let him get away with it. 'Moni . . . Mrs Noble was with you at the time I understand?' he pressed.

Graham began to look angry and took a deep, steadying breath.

'In fact,' Jason carried on remorselessly, 'from what we've been told, Celia flirted with you quite openly, and caused something of an embarrassment. I imagine it made Mrs Noble very angry?'

Graham shrugged. 'A little. But it was nothing. As I told you earlier, I hadn't seen Celia for twenty-five years or so.'

Jason leaned back in the chair and sighed heavily. 'So you didn't regard her as a serious threat to your marriage?' he asked bluntly.

Graham gaped at him. 'You're not serious,' he finally said.

Jason shrugged. 'You're in a very precarious position, aren't you? Being a vicar, I mean. It would take so little to start an avalanche of painful and dangerous gossip, wouldn't it?'

Graham laughed. It was half-angry — and who could blame him, Jason sympathized — and half-defiant. 'I assure you, Chief Inspector, nobody who knows me would ever accuse me of infidelity. Not my bishop. Not my parishioners. And,' he looked Jason very levelly in the eye, 'certainly not my wife.'

Jason felt as if someone had just kicked him in the ribs and quickly looked down. His hands, he was surprised to note, were curled up into fists on his knees. He saw, out of the corner of his eye, his sergeant cast him a quick, anxious look.

'I have to ask certain questions of certain people, Graham, whether I like it or not,' Jason Dury said, in what was as close to an apology as the vicar of Heyford Bassett was going to get.

Graham slowly but visibly relaxed. He nodded. 'Yes, of course you do,' he said quietly. 'I understand that.'

Jason let out a long, slow breath. 'Let's get back to the bag of peanuts. I have a witness who says that during Dr Grade's talk just before your lecture you offered the bag around. Is that so?'

'Yes.'

'So the bag must have been opened already?'

Graham hesitated. He shook his head slowly. He looked frustrated. 'I don't know,' he finally said. 'It's ridiculous, I know, but I can't seem to remember. I might have opened the bag when I first bought them. Or later . . .' He tried to cast his mind back, but all he could clearly recall was Celia's tight face and glittering eyes.

'It's probably not important,' Jason said hastily. 'What did you do with them then?'

Graham looked at him, frowning slightly in puzzlement. 'Hmm? Oh, the bag of nuts. I . . . yes, I took them into the lecture hall with me.' He laughed at his remembered embarrassment to find he was still hanging on to them. 'I put them on the little ledge that runs along the blackboard.'

'But you picked them back up again when you left?' Jason prompted.

Graham frowned. 'No, I didn't. I'm sure I left them there. To tell the truth, after giving the lecture I was so relieved that I hadn't made a complete fool of myself that I forgot all about them.'

Jason sat up abruptly. 'Are you sure?' And, at the cleric's nod, he turned to Flora.

'Sergeant, nip down to the lecture hall. See if they're still there.'

Flora got up quickly. For a long moment the two men were quite silent. Jason ran a tired hand across his face, whilst Graham watched him, unable to help. They were both relieved when Flora returned, panting slightly. Behind Graham Noble's turned back, she met the eyes of her superior and shook her head emphatically.

Jason nodded. He'd been expecting that answer. 'So, you finished your lecture and left. And that's the last you remember seeing of them?' he swept on.

'Yes.' Graham glanced at Flora as she retook her seat, but knew better than to ask what she'd found. He had a horrible suspicion that the bag had gone. That someone had used them to kill Celia Gordon. And he didn't really want to know that.

'Is there anything else you've forgotten to mention?' Jason asked, then jerked a quick hand gesture of apology. That had sounded more accusing than he'd meant.

Graham, however, merely smiled. 'No. I don't think so. And I would have told you earlier about the peanuts, I really would, if I hadn't been so . . . preoccupied. Celia's death has come as such a shock, you see.'

'Well, thank you for your co-operation,' Jason said somewhat flatly, and watched him walk to the door. He knows, Jason thought gloomily. Oh hell, he knows that I'm attracted to his wife. He closed his eyes briefly and wondered how he would feel if the situation were reversed.

'Damn!'

'Sir?'

With a jerk, Jason looked up and realized that he'd spoken out loud. 'Nothing. Show Monica Noble in, will you, Sergeant,' he said brusquely. 'And get Graham and a constable together. I want to know who else was at the shop when he bought those damned peanuts.'

'Yes, sir.'

Flora left, quickly catching up with Graham before he reached the lawn. She saw that he was making a beeline for his wife, no doubt to warn her, and beckoning a constable who was watching the garden party from the sidelines, promptly cut across to intercept him.

'Oh, Reverend Noble,' she said sharply, seeing Monica coming their way. 'If you could go with Constable Wainwright here and point out those clerics you recognize from the shop yesterday morning, I'd be very much obliged.'

Graham cast a quick glance at his approaching wife, then at Flora's determined face as she planted herself firmly in front of him, thus blocking Monica's path, and smiled in acknowledgement of her adroitness. 'Certainly,' he said.

'Ah, Mrs Noble,' Flora said, turning to give the vicar's wife a polite smile. 'Chief Inspector Dury would like another word with you if you don't mind.'

Monica followed her meekly, her mind working fast. She hadn't mistaken her husband's warning look. But what on earth could it mean?

She wasn't to be kept in the dark for long.

Flora left her at the door to the interview room, and when Monica sat down opposite Jason a few minutes later, he had a very tight, shuttered look on his face. His jacket was off, and the top two buttons of his shirt were undone. The sunlight had moved around during the afternoon and now shone through the windows just behind him, turning his hair into a golden halo. Monica caught just a whiff of his aftershave as she sat — something cool and refreshing. Her heart began to beat just a little faster than it should.

And, although she thought she was prepared for the ice-blue quality of his eyes, she wasn't. She quivered, just for a second or two, as he looked at her.

'Why didn't you tell me about the bag of peanuts your husband bought yesterday morning?' he shot out, far more brutally than he'd meant to. 'Did you think we wouldn't find out?'

Monica flushed. 'Of course not. I mean, of course I expected you to find out. And I was going to tell you later,' she said, clearly flustered. 'When you weren't so busy,' she ended lamely.

Jason smiled grimly. 'I see. And were you also going to tell me that Celia Gordon "draped herself around your husband," as one eyewitness put it? And that she was "all over him," as another would have it?'

Monica angrily rose from her chair then slowly sank back again. She stared at him, eyes wide. 'You don't seriously think that either Graham or I would kill her over something like that?' she demanded in disbelief.

Jason shrugged. 'Somebody killed her,' he said flatly. 'For some reason or other.'

Monica stared at him grimly. 'Yes they did,' she agreed. 'And I'm beginning to think that it will be in my best interests to find out who.' He was not, after all, the only one who could throw dramatic statements about.

'Now wait just a minute,' Jason yelled, getting to his feet and glowering down at her. 'Just because you were lucky twice before . . .'

Monica also rose to her feet. 'Lucky?' she echoed softly. Twice in the past she'd discovered the identity of a killer. And, if she remembered correctly, it had had far more to do with her reconstructing events, questioning witnesses and putting the pieces together than mere luck.

Jason sighed and ran a harassed hand through his hair. The gesture gave her a distinct pang deep in her stomach. 'Look, Monica, you have to keep out of this,' he began, in a much more reasonable tone.

Monica smiled savagely. She had Graham to think about — and in more ways than one. Hadn't this policeman just told her that they were both suspects? Graham, she thought, rather more so than herself.

'I'd love to keep out of this,' Monica said quietly. 'But I rather think that you've just dropped me right in it, haven't you?' And with a tremulous and defiant smile, combined with a devastating flash of those big blue eyes of hers, she turned and left him.

* * *

At that moment, in a bedroom above Jason's head, a killer paced the floor anxiously.

How had it all gone so badly wrong? Surely the police would begin to suspect . . . but perhaps not. With just a little luck, all might not be totally lost. Not yet.

I have to think, damn it! The danger is still so sickeningly close. I can almost taste it, it's almost tangible. It's unbearable — it's simply far too much for flesh and blood to stand. Oh if only . . .

The killer continued to pace desperately amidst the remnants of a perfect plan that had turned out to be anything but. After a few minutes of this, the pacing began to slow. The fevered and tortured mind began to clear.

Because, when all was said and done, facts just had to be faced. And the simple fact was — it wasn't over. It should have been, but it wasn't. Which meant that now someone else had to die. And soon. Before the conference drew to a close, and all the delegates scattered to the wind.

The killer slowly sank down into a chair and began to think furiously.

The nut allergy had seemed to be ideal, since it might have been passed off as an accident or been blamed on the kitchen staff's negligence.

But all of that was irrelevant now. If a second person died, the police would know beyond any reasonable doubt that they were dealing with murder. And it was vital that they have as wide a range of suspects as possible to choose from. Which meant striking now, when everyone was still under suspicion.

Fast action was needed.

But when? And how?

Once more the frustrated pacing began. How could someone kill a second time, right under the noses of the police no less, and hope to get away with it?

Could it possibly be made to look like an accident?

Or could somebody else be framed for the killing — someone who might have a motive? Oh, but that was impossible.

The killer began to despair, fighting back the urge to scream in rage and rant at the injustice of it all.

It was all so unfair. None of this should have been happening. They should have been feeling home and dry now, and celebrating their success. Instead, they were in more danger than ever. Things just shouldn't have been this way!

But they were. The problem wasn't simply going to go away — and the killer knew that it had to be faced.

Somehow, somewhere, and within the next twenty-four hours or so, the danger needed to be eliminated. Someone else had to die.

I have to think! I have to be clever — cleverer than I've ever been before in my life. I have to be strong. I can let nothing stand in my way.

I can do it.

I must do it. But how? How?

CHAPTER 11

'It's nearly five, sir,' Flora said, looking up from a forensics report, which had made dismal reading. As expected, the kitchen had yielded a plethora of evidence — but none of it had been useful. Besides, Jason was hardly in a position to ask fifty-odd clerics to submit to fingerprint testing.

'All right. But before we go, I want to interview one more suspect. The woman Monica Noble took to her house for coffee. She was there when Graham Noble bought the bag of peanuts and might have something interesting to tell us. What was her name again?'

Flora consulted her notes. 'Reverend Jessica Taylor, sir. She's a speaker, I think,' she added. 'A mum and babies liberationist by the look of it, too. I bet she's popular,' she added, sotto voce.

Jason heard her nevertheless and laughed outright. 'I'll bet she's Archdeacon Pierrepont's favourite,' he drawled.

Flora was still laughing as she headed out of the door.

Jason tiredly rubbed his hand across his face and reviewed the day. What had they got?

A murder. Well, almost certainly a murder, unless they could come up with some innocent reason for that damned

142

peanut paste getting into the orange gateau. And he didn't think that was going to happen. So: a conference centre full of clerics and one grieving host, and a female vicar for a victim who, though universally unpopular, was still an unlikely candidate for murder.

And motives? A probably senile old archdeacon who didn't like women; a local vicar who'd been flirted with against his will; and a museum owner who'd got a case of the twitches whenever his precious manuscript was mentioned.

And what else?

Jason groaned. Already he'd been thoroughly sounded out by his superior, who'd demanded a lengthy verbal report and had been ominously silent when he'd finished. A terse reminder that he was dealing with vicars and was to tread carefully around the two bishops especially was all the help he'd been given there.

He had no forensic help worth a damn, a manor full of very discreet clergy, and an angry Monica Noble on the prowl.

Verily, my cup runneth over, he mused wryly.

He hastily straightened up as the door opened and a tall, rather pretty redhead walked in. She was dressed for evening service by the look of it, in a sombre dark suit and dog collar. He rose with a smile. 'Reverend Taylor. I'm Chief Inspector Dury. Thank you for seeing me.'

'Not at all,' Jessica said smoothly. She took the seat offered, gave Flora a friendly, curious glance as the sergeant picked up her notebook, and looked back at Jason.

'As I'm sure you're aware by now, we're treating the death of Celia Gordon as . . . suspicious,' Jason began.

Jessica nodded alertly.

'First of all, what can you tell me about dinner yesterday?' Jessica did her best, but could tell them nothing new. 'I see. Now, going back to the beginning of the conference. Can you tell me anything about Celia Gordon that you think might be relevant? Did you see her having any arguments with anyone? Did she say anything to you that struck you as odd, or did you overhear her say something to anyone else that you didn't understand? Anything of that nature.'

Jessica looked at the handsome blond man in front of her for several long seconds, then sighed. 'Well, when we arrived, Celia Gordon was just ahead of me. I saw Sir Andrew greet her, the owner of the manor. That was rather odd.'

Jason leaned slightly forward. 'How so?'

Jessica sighed a little helplessly. 'I'm not sure. I think they recognized each other. Or perhaps it was just that there was an instant antagonism between them. I'm not really sure. Dr Carew was there, he might be able to tell you better what went on. But it seemed to me, to those of us who were in the foyer at the time I mean, that . . . well, something unpleasant passed between them.'

'They argued?'

'Oh no. No, nothing like that,' Jessica assured him quickly. 'It was much more . . . subtle than that. And perhaps I imagined it.' But she frowned.

Jason didn't think she was the type to 'imagine' things. The slender redhead came across to him as a down-to-earth, sensible, natural observer. 'I see. And you got no clear impression about its cause?' he pressed.

'No,' Jessica said firmly. 'I didn't.' She wasn't about to allow herself to be pushed into speculation.

Jason nodded. 'All right,' he sensed her mood and backed off instantly. 'What happened next? When did you next see the deceased?'

'Friday dinner. And I'm sure you've heard by now about Reverend Gordon's run-in with Archdeacon Pierrepont?'

Jason smiled. 'Yes. We've had several versions of that. Perhaps you could give us yours?'

Jessica's tale was very similar to that of Chloe Bryce's. Jason was rather miffed that no report had yet come in on Archdeacon Pierrepont's past indiscretions. Whatever it was he'd done, his bishop had certainly kept it very quiet.

'I see. And during that Friday night nothing else happened?' he continued.

Jessica hesitated then shook her head. 'No. Not that I'm aware of.' Nothing relevant, anyway, she amended silently to herself.

'I see. And then comes breakfast on Saturday morning. Were you there when Reverend Gordon made it clear that she loved oranges?'

'Oh yes,' Jessica said with a wry smile. 'Our table was right next to hers. But she had the sort of voice that carried.'

'So all of those sitting at your table would have known of her preferences?'

'Oh yes, the whole room did. As well as the fact that she was allergic to nuts.'

The room went suddenly and strangely still. Jessica, aware of it, flicked a quick, nervous glance from Jason to Flora and back to Jason.

'I'm sorry?' It was Jason who eventually spoke, his voice ominously quiet and neutral. 'What did you just say?'

Jessica frowned. 'Well, Celia ordered the cornflakes for breakfast, and when they arrived she demanded to know from the waiter whether or not they were the ones that have nuts and honey on them. The waiter told her they weren't, but she said she was very allergic to nuts and preferred not to risk it, and so she ordered a different breakfast instead.' Jessica looked down at her hands. She worried at her lower lip nervously, then asked in a subdued tone, 'Is it true that that's what killed her? That there were peanuts in the dinner she ate?'

Jason said nothing for a long, silent moment. Then he nodded. 'It seems so,' he said flatly. 'Tell me, who was present when she said this? About her allergy to peanuts.'

Jessica looked at him oddly. 'Well, nearly everyone. We were all at breakfast. The dining hall was full. Oh, wait a minute. I think Chloe Bryce had left to go to the powder room. And Graham Noble wasn't there either, of course, since he's not a resident.'

'And was Sir Andrew there?'

'No I don't think so,' Jessica said, frowning in thought. 'He had been going around the tables before, you know, chatting, the way they do. But I think he'd gone by the time the cornflakes incident took place. And, come to think of it, Celia's table was the only table he didn't stop at to chat. They seemed to me to be avoiding each other — Reverend Gordon made no effort to talk to him, either.'

Jason nodded. And you would have expected her to, he thought cannily. The type of woman that Celia Gordon appeared to have been certainly wouldn't have missed the opportunity to cultivate her host. Not under normal circumstances, anyway.

'I see. So it's your opinion that all your colleagues must have heard her make this statement?' he wanted to get that quite clear.

Jessica began to look distinctly uncomfortable, but nodded her head firmly. 'Yes. I'm sure of it.'

Jason nodded. 'I see. And later, at the village shop, you met the Nobles?'

Jessica's face brightened. 'That's right. A lovely couple. Monica took me back to their place for morning coffee. She's thinking of setting up a mother-and-baby group here in the village.'

'Were you aware that Reverend Noble had bought a packet of peanuts at the shop?' he asked calmly.

Jessica tensed. 'I don't think so, no,' she said. For the first time there was a trace of belligerence in her voice, but whether it was on her own behalf or that of the Nobles, he couldn't tell. Obviously she didn't like the idea of any of them being a murder suspect, and who could blame her?

'I see. And is there anything else you can tell me that might be useful?'

Jessica hesitated a split second. Then, 'No, I don't think so. She wasn't . . . well, she wasn't the kind of cleric who was particularly well-liked, which sounds awful, but . . . I'm sure no one wanted to harm her deliberately. I'm sure it'll turn out to be some kind of a nasty accident.'

Jason nodded and smiled. 'Of course,' he murmured noncommittally. She rose and Flora politely ushered her out. When she was gone he sat down slowly. Flora returned to her chair, her face tense and excited.

146

'Well, that blows it all wide open,' she said, with something suspiciously close to satisfaction in her voice.

'Doesn't it just,' Jason agreed dryly. 'And why are we only hearing about it now? There was nothing in our earlier interviews about her talking about her peanut allergy, was there?'

Flora shook her head. 'No, sir. People mentioned the oranges, but not the peanuts.'

'I wonder why,' Jason said. Then shook his head. 'No I don't. I know why. They were all being ostriches, sticking their heads in the sand.'

'A kind of mass self-denial, you mean?' Flora said.

Jason grunted. 'It happens. Believe me. Ask Harrison to go over the other interview reports so far. I want to know if anyone admitted to overhearing that nut allergy remark of hers.'

'Yes, sir.'

Whilst she was gone, Jason tried to organize his thoughts, recalling all those people that he'd interviewed that day. Dr Simon Grade had not been at breakfast, so he wouldn't have known about it. But that couldn't be said of Chloe and Arthur Bryce — although, according to Jessica Taylor, Chloe might have been absent at the crucial time. Which left Arthur — the three-wise-monkeys man. Of course, *he* would have heard no evil. And then there was Sir Andrew. Again, according to Jessica he hadn't been present at the time, but might easily have heard about the incident later from the waiter concerned. Surely it would have been human nature for him to grumble about the extra hassle caused by Celia Gordon? To be fair, Jason knew that the squire might not have been in the kitchens at the time, and might still be ignorant about it. And he knew for a fact that the staff were deliberately shielding him from any unpleasantness. So Sir Andrew might be in the clear.

And yet, according to Jessica, he and Celia had had a clash of some sort the day of her arrival. What was *that* all about? He'd have to have another word with Sir Andrew, like it or not.

Who else from his own bunch of interviewees? Archdeacon Pierrepont. No guesses why he wouldn't have mentioned

147

Celia's loud statement about her allergy to peanuts. He would be as unhelpful and as obstructive as possible just on principle.

No, on the whole it was perhaps not quite so surprising that this was the first he'd heard of it.

'Sir,' Flora came back a little grim-faced. 'We've found three reports of the incident. A verger, a canon and one other vicar admitted hearing her say that she was allergic.'

'Three out of nearly fifty odd.' Jason grimaced. 'They certainly know how to protect their own, don't they?' he added bitterly. Which put everyone at the conference firmly in the frame.

'Oh hell!' Jason snarled. Rather inappropriately, considering the circumstances.

* * *

The killer prowled the grounds, looking for inspiration, and was brought up short by the sight of a lovely old yew tree and its oddly shaped, conical red berries.

Yew berries were poisonous, everyone knew that.

If they were to gather some of the berries and crush them down into a juice and add them to a strong-tasting, already bitter drink — say black coffee, or strong spirits — would the taste of the poison be disguised enough for someone to drink it?

Then the killer gave a mental head shake. No, that was no good. For a start, how could you manage it? It was all very well on television and in books when pills or potions were 'casually slipped' into another person's glass, but you'd need to be very discreet to do that, and even then you'd be lucky not to be spotted.

No. It was too risky. All the delegates seemed to congregate around the bar come evening time, and there were bound to be eyes everywhere. Besides, everyone was hyper-alert now when it came to what they ate and drank — the appalling nature of Celia Gordon's death, indelibly and freshly imprinted on everyone's mind, had seen to that.

No, another poisoning simply would not do.

They would have to think of something else!

* * *

Monica pushed the salad bowl across the table towards Carol-Ann, who helped herself lavishly. Her husband's plate, she noticed, was barely touched. 'Have some potato salad, Graham,' she murmured, and watched him absently spoon some onto his plate.

Carol-Ann looked at them curiously. 'What's up with you two?' she complained. 'You're like a pair of zombies.'

'That's because we're murder suspects,' Monica said, unable to resist scoring off her fast-tongued daughter for once.

Carol-Ann's big baby blues widened appreciatively. 'Yeah! Neat! Oh, is it Jason again?' she gushed, leaning her elbows on the table and fixing her mother with a particularly beautiful smile. 'He's lush. Old, of course, but lush. Besides, Johnny Depp is really old, but he's still fanciable.'

Monica grinned. 'That's our daughter. We tell her we might just be hauled off to the cells at any moment, and she goes gaga over the man who'd be putting us there.'

Carol-Ann snorted. 'Huh. No one with a brain cell would ever think that either of you two would kill anyone. Besides, Mum, you always solve murders. You gonna solve this one?'

'No,' Graham said shortly. At the same time, Monica said, 'Yes,' just as firmly.

They stared at each other in confusion.

Carol-Ann said, 'Uhhh-ohhh,' in a long, drawn-out way, rife with meaning, and grabbed her plate. 'I'm gonna eat outside,' she said wisely, and promptly skedaddled.

'Monica,' Graham began warningly, but his wife quickly held up her hand.

'I know what you're going to say,' she said quickly. 'Keep out of it.'

Graham's lips twisted into a rueful smile. 'I was. I take it that you don't agree?'

149

'I don't, no,' Monica said. 'Look, I know it's not as if it happened in our house and to one of our neighbours, as it did the first time. And I know it's not a friend of ours who was killed, like the last time. But this time we're on the suspect list.'

'Which we were on the last two occasions, as I remember,' Graham pointed out with annoying logic.

Monica sighed. 'Oh yes, I know. Technically we were. But this time . . . well, this time, sweetheart, we really are up there with the others.'

Graham's eyes flickered. 'You mean because of the way Celia behaved towards me? And the peanuts,' he added flatly. It was clear that he thought the blame for their predicament rested entirely on his shoulders. Monica quickly got up and walked around the table. She wriggled her way onto his lap and looped her hands around his neck. She hadn't missed the guilt and strain in his voice.

'This isn't your fault,' she said, softly but firmly. She ran a hand through the dark hair at his temple and tenderly kissed the tiny blue vein that her action revealed. 'You didn't know she was going to be there or the fuss she'd make. Or that she'd die as she did. I know that, and so do you, so let's not have any recriminations, hmm?' she said firmly, but with a trace of real fear in her voice.

Graham was her rock, he always had been. And she needed him now. She felt his arms squeeze around her tightly, once, then twice, then he tipped his head back to look her in the eye. Monica sighed. 'I love you,' she whispered and kissed him gently on the lips.

'I love you, too,' he said, when she lifted her head at last. 'And you're right. No recriminations. So, Sherlock, what's your plan?'

Monica smiled. 'Well, we've got to find out what really happened of course,' she said, then laughed. 'Nothing like stating the obvious.'

Graham sighed as she got off his lap and watched her return to her place at the table. But since he was due in church soon for evening services, perhaps it was just as well she'd moved when she had.

'First we'll have to try and gather as much information as the police have by now,' she said seriously. 'Oh, not the scientific, technical stuff. But the rest.'

'And how do we do that?' he asked sceptically.

'By talking to people,' Monica said firmly. 'Dr Carew wants us there, so we've got the perfect opportunity to circulate. I'll tackle Jessica, you pump your boss. Then we'll go on to the others. Someone, somewhere, must have seen something.'

Graham continued to look sceptical. 'If you say so,' he muttered. But then remembered that twice before his wife had come up trumps. 'Monica,' he said slowly, picking up a lettuce leaf on his fork and letting it drop again. 'Did Jason ask you about the state of our marriage?'

Monica felt her stomach drop to her feet. She blinked. 'No. Why?'

Graham shrugged. 'Oh, nothing. It's just that he wondered how upset you were about Celia, and how vulnerable I was to gossip — about accusations of infidelity.' He looked across the table at her. 'I told him we were as solid as granite. That you knew I'd never cheat on you. You do know that, don't you?' he asked quietly.

Monica left the table at a run. She was back in his lap in a flash, the worried, afraid look in his eyes promptly sending tears to her own. 'Of course I know that, Graham,' she said thickly. 'I'd never, ever think anything else.'

Graham's hands tightened on her waist. 'Good,' he said simply. 'That's all I need to know.'

Monica lay her cheek against the top of his head.

Carol-Ann, coming back with her empty plate, eyed them with disgust. 'Oooh, yuck,' she said. 'Can't you do that somewhere else?'

CHAPTER 12

Monday dawned with a change in the weather; the trees dripped the previous night's rain onto Monica's shoulders as she walked underneath them to the village square, then crossed towards the shop.

'Morning, Phyllis,' Monica called gaily as she went through the door. 'Do you have any bacon left?'

She and Graham only allowed themselves bacon and eggs for breakfast once a week, usually on a Sunday. Yesterday, of course, they'd missed it, and Monica was feeling guilty.

'Course I have,' Phyllis called from her place at the till, and watched the vicar's wife add eggs, a white loaf and a pound of apples to her basket. As Monica opened her purse and counted out the change, Phyllis stacked the purchases carefully in a second-hand plastic carrier bag.

'Bit of a shock up at the manor, then,' Phyllis said casually.

'Yes,' Monica said dryly. She didn't need to be told to be careful about what she said around Phyllis. It was a lesson she'd soon learned.

'Poor Sir Andrew isn't looking well.' Phyllis was not about to be put off by monosyllabic answers. 'This is the last thing the poor duck needs.'

'I know,' Monica said, thawing in spite of herself.

'Fancy that woman who gave the village mums something to think about, dying like that. Sudden and nasty it was, they say.'

Monica blinked, feeling confused, then quickly shook her head. 'Oh no, it wasn't Jessica who died. It was another woman cleric. I don't think she'd been in the shop, had she? A blonde, rather businesslike woman in her late forties?'

Phyllis sniffed. 'No,' she admitted. 'But we had some queer sorts in, for all that,' the shopkeeper mused. 'One chap would keep wittering on about wagtails. And one miserable blighter tried to tell me my husband should be serving behind the counter, not me. Hah! I told him I've been on me own for years now and have been doing just fine, thanks very much. Lor! You should have heard him go on. I thought he was gonna take a swing at me with his walking stick at one point. If he 'ad a done, I'd have decked him,' Phyllis said flatly.

She was a grey-haired, lean woman, but looked at that moment perfectly capable of 'decking' anyone.

'Sounds like Archdeacon Pierrepont,' Monica murmured. 'He's a bit of a misogynist.'

'I don't care what religion he is,' Phyllis huffed. 'I'm surprised they don't lock him up.' She rang up the till, then hesitated, looking uncharacteristically shamefaced. 'I'm sorry about having to tell that flat-footed young constable about your husband buying some peanuts, Mrs Noble.' Phyllis, going a little red, launched into what was obviously a well-rehearsed speech. 'I had no idea they'd make such a fuss about it.' Then, rather ruining it, added avidly, 'Is it true that the lady died because she was allergic to them?'

Monica sighed. 'So it seems,' she said firmly, handing over the money and reaching for the shopping bag. And even Phyllis, given such a monumental hint, had to give it up as a bad job and let her go on her way.

* * *

153

The killer was also up early and was now staring thoughtfully down at the long rectangular azure-blue length of the indoor swimming pool.

At this hour in the morning, only a few of the more hardy delegates were taking advantage of it to get in a few pre-breakfast lengths. Several of these called out a vague but cheerful 'good morning' to the figure strolling casually around the pool, and were rewarded with a brief smile.

Surely there were possibilities here? After all, you heard of people accidentally drowning in private swimming pools every day, didn't you? True, they were usually either children or drunken celebrities, but those were the only ones that the media ever bothered to report. The police must come across fatalities of ordinary citizens every day.

But after one suspicious death already, nobody would be willing to believe that a second fatal accident had occurred. No, a simple, straightforward killing, with no pretences or fancy touches, might just have to be the way to go.

But even given that, how could you go about luring your victim down here when you could be sure that nobody else would be around to witness what happened next? A phone call might be recorded and a note might be retained by your target and found later by police.

And it had to be harder than you thought to actually drown someone in a swimming pool, didn't it? They would fight back and unless you could somehow manage to smash your victim's head on the side of the tiles in order to incapacitate them, the margin for error was simply too great. Anything could go wrong.

No, the killer thought, reluctantly abandoning the pool. As tempting as it might have seemed, there was no help here.

* * *

Jason had driven through the early morning rain hours ago and had already gone through yesterday's interview reports in

154

fine detail. So he was glad when Flora arrived with some fresh data. If he had to read again who said what to somebody else just before Celia Gordon began to choke, he'd start climbing the walls.

'Sir, something on our Dr Grade. Or at least about that rinky-dink museum he runs,' Flora said, depositing one specific folder in his lap. 'Not sure it's helpful though.'

Jason read it quickly. The report was of a break-in at the museum some time ago. 'Nothing much taken it seems,' he said, frowning slightly. 'Why bother breaking in, then only taking a couple of Renaissance snuff boxes or whatever the hell they were?' he demanded.

Flora shrugged. 'Probably thought they'd find something more worthwhile? Not all burglars are smart, sir. They might have thought a museum, any museum, would have valuable paintings or gold items or stuff like that, which I'm guessing he didn't have.'

'Hmm. I see his security arrangements weren't up to much,' he said, with a typical policeman's scorn for inadequate means of crime prevention. 'At least he had a better system installed afterwards,' he added, then snorted. 'Nothing like locking the stable door after the horse has bolted.'

'No, sir. Still, I can't see how it's relevant to our inquiry though,' Flora sighed.

'No, neither can I,' Jason admitted. Nevertheless, something about the report niggled him, and continued to niggle him all day.

* * *

Sir Andrew Courtenay walked through the water meadow, his old hand-made boots getting wetter and wetter. His head was down, his shoulders hunched, and he was oblivious to the brightening weather around him. Eventually he paused on the bank of the weed-strewn river and stared down into the water. Then he looked around vaguely.

No fisherman lined the bank, and beyond, no villager walked a dog. He cast a look behind him, but saw only cows chewing the cud and staring at him curiously. Nervously, and a shade reluctantly, he reached into his pocket and pulled something out. He stood looking down at it for a few moments, a bleak look in the depths of his eyes, and then with a violent gesture threw it overhand far into the river.

It floated for a short while in the current and then slowly sank.

Sir Andrew stood for a few minutes longer as the clouds broke up overhead and the first rays of sun began to shine through. Then he turned and tramped heavily back to the manor.

Breakfast was all but over when he stepped back into the lobby, and from the open French doors leading into the dining hall, the last scrapes of knives and forks on plates made his teeth tingle. As he made his way to the back of the hall and to the corridor leading to his private quarters, he noticed the lean, stooped old man who came out of the dining hall.

Archdeacon Pierrepont glanced up as Sir Andrew stepped back into the lobby. The old man glanced furtively around, then followed the squire into his private office.

'Got rid of it then?' Matthew Pierrepont asked gruffly, coming straight to the point.

As Sir Andrew studied the old man in front of him, a vague look of distrust and fear seemed to cross his face.

Sir Matthew Pierrepont didn't like the look of it.

'Yes,' Sir Andrew said shortly. 'And I suggest you never speak of it again. Not to me, or to anyone else.'

Sir Matthew gave a scornful laugh. 'I'm not likely to, am I?' he snorted. He had an egg stain on his shirtfront and ash in the turn-ups of his old trousers. He smelt of old man. With a hidden grimace of distaste, Sir Andrew moved behind his desk and sat down in a gesture of unmistakable exhaustion. He hadn't slept again last night.

'I'm not joking, Sir Matthew. You can't brag about this. Or joke about it. You can't mention it to any of your cronies,

no matter how much you trust them, or think they'll sympathize with our actions. You've got to keep your mouth shut.
Firmly shut. Do you understand me?' There was steel in his
voice now, unmistakable and threatening.

Sir Matthew straightened his stooped shoulders. His own
eyes glinted. 'You can rely on me, sir,' he said gruffly. 'I shan't
let you down.'

Sir Andrew smiled wryly. He wasn't much of a betting
man, but if he had been, he wouldn't have put much money
on the surety of Pierrepont's word.

* * *

Back in the incident room, Flora was busy taking notes. 'So,
we're building up a picture at last,' Jason was saying. 'The
killer hears at breakfast on Saturday morning that Celia
Gordon loves oranges and is allergic to nuts. There is both
duck à l'orange and an orange gateau on the menu for that
night. We've confirmed that the menus on the tables included
details for that evening's dinner?'

'Yes, sir. Geoff Banks said they always do that — give
out the menus ahead of time, I mean. He says it gives guests
a chance to say if they don't like the choices, and order something different. That way the chef has a chance to prepare
something else. Not that many guests do, it seems, since the
range of choices is quite wide.'

'Right,' Jason said, waving a hand impatiently. 'So our
killer is instantly presented with a relatively easy way to do away
with Celia Gordon. To make things even easier, he or she spots
Graham Noble with a bag of peanuts that very lunchtime, either
in the hall, when they're discussing that blasted manuscript, or
later in the lecture hall. We have confirmation of his story, right?'

'Yes, sir. A lot of people who attended the lecture said
they saw him put the bag of peanuts on the blackboard. And
no one recalls seeing him pick them back up again afterwards.'

'Hmm,' Jason said wryly. 'They're suddenly a very obser-
vant bunch, aren't they?' he drawled. But he was not really

angry. It put Graham Noble, if not in the clear, then at least further down the list of likely suspects. 'So, our killer waits until the hall is empty, then nips back and retrieves the nuts. That means the paste wasn't made and put on the cake until after the lunch hour, not during, as we'd previously supposed. The chef says the sponges were out and cooling until around three-thirty. Graham's lecture ended at three. That gives our killer half an hour. Come on, let's time it and just make sure that it's all feasible.'

Jason had a bag of peanuts on him, having bought some earlier and knowing that he'd be going through this reconstruction later. Together, the two police officers went upstairs to an empty bedroom that Geoff Banks had allocated to them for this purpose. It was a typical guest bedroom, with double bed, velvet curtains and attractive furnishings.

'Right. Here's the bag of nuts,' Jason said, holding it aloft and looking around the well-appointed room. 'Our killer needs to make a paste to go on a sponge. How easy would it be? There's a little mini-bar, for a start. When we've got the analysis back from the lab we'll know whether or not there was any alcohol mixed in with it. We'll say, for argument's sake, that there was. It would help disguise the taste. What else would he or she need?'

'Well, here's a big round glass ashtray, sir.' Flora picked one up. 'And a cup and saucer. We've got a kettle and sugar on the complimentary tea-and-coffee tray,' she pointed them out.

'Right.' Jason emptied some of the nuts into the glass ashtray, then using the bottom of the cup as a pestle, quickly ground the nuts to a fine mush. He then boiled the kettle, added some sugar and the hot water and a dash of spirits to the mix, and got to work with the teaspoon. Within a few minutes he had a fine peanut paste which could be easily spread onto a sponge cake.

'Time?' he asked.

Flora checked her watch. 'Just under ten minutes, sir.'

'Right. Plenty of time to go downstairs and into the kitchen. We don't need to go down there again — we've already seen what a mad house that is.'

Flora nodded. 'That little dogleg arrangement of rooms down there must have been a real bonus,' she added grimly.

'It's almost certain that the killer must have scouted the area earlier and already knew about the sponges cooling on the trays,' Jason was thinking hard, 'or else he or she would be going down there blind, just on the off chance that they'd be able to infect something. And that sounds too iffy to me — after all, they had to go with the gateau to have a fair chance of Reverend Gordon eating it.'

'Right. And they may have even gone in there to look for peanuts in the first place — after all, that would have made more sense than hoping to nab Reverend Noble's,' Flora ventured. 'So we know how it was done, and roughly the timing. We know Graham Noble unknowingly provided the murder weapon. We know they all knew about Celia's allergy.'

'With a few possible exceptions,' Jason reminded her carefully. It sounded good, but in reality . . . 'OK, what we need to do now is re-question the chambermaids. It's a long shot, but someone may have noticed something. I doubt we'll get much joy out of rifling the bins for empty booze bottles — I'll bet half the conference has got through the contents of their complimentary mini-bar by now.'

Flora grinned.

'What we need them to concentrate on is anything unusual — cups or ashtrays or anything else the killer might have used that were unusually dirty.'

'Or smelt of peanuts?' Flora put in.

'Hell no,' Jason said quickly. 'Ask them that and they'll suddenly be "remembering" how everything smelt odd, from so-and-so's shoes to somebody else's aftershave lotion. No, let's keep it simple.'

'Sir,' Flora said. Then, 'But surely the killer will have cleaned up after himself? I mean, he'd hardly be likely to leave traces of peanut paste in his or her room.'

Jason sighed heavily. 'I know. If we could just get forensics in! But we can't do that until we know whose room to concentrate on. We'd never get a judge to give us a warrant to search every room. Damn, I wish we didn't have to tread so carefully around these people.'

'Civil rights apply to vicars, too, sir,' Flora muttered sympathetically. 'I can just see the newspaper headlines now if we get it wrong.'

Jason laughed. So could he! 'Mind you, I can't see anybody suing us for wrongful arrest. They're more or less obliged to turn the other cheek, aren't they?'

Flora laughed again. 'I knew there had to be a plus side to all this somewhere, sir.'

Jason scratched the side of his nose thoughtfully. 'It still seems fantastic to me,' he muttered, suddenly sombre again. 'This whole thing, I mean. Vicars killing vicars. And let's just picture the scene down in the kitchen for a minute. The killer has the paste. He or she has to sneak down to the kitchen without being seen. Has to get into that little side room and apply the paste. The killer must have heard them all in the kitchen just yards away, and knew someone could walk in at any minute.'

'There were plenty of places to hide though, sir,' Flora pointed out. 'You said so yourself.'

'Yes, but even so. The sheer gall of it. The risk. The killer must have been desperate. And why were they so desperate?' Jason stared at his sergeant in frustration. 'That's what I can't get hold of. What was it that Celia Gordon did, or said, or knew that made her so dangerous to somebody?'

Flora scratched her head with the end of her ballpoint pen. 'It might have been brewing for some time, sir,' she said, but without much conviction. 'Something in her past perhaps?'

Jason sighed. 'In which case, why wait until now to kill her? This peanut business has all the hallmarks of a hastily constructed, ad hoc killing to me. Especially if it was Graham Noble's peanuts they used. But even if the killer knew before coming here about her allergy, why wait until now to do it?'

'Because he'd have a house full of other suspects to divert suspicion from himself perhaps?' Flora hazarded, but again without much conviction.

Jason sighed. 'Perhaps. I don't know. We have no one here from her past on hand to kill her, right? We've got someone down in Bath checking that that's so?'

'Yes, sir. No one who knew her down there has followed her up here as far as we can tell.'

'Right. So it's not likely to be something to do with her life or work in Bath. But on the other hand, we've got no motive for anyone here to want to kill her either — they are all relative strangers to her. Except our old friend, the archdeacon, who may or may not be senile.'

'Reverend Noble fits the bill,' Flora said quietly. 'He knew her before and he was here on the spot.'

Jason shook his head. 'Too tenuous. Besides, he might not be the only one. Jessica Taylor said she thought there was something going on between Celia and Sir Andrew. Could they have had an affair in the past? Something that turned sour? He's been a widower for quite some time. And Celia was an ambitious sort of woman. She might have seen herself as lady of the manor as a means of climbing the old ecclesiastical ladder.'

'I don't know, sir,' Flora said dubiously. 'It seems to me like we're clutching at straws here.'

'And how,' Jason agreed ruefully. 'Nevertheless, get those chaps who are running down the background on Sir Andrew to dig a little deeper. There's more going on here than meets the eye.'

Flora wasn't about to argue. She'd seen the chief inspector prove himself right far too often to ignore his gut instincts now.

* * *

The killer stumbled upon the old boathouse more or less by accident. Disconsolately wandering around the grounds in search of inspiration, the side of the weathered timbered wood had peeped through the greenery.

It had obviously not been in use for some time, for stinging nettles were growing around the door that had once been securely padlocked, but time, warping the old wooden doors out of shape, now rendered such security pointless.

The killer eased between the gap and found another world inside — a green-dappled, dank-smelling world, where precarious decking led out to an entrance onto the river and old, mouldering canoes and kayaks lay rotting, scattered around the base of the lichen- and moss-covered walls.

What a pity the conference centre didn't have this place up and running. There had to be possibilities in a boating accident, surely?

And then the killer thought. Did there really though? Even supposing the boats were in good working order, and the facilities did include river trips, what good would it have done? You could only fit two to some canoes, and even in the bigger boats, three or four at most. Which meant that if you managed to get your victim into a two-boat canoe and only one of you came back, you might just as well hand yourself over to the police then and there. After all, who else could be responsible?

And if you got into a bigger boat, how on earth did you manage to hoist someone overboard and drown them without your fellow passengers noticing?

With a cry of rage, the killer stormed out of the boat-house and tramped alongside the river, hands clenching into fists, impotent rage making purple and red lights flash across eyes screwed shut in frustration.

Time is running out! I have to think of something. I have to do something.

The killer opened their eyes, which alighted once more on the river. It was a pretty river, and looked deep in places. Lime-green weed swayed like a maiden's hair in the current. White-flowering water-crowfoot littered the surface and dragonflies darted everywhere. It was a picturesque, delightful place.

Slowly, tentatively, the killer began to smile.

* * *

Monica smiled across the table. 'Have another biscuit.'

Jessica laughed and patted her flat stomach. 'Better not. They're lovely though, did you bake them yourself?'

'Good grief no,' Monica laughed. 'I'm no whizz in the kitchen. I wasn't the homely sort until I met Graham — I used to work in advertising!'

For the next half hour, they talked about Monica's previous life in London and the way she'd coped, exchanging that lifestyle for a totally different one as a rural vicar's wife. From there it was a short step to Jessica's own married life, her work in her mother-and-child clinic, and thence to her lecture for the conference and the events there during the last forty-eight hours.

When Jessica left an hour later, she didn't realize it, but she'd given Monica huge chunks of information that she didn't have before. Information about what was said and done from the time Celia arrived until the fateful dinner that Saturday night, about the rumours of Sir Matthew Pierrepont's past sins, about the constraint between Celia and Sir Andrew. And, although Jessica had no idea that she'd given this impression, her own dislike of Arthur Bryce and his very attractive wife, Chloe.

The trouble was, Monica now seemed to have so many leads that it was hard to know where to start. She wasn't about to give up now, though. She needed to succeed, if only to get Jason off their backs. At the thought of the handsome blond chief inspector, Monica flushed hotly and stomped into the kitchen to put a load into the washing machine. It was annoying the way that man kept intruding into her thoughts, and at the oddest of moments.

Well, too bad. She had some hard thinking to do, and Jason Dury could just go and jump in the river.

CHAPTER 13

'Sir, I think you'd better talk to this witness.'

The young police constable who stuck his head around the door had previously been the one watching the 'garden party' outside, and had consequently been in just the right position to overhear a private conversation between two unwary vicars, lurking, as he had been, behind the massive trunk of a cedar tree. He looked both excited and pleased with himself.

Jason regarded the middle-aged cleric who crept in, looking nervous and very much out of his depth, with interested eyes. He stood up and held out his hand, smiling amiably, trying to put the witness at his ease.

'Chief Inspector Jason Dury. And you are Reverend . . . ?'

'Smith. Christopher Smith,' the man said, taking a few quick steps forward to take Jason's proffered hand and shaking it firmly. The vicar looked to be in his early fifties, and had the beginnings of a potbelly. 'Chief Inspector, my word,' he murmured. 'Rather a high rank to be working on the shop floor, so to speak?'

This rather astute statement had Jason rapidly reassessing the man's character.

'Yes, I suppose so,' Jason said casually. 'But we're very short-staffed, and I know this area.' Both of which were true, but were not the main reasons that he'd been assigned to this case. As he rather suspected Reverend Smith already knew. Or had surmised. 'The constable tells me that you have some information for us,' Jason prompted.

'Oh, yes,' Reverend Smith said, shooting the constable a rather unhappy look. He'd never have been discussing the matter with old Jenkins if he'd known a policeman was snooping about.

'It's about the lady who died,' he began, tactfully. 'It concerns Saturday afternoon — when nearly everyone was still at lunch. I'd finished very early. I'm not allowed to eat sweet stuff anymore,' he added, looking down at his protruding belly with a look of acute misery. 'So I left before the puddings, to avoid temptation. And I saw Reverend Gordon bent almost double over that manuscript case and demanding that the chap watching over it should open it up for her.'

'Oh?' Jason said blandly.

The cleric flushed and began to look uneasy. 'The thing is, they seemed to be having a bit of an argument. Reverend Gordon wanted to study the parchment, or the colour of the ink, or something rather technical. She said it was impossible to do so under glass and electric light. But the chap was out and out refusing to remove it. Can't say I blame him. Even I know you can't take chances with such delicate and perishable things like that.'

'And Reverend Gordon would have known this too, presumably,' Jason pointed out. 'I wonder what made her so adamant?' he mused craftily.

Again the good reverend flushed. 'Well, she er . . . well, she seemed to be casting aspersions of some sort on the authenticity of the piece, as far as I could tell.'

'And did Dr Grade remove the manuscript for her?' Jason asked, although he already had a good idea of what the answer to that question was going to be.

'I don't know,' Christopher Smith admitted. 'I didn't linger,' he added quickly. 'I didn't want to get drawn into it. And, frankly, I found Reverend Gordon rather alarming.'

Jason could quite understand that. 'Well, thank you, Reverend Smith. You've been most helpful.'

The vicar beamed with relief and the constable, with an air of palpable pride, ushered his 'find' out of the room. Flora looked at Jason with glinting eyes. 'Well, you said you wanted something more on Dr Grade, sir,' she pointed out. 'By the way, did you note that little titbit of information in the report about Dr Grade's less than impressive "doctorate"?'

Jason nodded. 'I did, yes. A bit of a pseudo-intellectual, our Dr Grade. But in Celia Gordon he met the real thing.'

Flora nodded. 'You think she spotted something a bit off?'

'Seems so.'

'Shall I get Dr Grade back?'

'Yes. Take a car and fetch him. And I want you to put the wind up him a bit before he gets here,' Jason ordered pitilessly.

* * *

As a strategy, it obviously worked well, for when Flora returned with the good doctor nearly half an hour later, he was looking distinctly queasy.

'Dr Grade, thank you for coming back,' Jason said, superbly ignoring the fact that he'd hardly had any other option. 'I thought I should let you know, as a matter of courtesy, that an expert is going to be sent to your museum tonight to examine the St Bede's manuscript. I hope you have no objection to that?'

Whilst Flora had been gone, he'd sent out feelers for a local man with the necessary expertise. Being so close to Oxford University, of course, there'd been no trouble finding one both willing and indeed eager to examine the manuscript.

But it was absurdly obvious from the way that Dr Grade swayed and almost fell into the chair facing the policeman that he had many objections indeed to this state of affairs.

The big, haunted eyes stared at Jason, reminding him of a mouse looking up at a cat.

'What?' he finally said faintly. 'What for?'

'We have a witness who claims that Reverend Gordon . . . well, not to put too fine a point on it, Dr Grade, it appears that she cast some doubt on the authenticity of the manuscript,' Jason explained blandly.

'But that's ridiculous,' Simon said, beginning to rally a little. 'It was fully authenticated by an eminent man in the field before the bishop purchased it.'

Jason blinked. 'The bishop?'

'Dr Carew. Strictly speaking, the St Bede's manuscript belongs to his diocese.'

Jason couldn't remember whether he'd been told that before. He took a moment to see if it could possibly make any difference, and didn't see how it could. 'I see. Then I'm sure you have nothing to worry about,' he said smoothly. 'Oh, do you have the keys to the museum on you, Dr Grade?' he asked, very casually.

Simon mutely shook his head.

Flora coughed. 'I picked you up at the museum, Dr Grade. Surely you remember locking up behind us?' He must do, she thought sourly. He'd objected to closing the museum long and hard enough!

'Then I'll take care of them for now,' Jason said, and held out his hand remorselessly.

With the expression of a man who's suddenly found himself sinking in quicksand, Dr Grade grudgingly handed them over. 'But I don't see why you want them,' he muttered helplessly.

'As I'm sure you'll appreciate,' Jason responded coolly, 'we don't want any . . . er . . . accident to happen to the manuscript before the expert has a chance to look it over.'

Simon Grade went white, then red, as the implication washed over him.

'But look here, I can't just have strangers trampling about all over my museum,' he began to huff and puff, but Jason held up a silencing hand.

'Professor Sidney Wyatt will have a police constable present throughout his inspection, I assure you. And he'll oversee the locking up of the museum afterwards and make sure the security system is operating properly before he leaves.'

'Professor Wyatt?' Simon Grade mumbled, appalled, having scarcely heard the rest of the policeman's statement.

Jason smiled beatifically. 'Yes, you've heard of him I expect? A top man in his field, so I understand,' he finished cheerfully.

By now, Dr Grade was looking positively green about the gills. 'Well that's all for now,' Jason said briskly, standing up and watching the man as he stumbled to his feet and sleep-walked to the door.

Flora looked at her boss in awe. 'Crumbs, that was brutal,' she said admiringly. 'You're sure it's a fake then?'

'Oh I don't think there's much doubt about it,' Jason said. Not after that performance. 'All along, that report about the break-in last year at the museum has bugged me.'

'You think he faked it? The break-in, I mean?'

Jason nodded. 'I think he faked it, removed a few items to make it look good, and then substituted a counterfeit for the original St Bede's manuscript, thus covering himself if it ever came to light. He can always claim the "intruders" did it.'

Flora nodded. 'He probably sold it on to an avid collector. Wanted a little nest egg for his retirement, d'you think?'

Jason nodded. 'Perhaps the collector even supplied him with the fake to take its place. Collectors are amongst the most fanatical human beings to be found on the face of the planet, Sergeant, remember that,' he added grimly.

Flora looked suitably impressed. Jason sighed. 'We'd better have Dr Carew in and tell him what we suspect.' He shook his head. 'He's not going to be best pleased with us, methinks,' he added drolly.

* * *

That lunchtime a large proportion of delegates gathered around the bar for an aperitif.

The Bryces were sitting beside one another on bar stools, sipping Pimm's; they smiled an invitation to join them to Archdeacon Pierrepont when he arrived. The curate from Bangor hovered on the periphery and drew Jessica in, the two of them starting a conversation on a project Jessica was working on, which involved taking mainly unloved, unused churches and using them as social gathering places for all sorts of community activities. Sir Andrew Courtenay, playing host to the gathering throng, joined them and the talk turned to sporting activities.

And somehow, from there, ventured onto the new fad for 'wild' swimming.

Jessica, who'd never come across it, listened with interest. Apparently, people discontented with the loveless, chemical tyranny of swimming pools had taken to swimming more naturally, in rivers and lakes. It was about getting back to nature, and enjoying a less manicured experience.

Sir Andrew, when questioned about possible local sites for this phenomenon, somewhat reluctantly conceded that the nearby river was ideal for this, being not too wide and neither too shallow nor too deep. He was quick to point out that neither he nor the conference centre could ensure the health and safety of anyone taking part in something like this, and that he was sure his insurance didn't cover such an activity. However, everyone assured him that they understood that they would be undertaking this at their own risk, and would sign a blanket waiver stating so.

Later, when people were asked about it, nobody was quite able to say exactly who it was that had first suggested that anyone interested should gather on the banks of the river not far from the old boathouse, and participate in this new adventure. But it was a popular idea, and since nearly everybody had brought their swimwear for the pool at the manor, it presented no practical difficulties for anyone. Especially since the overnight rain had turned to bright sparkling sunshine and the weather looked set to remain fair for the rest of the day.

And so it was that, throughout lunch and some of the early afternoon sessions, the idea spread, until nearly a score of people had intimated that they were up for the new experience.

Jessica called Monica and invited her to join them, and Monica accepted at once, asking if Carol-Ann wanted to come along, too.

Archdeacon Pierrepont, declaring that he was too old to swim, nevertheless informed Dr Simon Grade of the event, and promptly invited him. He had been amused by the man's obvious social climbing, and knew his kind well enough to predict that he would be unlikely to want to cause offence by declining. Dr Grade clearly wasn't that keen on the idea — in fact, he sounded downright distracted and not at all his usual affable self — and the archdeacon wasn't particularly surprised. He didn't have the look of a natural athlete about him, and was probably scrambling to come up with some imaginary urgent appointment elsewhere. But he was secretly looking forward to seeing the dapper pseudo-academic cold and shivering and looking like a drowned rat, and made it clear that he wouldn't take no for an answer.

The Bryces both agreed to go, since it would have made them look standoffish if they'd declined, and the bird-watching curate was more than happy to join in, if only in the hope of getting up close and personal with moorhens.

Many of the older delegates, of course, had swum in rivers when they were children, and nostalgia was a strong draw.

And so the afternoon drew on with a great many people happily anticipating a new and refreshing experience.

And the killer looked forward to it most of all.

* * *

Dr Carew sensed trouble the moment he walked in. Jason Dury rose from his seat and ushered him to a comfortable armchair.

'I'm afraid we've run into something of a problem,' Jason began tactfully, 'that may, or may not, have any bearing on the case.' And, not wanting to prolong the agony, he gave the stone-faced bishop the facts about the St Bede's manuscript.

When he was finished, David Carew sighed heavily. 'But so far it's only a suspicion?' he asked hopefully.

Jason nodded. 'By tomorrow we'll know for sure. Professor Wyatt said he'd be able to give us a preliminary assessment. Of course, he said more detailed chemical testing would take time but . . . well, the man's an expert. I think we can safely take his word for it if he says it's genuine. Or not.'

David Carew sighed. 'I have to tell you, Chief Inspector, that there was a lot of opposition to our diocese acquiring the manuscript. If it turns out to be a fake . . .' He shook his head and sighed. 'But that's my problem,' he said stoically. 'You, of course, have problems of your own. Oh, and speaking of those,' he pushed the thought of his own woes firmly aside for the moment, 'I've thought of something that I didn't mention before. I can't see how it could possibly have any bearing on the . . . er . . . death of Reverend Gordon, but you did say you were interested in anything at all to do with her?'

Jason nodded, noting yet another cleric who had trouble saying the word 'murder.'

'Well, she and Bishop Bryce were both candidates for the chair of a large and important conference scheduled for next year in London. A very important conference,' he added, in case it hadn't been quite clear.

'I see,' Jason said thoughtfully. His first instinct was to give a silent cheer that the handsome and annoying bishop from Yorkshire had been brought back into the picture, but his second and more cautious instinct warned him not to jump to conclusions.

'Whoever was elected to chair the conference could almost certainly be guaranteed . . . well, if not an outright pro-motion, then at least to have a great big tick marked up against their name,' Dr Carew carried on carefully. 'In Arthur's case, it would almost certainly put him in the running to become Archbishop of . . . well, a very impressive minster, shall we

171

say, when the present incumbent retires. And in Celia's case . . . well, I think it was common knowledge that she had not given up her hopes of a bishopric at some point in the future.'

Jason began to look much more interested. Now these were what he called big stakes! At last, something worth killing over? 'I see,' he said again.

'And Arthur Bryce has, unofficially, been chosen to chair the conference,' David Carew finished quietly. 'But as I understand it, neither of them knew this. In fact, I'm breaking a confidence in telling you. The announcement isn't officially due to be published until next month.'

'I'll be discreet,' Jason promised. 'But it's obviously already known, amongst a certain number of you anyway, who had won the chairmanship, I mean? Is it possible that Reverend Gordon or Bishop Bryce might also have heard about it? If only as nothing more than a rumour?'

David Carew gave it some serious thought. Eventually he sighed and shook his head. 'I'd like to think not. We tend to keep things like this very much under our hats. I only know because I was on the selection committee.'

'Did you vote for Bishop Bryce?' Jason asked curiously.

Dr Carew smiled. 'No.'

'For Celia Gordon then?' Jason asked, raising his voice an octave in surprise.

Again, the bishop smiled. 'Not her either. There were two other nominees.'

'I see,' Jason said, and wondered. With the advent of the possibly fake manuscript, and now this committee thing, he seemed to be drowning in motives all of a sudden. It had the unfortunate effect of making him feel distrustful of both, when, in point of fact, either motive might hold good. 'Tell me a little more about how Bishop Bryce came to be chosen,' he said cautiously. 'I understand that Celia Gordon wasn't very popular . . .'

'Oh, I wouldn't say that,' Dr Carew put in quickly. 'She had a lot of big guns behind her. A woman chairperson would have been a first. And there are always those who like to see history being made. And there was no doubt that she was a very competent administrator. Sound. An academic, as you probably know. And there are a lot of advocates for women clergy, more than you might think.'

'But not enough to secure her the seat?'

'Not in this case, no. Even with the rumours . . .' Dr Carew snapped his mouth shut comically, then, realizing it was too late, smiled ruefully. 'Even with the rumours about Arthur Bryce going around, many thought he was a better choice. Well, perhaps a safer choice is the word to use. I suspect a lot of manoeuvring had been going on behind the scenes.'

Jason didn't doubt it. It was his experience that wherever power — of whatever kind — was being brokered, there were always dirty dealings of some kind lurking about in the background.

That wasn't what interested him.

'What rumours, Dr Carew?' Jason asked bluntly, making no apology for getting right to the heart of the matter.

David sighed, but he'd obviously been expecting this. 'First, let me make it quite clear that they are only rumours, Chief Inspector. It's being bandied about that Arthur had an affair a short while ago with one of his parishioners. There was absolutely no proof of it, and no woman ever came forward to complain or, as is more likely the case nowadays, to sell her story to the Sunday papers. And Chloe Bryce certainly seems to be standing by her man, so even if there was any substance to the rumours, there was obviously no real harm done.'

'And is the affair still going on?' Jason asked, then seeing the disapproving look on the bishop's face, added hastily, 'supposing anything had been going on at all, I mean?'

Dr Carew smiled wryly. 'No. According to the grapevine, it's all over, and has been for some months.'

'I see.'

Now Jason could understand why he'd touched such a nerve with both the Bryces when he'd asked if there'd been any nocturnal wanderings during the night. Talk about putting his foot in it!

'I hope you won't mention this more widely, Chief Inspector,' Dr Carew suddenly spoke up sharply and Jason wondered if any of his less than sympathetic feelings had been showing on his face. 'The last thing the Church needs is a scandal.'

And if the St Bede's manuscript turns out to have been stolen and replaced, you'll already have enough scandal on your plate, Jason thought sympathetically.

'No, of course not. We can be very discreet when we need to be,' Jason hastened to assure him.

Flora showed the unhappy bishop to the door. When she came back, she looked at her boss thoughtfully. 'At least the case seems to be opening up a bit, sir,' she said.

'Hmm,' Jason said, somewhat doubtfully.

'Do you think the Bryces knew they'd got this committee thing in the bag?' Flora asked. 'Or Reverend Gordon, for that matter?'

Jason sighed. 'No knowing. If they did, they'd have kept it to themselves. It wouldn't have been a very Christian thing to do, would it, to go about either boasting or moaning about it. But I can't see our Reverend Gordon taking it lying down, can you?'

Flora shook her head, then looked around as the door opened and the constable on guard in the lobby stuck her head around the door.

'Sir, there's a man here wants to see you. Says he's from *The Times*.'

Jason looked up in astonishment.

'He's not here for a story, sir,' she added hastily, seeing her superior's look. 'Or at least, he assures me he's not,' she added more darkly. 'He says he's got genuine information.'

Jason glanced at Flora, who was looking dubious. Jason sighed heavily. Like his sergeant, he'd seen the press get up to all manner of things for the sake of a story. Nevertheless . . .

'You've checked his credentials? He is from *The Times*?'

The constable nodded firmly. 'Yes, sir.'

Jason shrugged. 'Then show him in.'

* * *

The journalist who came through the door was dressed, of all things, in tweeds. A man in his late sixties, he was trim and fit-looking and when he spoke it was with the sort of upper-class accent that Jason would have expected. Some things, he mused, never change.

'Mr Smith, sir,' the constable introduced.

'Bretton-Smith, Chief Inspector,' the journalist rectified, shaking the proffered hand and sitting down without being asked. He reached at once into his jacket pocket for a notebook.

Jason flushed. 'I hope you don't think I've consented to give an interview . . .' he began hotly, then felt foolish as the journalist produced a sheet of paper from the big notebook and gave him a slightly hurt, slightly amused glance.

'I received this by this afternoon's post.' The journalist handed it over, making Jason glance surreptitiously at his watch. It wasn't yet 3:30. He certainly hadn't wasted any time!

Jason read it, his face registering a certain amount of surprise even though he tried to keep a poker face. Flora was hardly able to sit still. Without a word, he handed it over to her when he'd finished.

The letter was brief, but to the point. Sir Matthew Pierrepont had written to someone who was obviously an old friend at the paper, wanting to know if he'd be interested himself, or more likely, would know of anyone from a tabloid paper who'd be interested in a female-vicar scandal. If so, he was to get in touch with Matthew by phone right away.

'The man he wrote to, the addressee,' Mr Bretton-Smith said sardonically, 'has been dead for nearly six years. I inherited his desk. Naturally,' here he paused to smile slightly, 'I was curious.'

And so was Jason.

It went without saying that the journalist had tracked the archdeacon down to this conference, and then noted the death of a guest and the presence of a chief inspector with a gurgling of journalistic juices.

'Thank you for bringing this to my attention, Mr Bretton-Smith. If . . . anything comes of it, I'll see what can be done about giving you an exclusive,' Jason dismissed him, somewhat clumsily, he felt.

Bretton-Smith looked rather offended, as if Jason had just offered to give him a 'bung' under the table, but he rose and nodded politely.

Jason waited until he was well out of earshot behind the closed door, then said to Flora savagely, 'Get Pierrepont back in here.'

* * *

Sir Matthew Pierrepont came in, looking alternately gleeful, belligerent and curious.

Jason watched the old man walk stiff-legged to a chair and fold himself painfully into it. He looked slightly drunk.

'I want to know what you meant by this,' Jason said without preamble, his voice hard and cold as he pushed the piece of paper across the desk towards the archdeacon.

He noticed, approvingly, that Flora had come to stand close behind the cleric, just in case he tried to do something silly — like destroy the letter.

But Sir Matthew was not that foolish. He simply read the letter with a sneer then shrugged. 'Never seen it before,' he said flatly.

Jason smiled. 'Are you denying that it's your handwriting?'

Sir Matthew looked at him, blinking his rheumy grey eyes.

'It looks like my hand,' he admitted. 'But nothing a good forger couldn't copy.'

'Oh come now, Sir Matthew,' Jason said. 'You're surely not going to deny writing this letter?'

'I do, and I dare you to prove otherwise,' the old man snapped, getting to his feet. 'Now, if that's all.'

'It isn't,' Jason rasped back. 'I want to know exactly what kind of scandal you had in mind—'

'I told you before,' Sir Matthew interrupted rudely. 'If you want to speak to me, you'll have to do so through my lawyer. I only came in at all to see what you wanted this time.'

'If you know of any scandal involving Celia Gordon it's your duty to tell us,' Jason said, then realized just how ridiculous that sounded. 'We can get experts in to verify that this is your writing, Sir Matthew,' he tried instead, his voice distinctly threatening now as he watched the old man head towards the door.

Sir Matthew shrugged without turning around. 'Go ahead.' He sounded more pleased than put out, and Jason realized that the old sod probably would enjoy a good legal wrangle.

Flora all but slammed the door after him, her colour as high as her temper. 'I'd like to lock him up in a cell with a couple of Hell's Angels in a bad mood.'

'What have you got against Hell's Angels all of a sudden?' Jason asked, making Flora grin, if a shade reluctantly. 'What I'd like to know,' Jason continued glumly, 'is why we're suddenly being inundated with all this new information.'

And he wasn't put in any better a mood by the feeling that he was missing something. Something important.

What's more, he was worried about Monica Noble. Just what was she up to? He found her absence very suspicious indeed.

CHAPTER 14

'You're not wearing that!' Monica Noble said firmly to Carol-Ann, as she watched her teenaged daughter admiring her reflection in the mirror.

'What? Why not?' Carol-Ann demanded, turning around and mimicking her mother by standing with her hands aggressively on her hips. She was wearing a minuscule lem-on-coloured bikini and a faded pair of pink flip-flops.

Monica, pulling on a long-sleeved dress over her own modest turquoise one-piece, sighed elaborately. They were in her bedroom, getting ready to depart for the swimming party. 'Because, Carol-Ann,' she said patiently, haphazardly shoving two fluffy towel-like wraps into a large wicker bag, 'there will be a lot of your father's clerical colleagues there, and . . .' she swept on quickly, as she saw her rebellious daughter open her mouth, no doubt about to say something pithy, 'we're swimming in the river, not a heated swimming pool. Just think about that for a minute, why don't you?' she cautioned ominously.

Since her only child was at home that day, due to the mysterious workings of a 'teacher training day,' she'd invited Carol-Ann to come with her, not really expecting her to accept. After all, an hour or so splashing about with much older strangers could hardly rate highly on a modern young girl's wish list. But it turned out that she had underestimated the teenager's boredom threshold, since a planned shopping trip with her best friend had to be cancelled due to the so-called best friend getting a better offer of a day trip to the coast.

And to save herself from hearing, at length, about this particular tale of earth-shattering treachery, she'd rather impulsively invited her daughter to accompany her to come swimming and was fast beginning to wish that she hadn't.

Carol-Ann, long blonde hair streaming over her shoulders, now scowled at her mother uncertainly, fearing some sort of a trick. She'd bought the bikini at the tail end of last summer and had hardly had a chance to wear it, and she was looking forward to strutting her stuff. Doing so in front of a load of old fuddy-duddy vicars had appealed both to her vanity and her sense of iconoclastic daring. Naturally, she'd suspected her mother wouldn't particularly like this plan, and as a consequence she was exceedingly wary. For her mother, she had long since learned, had a habit of being rather crafty when it came to thwarting her. And she was not about to let reverse psychology do her out of her fun.

'What do you mean?' she nevertheless felt compelled to ask.

Monica sighed a shade wearily. The last thing she wanted was a prolonged argument with her daughter. They were already running a little late. 'Well for a start, it's only May, and the river, unlike a swimming pool, won't exactly be heated, will it?' she pointed out reasonably. 'And even though it's been sunny all day, the temperature will still be enough to give us goosebumps, I expect. That's part of the thrill of the experience, or so Jessica was saying.' Monica realized that she didn't sound particularly convinced of this herself and tried to push the thought of shivering, blue-tinged flesh to one side. They were bound to feel warmer once they started exercising, weren't they?

Carol-Ann shrugged one shoulder negligently at this, clearly less than impressed by her mother's opening gambit.

After all, she didn't mind a little physical discomfort so long as she looked good and set middle-aged and elderly jaws comically dropping.

'But more than that,' Monica, who knew her daughter very well indeed, added shrewdly, 'there will be the wildlife to contend with.'

Carol-Ann's head whipped around. From over her shoulder, she had been admiring her slim derriere in the mirror's reflection. Now her eyes widened visibly. 'Wildlife?' she echoed uncertainly.

Trying not to look triumphant, Monica nodded solemnly. 'Of course. It's a river — there'll be fish, and crayfish, and frogs and . . . er . . . newts,' she added with a flourish. 'Are you really sure you want to be showing so much bare flesh around slimy newts?'

Carol-Ann's eyes narrowed. 'You're just trying to put me off,' she said. But she was clearly thinking about it. And, in the end, the newts won. 'Oh all right,' she shrugged dramatically. 'I'll wear something else.' She stomped exaggeratedly across the room to go back to her own bedroom, where she could change.

'What's wrong with that navy blue costume — the one you wear to sports day?' Monica called the suggestion after her hopefully. It was long in the leg and high in the neck, and covered all the bits in between.

'Oh, Mum! That's just for serious swimming, when we do games at school. It's really naff otherwise. It's practically a part of the school uniform! No, I'll wear the red one,' she said, in a tone that brooked no further discussion.

Although she was, in fact, a very good swimmer and liked competing with her fellow students when it came to races, she didn't think she'd be doing anything so strenuous this afternoon that it would require the professional swimsuit. Besides, wasn't red the colour of the good old-fashioned 'scarlet woman' so beloved of the Victorians?

Monica supposed that, as a compromise, it would have to do. At least it was a one-piece and had a reasonably high, scooped neck. 'All right, love. But get a move on will you, we're rather late!'

She threw some more towels into the basket and then, as an afterthought, a paperback novel that she'd been reading, and within a few minutes, mother and daughter were ready to go.

The walk to the river was a short one, and like her mother, Carol-Ann had donned a long summery dress over her costume, since neither were sure whether someone had thought to provide a changing room at the conference centre.

As they approached the banks of the river, it became obvious that they were among the last to arrive. Already several swimmers were splashing about in the inviting-looking dark river water, and many more were disrobing, ready to join them. There was plenty of pale-coloured flesh on view, but with everyone in the same boat, the atmosphere was cheerful and determinedly light-hearted. It was a beautiful afternoon, with butterflies, and dragonflies flitting about the pink rosebay willowherb and the spikes of purple loosestrife. Swallows swooped along the river course, dipping their beaks into the water to scoop up water to mix with mud, which they would then use to form their dome-shaped nests under the eaves of the older houses in the village.

Walking slowly along the riverbank, Monica noticed that the elderly Archdeacon Pierrepont had found some sort of very long rod with a hooked loop on one end. Was it a bargepole? Although she, like everyone else, had grown up with the old saying 'I wouldn't touch it with a bargepole,' she'd never actually known what a bargepole looked like.

As she claimed her own bit of grassy bank by laying out their towels, she noticed that the old man was slowly walking along the bank, prodding and poking about, and at one point, dragged the pole into the side, dislodging rather a lot of mud into the river. He was also smirking in a rather superior manner at his fellow conference-goers, who were either energetically swimming along in the current or were shivering pathetically on the outskirts, trying to look interested in the ducks and moorhens. These feathered creatures were staring at the unexpected human invaders in some alarm from a patch of bulrushes, and didn't look particularly impressed.

The female delegate from Bangor gave the elderly cleric a distinctly less than charitable look as he went by her. He was swirling up a lot of silt that was washing her way and beginning to stain her pristine white costume.

He stopped to give a patch of river weed a particularly vicious prod, and twisted the hook around a lime-green clump, pulling it free and letting it float into the current. There it overtook one of the more lethargic swimmers, who watched it go past with a surprised double take.

'The squire's here, I see,' Carol-Ann said a shade sardonically, and Monica turned just in time to see Sir Andrew Courtenay execute a rather neat little dive from low down on the river bank and surge strongly out into the middle of the river. He alone of the company looked to be very slightly tanned, and wore a pair of plain black trunks. He also displayed a fair amount of muscle in his upper arms, indicating a fit and healthy lifestyle. 'Hmmm, he's rather fit, isn't he, for a wrinkly?' Carol-Ann said, with grudging admiration.

Monica hoped Carol-Ann wouldn't try flirting with him. She'd have to keep an eye on—

'I think Sir Andrew is a little worried about our health and safety,' a voice said behind them, and Monica turned to find Reverend Jessica Taylor walking up to them. She'd already changed into her costume which, Monica noticed with some dismay, was distressingly similar to her own.

'Oh?'

'Yes. I think he's here to keep an eye on us and make sure one of us doesn't drown and then sue him,' Jessica laughed.

'Rather hard to do if you've drowned,' Monica grinned back.

Jessica laughed and then frowned slightly as she saw Monica give her costume another look. 'What? It's not too young for me, is it?' she asked with some alarm. 'Only I do so like the colour.'

Monica grinned, pulled off her own concealing dress, and said drolly, 'Me too.'

The two women eyed their almost identical costumes and burst out laughing. 'Is it as bad a faux pas as wearing the same dress?' Jessica asked, giggling slightly.

'I hope not,' Monica said. 'Come on, quick, let's get in before anyone notices.'

'Right, and before I lose my nerve. My friend went in five minutes ago, and assured me it wasn't too cold. Mind you,' Jessica said wryly, 'it was rather hard to tell, since she was a bit breathless at the time.'

'Oh don't,' Monica groaned. 'Come on. It can't be that bad.' Bravely, the two women scrambled down the river bank, where the others who had gone before had thoughtfully created a bit of a path through the vegetation, and almost simultaneously put one foot cautiously into the water.

Soft silt and mud squeezed instantly between Monica's toes and a cold shiver shot up her spine.

'Oh crikey!' Jessica said beside her, clinging onto the grass on the bank, precariously half in and half out of the water.

Monica found herself laughing helplessly. From the riverbank, Carol-Ann watched them suspiciously. 'Mum, is it really cold?' she asked anxiously.

'Er . . . no, sweetheart,' Monica lied shamelessly. 'It's what's called bracing.'

She caught Jessica's rolling eyes and hastily looked away. 'They say it's best to do it all at once,' Monica said helplessly. 'Just throw yourself in and submerse yourself all in one fell swoop. Apparently it's harder doing it bit by bit.'

'Oh yeah?' Jessica muttered. The two women looked at each other, then turned and saw a white-haired lady cleric swim serenely by (who must have been seventy if she was a day), and suddenly rather shamefaced, the two women pushed away into near identical breaststrokes.

Monica managed to refrain from swearing like a trooper, but only by biting her bottom lip — hard! Beside her, Jessica began saying the Lord's Prayer under her breath.

'Here I come!' Carol-Ann said, and Monica turned just in time to see her daughter take a running jump and do a cannonball, landing between them. In her defence, she didn't have the breath to cry out a warning, and besides, it would have been far too late anyway.

Carol-Ann's sleek silver-blonde head popped up between them and her shuddering daughter promptly showed that she had no trouble in swearing at all. Behind her, a large, florid-faced, middle-aged canon from Northumberland lazily interrupted his amateur crawl to grin over at her admiringly.

'Haven't heard language like that since I was a padre in the navy, young lady,' he complimented her.

Monica felt herself go scarlet. 'Carol-Ann!' she finally found her breath.

'Well! It's p-p-perishing,' Carol-Ann shot back.

'Start swimming then and warm up,' Monica said tartly. 'In fact, that's probably good advice for all of us,' she added to Jessica, who needed no prompting.

And so for the next five minutes the three of them proceeded to swim about twenty yards downstream before turning and fighting their way back up against the current. Luckily all the self-respecting fish, toads and newts had long since departed for a less noisy part of the river, and they were left with just the emerald dragonflies and a very curious orange-tip butterfly that almost landed on Carol-Ann's nose.

They carefully skirted a large patch of lime-green floating river weed as Sir Andrew cut past them, doing a very fast and rather professional-looking crawl.

Up on the bank, Monica saw Bishop Bryce and his wife arrive. She was not surprised to notice that Chloe Bryce was wearing a streamlined, professional-looking black swimming costume, and watched as the elegant woman effortlessly tucked her hair into a sleek black swimming cap and duck-dived cleanly into the water with barely a ripple. She swam several yards below the surface before coming up for air, and didn't seem at all affected by the sudden drop in her body temperature.

Her husband, chunkier around the middle, but also clad in black, slid more cautiously into the water and swam much more hesitantly out to join his wife.

'Oh you finally made it, then,' Monica heard an old man's voice say, and from where she and Jessica were treading water whilst waiting for a pair of swimmers to pass them by, she looked up to see Archdeacon Pierrepont greet another man.

The newcomer was vaguely familiar — silver-haired, and like Arthur Bryce, looking rather chunky around the middle in a pair of white swimming trunks. She finally placed him as the man from the museum — the one who was overseeing the loan of the famous old manuscript.

Dr Simon Grade, Monica thought with a look of surprise and concern, looked almost ill. He was pale and sweating and the smile he managed to summon up for the archdeacon was pitiful indeed. 'Oh yes, I wouldn't miss it for the world,' Simon said. 'Thank you so much for inviting me. Er . . . you're not swimming yourself I see,' he added, rather unnecessarily, since the archdeacon was wearing a long, scarlet-trimmed black cassock.

The elderly cleric waved his curious long hooked pole in the air. 'No, no. Rheumatism and all that,' the older man said. 'But don't let me keep you, young fella. Have at it,' he said, with a rather cruel smile, sweeping his hand out encouragingly towards the water.

Monica could clearly see that his companion looked at the river with a distinct lack of enthusiasm, and she could well imagine that the academic was probably one of those men who probably abhorred all sports; hearty, healthy, outdoor sports most of all.

'Oh, er, yes, of course.'

Not wanting to watch the poor man struggle down the bank and then flop about like a stunned fish when the temperature of the river water registered, Monica turned and swam fast to catch up with Jessica, who was now just a little ahead of her.

Carol-Ann swam briskly and competently past, quickly outpacing her mother. Monica didn't mind. Now that she'd had a chance to acclimatize to the river, she was beginning to enjoy herself. As were those around her. A makeshift game of water polo seemed to be taking place a little further downstream and she noticed that Sir Andrew was still swimming steadily up and down, having clearly delegated himself as a lifeguard.

Monica had just caught up with Jessica by the large patch of river weed again when it happened. One moment she was doing her usual, less than efficient overarm crawl, and the next she was suddenly pulled underwater. She was so taken aback that, luckily, she gasped automatically in surprise as she went down, and thus took in a good lungful of air. Finding her head suddenly underwater, she panicked a bit and instantly closed her eyes. Not the best of swimmers, she thrashed her legs about spasmodically as the water muted the sound of the other people around her, but amplified the fast thud-thud-thud of her own elevated heartbeat.

She could feel something slimy and cold around her calf and realised that she must have got too close to the river weed, which had entangled her legs and must be pulling her under.

For a moment, it seemed as if she simply couldn't break free, and she knew a moment of stark, primordial terror. Then, all at once, it was as if the river let her go, and her head broke the surface. Opening her eyes again she took a deep, shuddering breath. The sunlight had never looked so bright or so welcome. Using a shaky hand, she brushed her dark hair out of her eyes.

'Mum, are you all right?' It was Carol-Ann's voice, and she turned with relief to see her daughter's concerned face as she swam up to her. 'I saw you suddenly disappear. Did you mean to do that?'

Monica gave a shaky little laugh. 'I'm fine. And no, I didn't. I think some weed . . . Jessica!' she broke off as her friend, who'd been alerted by Carol-Ann's sharp call to her mother and had come swimming over, suddenly likewise abruptly disappeared from view.

'Bloody hell, what's going on?' Carol-Ann muttered, and taking a deep breath, quickly bobbed down out of sight. Since Monica knew that her daughter swam like a fish and liked going underwater, she didn't panic. Besides, Carol-Ann had clearly done so of her own free will.

She did a quick full-circle turn, anxiously scanning for her friend's head, and a moment later, both Jessica and Carol-Ann popped up again. Carol-Ann was holding on to Jessica Taylor firmly. The older woman started to cough.

Monica somewhat clumsily splashed over to them. 'Are you OK?' she asked her friend.

Jessica looked pale, and coughed up a bit more river water.

'Yes, I'm fine,' she croaked, obviously lying. 'I felt something cold and slippery around my leg, and then I was underwater. It felt like something was deliberately pulling me down! It was scary, I can tell you.'

'I know just how you feel,' Monica said with feeling, and looked at her friend anxiously. 'There must be a really bad patch of weed around here. Perhaps it's time to get out now anyway,' she added, seeing Jessica was struggling for breath.

'Good idea,' her friend agreed.

Carol-Ann gave her mother a long look as together, with Jessica between them, they slowly made their way to the bank. They let Jessica get out first, helping her up the bank, as her legs were clearly feeling a bit wobbly, and then followed her to where she'd left her towel.

'Oh, the sun's lovely and warm,' Jessica said, still a little shakily. 'I think I'll lie down and sunbathe for a bit.'

'Good idea. Is there anything I can get you?' Monica asked. 'Some lemon squash? I brought a flask with us.'

'Thank you, I think I might just take you up on that. That river water tasted foul!' Jessica laughed.

'We'll be right back,' Monica promised, moving away to find her own spot and the wicker basket she'd left by the towels.

As she did so, Carol-Ann, loping alongside her, said quietly, 'You know, Mum, when I went down after Jessica, I could have sworn there was another swimmer down there with us.'

Monica, reaching for the flask of lemon squash in her basket, looked across at the teenager with a flash of concern. 'What do you mean? Someone else caught in the weeds?' she asked sharply. 'Carol-Ann, we need to—'

'No, no, don't panic. I don't mean anyone else in trouble. Just someone else swimming away from us. It was hard to tell — the silt had been all churned up. So I might be wrong.' Carol-Ann shrugged, but her mother could tell the young girl looked both puzzled and faintly perturbed.

Monica thoughtfully returned to her friend, and poured out a drink. As she did so, she let her eyes drift around.

Over by the riverbank, Chloe Bryce and her husband were now sitting close together, but she noticed that neither of them was talking to the other. A little further away, Dr Simon Grade had also climbed out and was forlornly rubbing himself down with a towel. He still looked grim and now thoroughly depressed. Archdeacon Pierrepont was at the side of the bank, and the hook on his long pole was dripping wet. As he turned, Monica could see that a little green wisp of river weed was still clinging to the metal. And still swimming up and down, keeping careful watch, was Sir Andrew Courtenay. Who obviously couldn't have noticed that first Monica and then Jessica had run into a bit of trouble. Which was odd, when you thought about it.

Telling herself not to make a drama out of a crisis, Monica began to talk to Jessica about husbands, and the perils and pitfalls of trying to combine church work with the modern world.

But beneath the laughter, she was worried. Very worried.

CHAPTER 15

The blackbirds were singing in the shrubbery as Graham opened his front door to a reddening sunset, and followed David Carew out onto the gravel-lined path.

'Well, the conference is breaking up tomorrow,' the bishop said, with more than a hint of relief in his voice. 'Not that that'll mean the end of things, of course,' he added flatly. 'The police . . .' he let the sentence trail off with a heavy sigh.

Graham knew how he felt. 'The police, I suppose, asked everyone to stay on another day?' The conference had, he recalled, originally been due to break up that afternoon.

'So it seems,' the bishop agreed, then held out his hand. 'Well, Graham, take care.'

Graham shook his bishop's hand with a smile and a promise to do just that, then waited until he'd disappeared from sight before going back inside. There he found Monica sitting in the lounge, the television on, but her mind obviously not on the programme. She looked up swiftly.

'Are you sure you're feeling all right?' he asked, and not for the first time. When she'd returned home and told him what had happened at that afternoon's impromptu wild-swimming event, he'd been deeply worried. In spite of her protestations that both she and Carol-Ann were none the worse for their bit of fright, he wasn't convinced.

'I'm fine,' Monica said, giving him a mock-scowl. 'Don't fuss. How did things go with the bishop?' she asked, deliberately changing the subject.

Graham sighed heavily.

'Problems?' she interpreted sympathetically.

Graham smiled. 'Where do you want me to start?'

It didn't strike Monica as at all odd that David had chosen her husband to come and tell all his woes to. So she listened gravely as he told her about the possible question mark hanging over the St Bede's manuscript.

'And if it is a fake,' Monica said sadly, 'won't his critics crow?' She knew the manuscript had been very much David Carew's baby.

'Not if they get it back,' Graham said, and wondered, even as he spoke, how realistically that could be hoped for. 'And there's something else worrying him. The big conference next year . . .'

Again Monica listened intently as he told her about the competition for the chair between the murdered woman and Bishop Arthur Bryce, and about the rumours circulating about Arthur Bryce's affair with one of his parishioners.

'Do you really think Jason suspects him? Bryce, I mean?' Graham asked when Monica had had time to digest this bit of news in silence.

To his consternation, she merely shrugged. 'It's possible.' It hadn't been what he wanted to hear.

'But, Monica, it's just so . . . preposterous. Churchmen simply don't go around killing off rivals in order to get promoted. Or at least, not in this day and age they don't,' he added darkly.

Monica smiled. 'No, it does seem a bit drastic,' she agreed. 'But Chloe Bryce would make a rather fine Lady Macbeth, don't you think?' she teased.

Graham smiled. 'Well, she's obviously one hundred per cent behind her husband's career,' he agreed cautiously. 'But even so . . .'

Yes, even so, he was concerned and she understood that. Any major scandal affecting a member of his church was bound to shake him to the core. Monica reached for his hand and squeezed it comfortingly. 'I know and I agree. I don't think we've discovered the real motive yet,' she said firmly, watching the worry lines that had creased his forehead slowly ease away.

She kissed him gently and ran a finger across his cheek. 'But we should have discovered the real reasons behind it by now,' she added fretfully.

Graham frowned at her, turning on the settee to look at her more fully. 'What do you mean?'

Monica shook her head restlessly. All day long she'd been going over all that she knew, which, due to her various sources, was most of what Jason and his team also knew. And something told her that she should have some sort of a glimmering by now. So what was she missing? Or not seeing? Or at least, not seeing in the right way? She knew this feeling from the past. Twice before, she'd had this sort of tingling in the back of her mind that told her that she knew the identity of a killer, if only she would think about it.

And, what's more, someone had said something important to her only recently. Jessica Taylor, perhaps? Apart from the people she'd talked to on the manor house lawns for the past two days, she'd spoken to Jessica the most. No. Perhaps it wasn't Jessica after all. But somebody, somewhere, had said something that . . . Oh, it was no use. It just wouldn't come.

Monica sighed heavily and hoped Jason was having better luck than she was.

Just so long as he wasn't building up a case against them.

* * *

As it happened, Jason was building up a case against someone, but it was not the Nobles. It began with yet another routine report. It was Flora, going over the latest batch, who had suddenly caught her breath and stood up excitedly. 'Sir, look at this.'

Jason, who'd been staring at the clock and thinking about going home to a ready meal and the latest James Bond DVD, felt his stomach clench at the excited tone in his sergeant's voice. He held out his hand and quickly skimmed the report, surprised to discover that it was on Sir Andrew Courtenay, then found his eyes skidding to a halt at the mention of a certain name, as had Flora's before him.

There, in a dry-as-dust report about the death of the squire's daughter, was the information that she'd been married in Bath, by one Reverend Celia Gordon.

Jason stared at the stark piece of information for several seconds then looked up at his sergeant. 'Well, he kept quiet about that, didn't he?' he said softly.

He supposed he should be feeling good right about now, or at least gratified. But he didn't. A picture of the grieving man they'd met only briefly flickered at the back of his mind and haunted him, in some strange way.

Flora nodded. 'He did, sir,' she agreed grimly. Something in her tone made Jason wonder if she was feeling as deflated as he was. Absurd as it was, he knew that neither of them wanted it to be Andrew Courtenay, but as police officers investigating a murder, such an attitude had to be stamped on. And quickly.

'He said he'd never met her,' Flora said flatly.

'Not quite,' Jason replied, recalling now what had struck him as so strange when they'd first asked Sir Andrew if he'd met Celia Gordon before. 'Didn't he say something like . . . "I don't know her" or "I never knew her"?'

Flora shook her head. 'I can't remember. I can look it up in the notes, sir,' she said, but Jason was already shaking his head and getting to his feet.

'No. But look out that report on his daughter's accidental overdose again, will you?'

For a few minutes, both of them reread the report on the death of Sandra Jane Simmonds, née Courtenay, and that of her husband, Clive. The stark facts stated at the inquest hadn't changed. It was the considered opinion of the police investigating the case that Clive Simmonds, a well-known user and sometime pusher, had procured a fatally large and unusually pure dose of heroin and that the consequent deaths of him and his wife had been recorded as an accidental overdose, rather than suicide. They'd both been found dead in their beds in the rather run-down semi that Clive's parents had bought for them as a wedding present.

'Sounds as if the Simmonds were fairly well-to-do, sir,' Flora commented. 'If they could afford to give their son a house, I mean. Even if they did then let it go to rack and ruin.'

'Hmm. And we already know that Celia Gordon's church is in a wealthy, upper-crust area,' Jason reminded her. 'And Clive went to a public school, you'll notice.' He tapped the piece of paper listing Clive Simmonds' CV.

'I dare say that's how he could afford his habit,' Flora said bitterly. 'Mummy and Daddy kept him in funds.'

'No wonder Sir Andrew opposed the marriage so fiercely,' Jason said, real pity in his voice now. 'What father wants his daughter to marry a drug addict?'

'He was supposed to be clean, sir.' Flora pointed out the social reports on Clive Simmonds, but without much enthusiasm. 'Drug rehab, regular doctor's check-ups. His family were convinced he was cured. So, I would imagine, was Sandra Jane Courtenay.'

Jason said nothing. No doubt Sir Andrew too had had his doubts. He'd even disinherited Sandra in an attempt to make her see reason. And still she'd married her drug addict. In Celia Gordon's church. With Celia Gordon presiding.

'Let's go,' he said grimly, leading the way not to Sir Andrew's study, as she'd expected, but to the kitchens.

There all was organized bedlam — not surprising when Flora realized how close it was to dinner time. The smells were delicious, the staff harried, but Jason ignored it all. He beckoned Rory Blundell across to him. The head chef cast the two police officers an impatient and jaundiced look, but turned away from the hollandaise sauce he was overseeing and met them in the doorway. He made a show of looking at his watch.

Jason ignored him. 'Can you tell me if it's usual for Sir Andrew to be in and out of the kitchens often during the course of a normal working day?' he asked, his voice bland and casual, but causing shivers of unease to ripple through the chef.

'I suppose so,' Rory Blundell said reluctantly.

'Was he in and out on Saturday?'

'Yes,' the reply was terse in the extreme. 'But I never saw him near the sponges, if that's what you're after,' he added aggressively.

Jason had expected the belligerence and didn't take offence. 'Of course not. You'd have told us at once if you had, wouldn't you?' he agreed mildly.

Rory didn't bat an eyelash. 'Anything else? As you can see, I'm busy.'

Jason shook his head and felt the chef's eyes boring into his back as he turned and pushed open the swing doors.

This time he went to the squire's study and knocked loudly. After a moment he heard a summons and pushed open the door. Sir Andrew was seated behind his desk, listlessly fingering a paper knife. He looked up dully as they walked in and motioned them to a pair of chairs, then nodded towards the drinks cabinet. 'Sherry? Port?'

'No thank you, Sir Andrew.' Jason sat down, and got straight to the point.

'Is it true that Celia Gordon was the vicar who married your daughter Sandra Jane to Clive Simmonds nearly three years ago?'

Sir Andrew slowly nodded. He didn't look surprised, or make any startled movement. He didn't even look annoyed. 'Yes. She not only married them, she actively encouraged Sandra in her choice of groom. His parents were cronies of hers, or so I understood. The Simmonds are big in Bath apparently,' he added with a strange, sad smile.

'And you knew all this?' Jason prompted, not angry, but not elated either.

'Of course,' he shrugged, as if it was all so unimportant now. 'In the beginning, when she first announced her engagement, Sandra and I were still speaking. It was only after I learned about Clive and saw for myself what kind of a useless and dangerous bastard he was that I put my foot down. Sandra pointed out how respectable his family was and how even their vicar spoke up for him. Sandra thought that Reverend Gordon was . . . well, she looked up to her. Admired her,' Sir Andrew said helplessly. 'What could I do?'

'I see. And Celia Gordon took Sandra's side when you objected to the marriage?'

Sir Andrew nodded. 'Oh yes. She would, wouldn't she? The Simmonds were significant donors to her various pet projects and they saw their son's marriage as another vital step towards getting him to "settle down" and keep on the straight and narrow.'

'I see. So you were lying when you said you'd never met her?' Jason accused, wondering what he'd say to this.

But Sir Andrew merely sat there, looking at him in a vaguely puzzled way. 'Did I say that?'

Flora stirred restlessly beside her boss.

'Sir Andrew, I think at this point I should warn you . . .' and Jason recited the legal warnings he was duty-bound to give when questioning a suspect. Flora very carefully wrote it all down. Sir Andrew listened to the warning in silence. He didn't look particularly alarmed. Or even interested. As he made no demur, Jason carried on quickly, before he had a chance to change his mind.

'Sir Andrew, did you blame Celia Gordon for encouraging your daughter to marry Clive Simmonds?'

'Of course I did.'

Even Jason was a bit surprised by this blank admission. Did the man have no conception of how bad this all sounded for him? 'And you resented her even more for performing the ceremony?'

195

'Yes. I wasn't present at the wedding, naturally, but I heard it was quite a social event in the city.'

Jason was getting a bit worried about Sir Andrew's attitude. His voice was absolutely toneless. It was like talking to a robot. And the way he kept turning the paper knife over and over in his hands was also distracting and worrying. Jason would have bet any amount of money that the squire wasn't even aware that he had anything in his hands. He began to wonder if he should call in a medic of some kind, someone with specialist psychiatric experience — or the police surgeon at the very least. On the other hand he didn't want to interrupt the momentum of the interview.

'Did you know that Celia Gordon was among those invited to this particular conference, Sir Andrew?' he asked, and tensed, thinking that surely now the man would put up some kind of defence. But it didn't happen.

'Yes. They always send me a guest list in advance. It helps us to make sure everything runs more smoothly,' Sir Andrew explained patiently.

Jason glanced at Flora, reassured to see that she was getting it all down.

'And how far in advance were you aware of Celia Gordon's imminent arrival? A few days?'

'Something like that,' Sir Andrew agreed. He was looking straight at the chief inspector as he spoke, but Jason had the uncomfortable feeling that he wasn't seeing him at all. Perhaps it was shock? Some murderers, when confronted with the sudden possibility of being found out, went into a kind of numb disbelief.

'So you knew Celia Gordon was due to come to your home. By your own admission you hated her and blamed her for your daughter's death. Is that so?'

Sir Andrew sighed heavily. 'If it hadn't been for Celia Gordon, Sandra might not have married that bastard. I might have been able to bring her around. She never was very strong-willed, you know. If she'd had less support from those around her at the time . . .' Sir Andrew shrugged helplessly again.

'And on the Saturday morning, the first full day of the conference, were you present when the waiter who'd served Celia Gordon commented on her being allergic to nuts?' Jason asked.

And then at last — and for the first time — he saw something flicker in the squire's eyes. Sir Andrew Courtenay seemed to stiffen just slightly in his chair. His eyes widened a little in surprise. 'Sorry?' he said, his voice definitely holding a note of surprise now. 'Was I what?'

Jason was glad the monotone was gone, even if it did signal the possible end to Sir Andrew's obliging answers. 'Did you know that Reverend Celia Gordon was allergic to peanuts?' Jason repeated clearly.

Sir Andrew flushed a slow, creeping tide of red. His mouth opened, but no sound came out.

'I understand you're in and out of the kitchens all day,' Jason pushed on. 'You were in the dining hall that morning. The morning Celia Gordon rather loudly proclaimed her fatal allergy to nuts. Did you know about that, Sir Andrew?' Jason demanded, being careful to keep his voice clear and calm.

Sir Andrew's flushed face paled to a strained greyish-yellow. His look went from the scribbling Flora to her superior, back to Flora and then finally rested on Jason. 'Bloody hell,' he gasped. 'You think I killed her?'

He sounded absurdly surprised.

'Please answer the question, Sir Andrew,' Jason said, ignoring the shaft of worry that was now slithering down his spine. He reminded himself that the squire might be a brilliant actor, or that the stunned disbelief was indeed real, but not as a result of his innocence, but just at his inability to believe that Jason would have the temerity to accuse one of his rank of murder.

'I think,' Sir Andrew said, beginning to sound angry and just a little shaken, 'that I shall take your earlier advice and have a solicitor present.'

And with that he reached for the phone.

Beside him, Jason heard Flora sigh with regret and real-ized that his sergeant, at least, had no doubts that they'd got their man, even if she was sympathetic towards him. And who could blame her for that belief? Sir Andrew had a proper motive. He'd had plenty of time to plan the killing, or if not plan it, at least to work himself up into a state whereby he'd be ready and willing to commit the ultimate crime. He'd had access to the kitchens. In fact, it all fitted nicely into place.

So what was wrong with it?

Because Jason, instead of feeling relief at having a prime suspect and some real hard evidence to build on at last, was beginning to feel downright uneasy.

'I think you should ask your solicitor to meet you at the police station in Kidlington, sir,' Jason said, interrupting the squire's terse conversation on the telephone, and standing up slowly. Although he had enough to go on to charge Sir Andrew then and there, he rather thought he'd leave it until they got to Thames Valley HQ.

Besides, he needed to have a word with his own superiors. It didn't take a genius to know that they were not going to like this.

Any of it.

* * *

That night the killer prepared for bed in a state of near exhaus-tion and emotional collapse. It needed an extraordinary dis-play of iron-clad self-control and willpower to carry on and look as if everything was all right.

How could things have gone so wrong again? It was almost as if divine providence . . .

No, I mustn't think like that. I mustn't be defeatist.

I just have to try again, that's all. The conference will break up soon, so it has to be tomorrow. And this time, it can't be anything fancy. I'm just going to have to get the job done, whatever it takes.

As the killer climbed into bed, mind whirling, time seemed to drag as a feverish, desperate mind dreamt up scenarios and was forced to disregard them.

How can I do it? When? With what?

The task ahead loomed as large as a mountain, but it was impossible to plan anything specific. And as the hours dragged, the killer realized that it simply boiled down to watching and waiting for an opportunity.

And the determination to succeed, no matter what the risk.

* * *

Tuesday morning and Heyford Bassett awoke to a storm of disbelief and dismay. Phyllis Cox, the owner of the village shop, was, as always, first with the news and soon the entire village had learned of the arrest of Sir Andrew Courtenay for the murder of Celia Gordon.

Graham came back with the news, grim-faced and tight-lipped, and told Monica all about it.

'But, Graham, they can't!' she said, aghast. 'I mean, well, obviously they can, but . . . why?'

Graham shook his head worriedly. 'Phyllis hadn't got all the details. Give her time,' he added wryly.

Monica sat down with a bump onto the settee and shook her head. Sir Andrew? She'd never even considered him. He wasn't even on her mental list of possible suspects. Suddenly she was aware of how big the gulf must be between what she knew, guessed, surmised or suspected, and what the police must know.

Could it be possible?

There was nothing, really, apart from her shock and natural disinclination to believe it, to say that Sir Andrew wasn't the killer. And unless she came up with a better theory, and one, moreover, that could be proved, who was to say that the police hadn't got their man?

Graham watched his wife's face, seeing the shadows and thoughts flickering behind her lovely blue eyes, and sighed. He knew that she wanted to be alone to think. And he didn't doubt that his wife could think very well indeed when she needed to.

'I'll be in the study,' he said quietly. There was nothing for him to do right now. Sir Andrew had no immediate family in need of support or counselling, and the last thing Graham wanted at this point, especially considering his own role in the affair, was to get under Jason's feet.

* * *

Jason was, at that moment, sitting in the incident room, moodily watching some constables packing things away.

Last night he'd laid all the facts before his immediate superior, who'd had a hurried phone call with *his* superior, and had finally been told to go ahead and make the formal arrest. Jason had done so, in the presence of Sir Andrew's grim-faced lawyer. The squire was to be up before the courts later on that day in an effort to obtain bail. Jason supposed he should be there, but had already decided to wriggle out of it and delegate that privilege to a junior. Delegation was one of the few perks that went with a promotion, as he'd quickly discovered.

Besides, if nothing else, there were still some loose ends that he needed to tidy up here. Not least of which was the expert's report on the St Bede's manuscript.

All Sir Andrew's legal team needed to find out was that the police had another hot suspect, with another compelling motive, and all legal hell would be let loose. Besides, Jason still wasn't sure that they had the right man. Not that he'd be willing to say so out loud.

'Sir, Professor Wyatt is here,' Flora said, walking in then stepping aside to allow a surprisingly young-looking man to precede her.

Jason rose and held out his hand. 'Professor Wyatt.'

'Are you Chief Inspector Dury? The man I spoke to on the phone yesterday?' He glanced around the office-cum-country-house-study and smiled rather sadly. 'Nice place this. Never met Sir Andrew,' he added vaguely.

'Did you get a chance to study the manuscript last night, Professor Wyatt?' Jason asked, in no mood for pleasantries.

'Yes indeed. A most remarkable forgery,' he said at once, watching the chief inspector closely for his reaction.

Jason nodded. 'I see,' he said, keeping his face bland. 'You're sure?' he asked smoothly.

'Oh as sure as I can be without the chemical analysis to back it up. But I have no doubts whatsoever that the tests will eventually confirm my findings. The forgery is first class, mind you, but I have no doubts at all that it *is* a forgery. You can have a full written report in due course, naturally.'

Jason, not wanting to have to field any awkward questions, rose quickly to his feet. 'Well, thank you very much for doing this on such short notice, Professor. I hope it hasn't inconvenienced you too much?'

'Oh not at all, not at all. Always glad to look at new material. Even fakes. In fact, sometimes the fakes are downright more interesting than the real thing!' he laughed, and beaming widely, the professor left.

'You want to see Simon Grade again, sir?' Flora said, more as a statement than a question.

Jason nodded, and Flora dispatched a constable to pick him up. She only hoped that he hadn't done a runner when he'd realized that they were on to him. Sometimes they did that, and the more inoffensive and respectable the perp seemed, the more likely he was to bolt.

'Sir,' she began, a nervous quality in her tone making him look at her intently. 'You don't think . . . well, this isn't going to throw a spanner in the works when it comes to our case against Courtenay, is it?'

Jason rolled his shoulders, not surprised to feel them tense and aching. 'I don't know. I don't see why it should.

There are still more factors pointing to Sir Andrew than to Grade. For instance, how would Simon Grade know that Celia was allergic to peanuts? He wasn't at the breakfast when she announced it to the world. And during the afternoon he was in the hall with his precious manuscript. When would he have had a chance to reconnoitre the kitchens?'

Flora nodded, apparently satisfied. Jason just wished that he could be so sure.

* * *

Graham looked up as a soft tap came on the study door. 'Come in, darling.'

Monica walked in, smiling broadly. 'And how did you know I wasn't old Mrs Thistlewaite, come to tell you her dreams about angels again? What would she say to being called darling?'

'She'd be over the moon,' Graham said drolly, pushing aside the book he'd been reading.

Monica was dressed in jeans that hugged her figure like a Latin lover and a plain white T-shirt. She had her hands slipped into the jeans pockets and her shoulders were slightly hunched forward. She also looked a trifle shamefaced, a little excited, but mostly worried.

Graham sighed and got up, walking around to meet her in front of the desk. He leaned back against it and held out his arms. Instantly she came into them and rested her cheek against his shoulder.

'You think you know who did it, don't you?' he asked softly. Against his breast, he could feel her head nod. He sighed. 'It's not Sir Andrew?' The head shook. He felt the tension slowly ease out of him. Then, 'Is it anyone we know?' he asked, holding his breath.

'Oh, Graham,' she merely said helplessly.

'What do you want to do?' he asked simply.

Monica sighed and pulled her head away to look at him. Her blue eyes were troubled, but resolute. 'Well, first I just want to go and see someone . . .' Graham looked concerned. 'No it's all right, they're in the village. It's broad daylight and I'm not going to do anything silly. I'm not going to confront anyone or anything. I just need to be sure of something first.'

'And then we go to Jason,' Graham said firmly.

Monica nodded. 'And then we go to Jason,' she agreed.

* * *

Dr Simon Grade seemed to have shrunk several sizes as he was ushered into the fast-clearing office. The files had been packed and loaded into police vans, as had the computers and most of the ugly, utilitarian furniture that came with it. Consequently, Jason was seated behind Sir Andrew's original, handsome, leather-topped desk when Dr Grade walked reluctantly across the room to shake hands.

'Chief Inspector,' he said, his voice weak and lacking in confidence. 'I take it this is about Professor Wyatt's findings?'

'Yes. As I'm sure you know . . . Please sit down, Dr Grade.' He waited until the museum owner was seated before continuing. 'The manuscript currently displayed at your museum is a well-executed fake,' he stated flatly.

Simon didn't go any paler than he already was, but his tongue flickered out to wet his lips. 'Really, I don't know what to say. I'm so surprised,' he managed to gasp.

Jason leaned back in his chair and sighed loudly. 'I don't think you're at all surprised, Dr Grade,' he contradicted grimly.

Simon twitched in the chair. 'Oh well . . . yes, I suppose after the break-in, I might just have thought . . . well, suspected that I . . . noticed tiny differences in the lettering . . .' he trailed off, as Jason was already shaking his head.

'No, Dr Grade, that won't do. How long do you think it'll take us to do a complete financial background check on you? How long do you think it'll take our expert accountants and fully trained fraud squad officers to find out where you have the money stashed?'

'I beg your pardon?' Simon Grade squeaked.

'It won't even take us long to find the collector you sold the real document to, will it? I doubt there can be that many . . .'

Jason stopped speaking as, before his astonished eyes, Simon Grade slowly toppled sideways out of his chair and fell gracefully onto the floor in a heap. Flora, who'd been taking notes, stared at the unconscious man, her mouth agape.

'Bloody hell,' she said.

* * *

In the kitchens, the chef was preparing scallops. Lunch was to be a light but tasty salad, and the room was full of kitchen staff preparing vegetables. None of them noticed the rear door opening which led into the smaller half of the dogleg room.

They certainly didn't notice that a sharp paring knife, left on the workspace near the storage cupboards, had been removed.

And when the door closed quietly behind a frantic killer, nobody heard it.

* * *

It was nearly an hour later before the last of the police equipment was finally loaded into the vans, and Flora and Jason, still in the incident room, were drinking their last cup of coffee at Heyford Basset Manor.

'So, do you want to charge Dr Grade now, or wait?' Flora asked.

Between them, they'd managed to manoeuvre Grade's dead weight back into the chair, and Jason had called in the police surgeon. By that time he'd come around and had clammed up. Jason, reassured by the medic that he hadn't suffered a heart attack or anything else serious, had allowed him to go home, knowing that they didn't have enough proof, as yet, to charge him. Like Flora, he had a sneaking suspicion that Dr Simon Grade might just do a runner, which would be a damned nuisance.

'We have to wait,' Jason said unhappily. 'Until we can find the collector who . . . Yes?' he snapped as a young police constable looked in through the open door.

'He's in here,' the young copper said, obviously not to Jason, and stood aside. Jason saw Graham Noble enter first, and then a moment later, Monica.

And Jason experienced an instant rush of déjà vu.

Twice before this couple had come to him, with just these identical looks on their faces, and within minutes had revealed the identity of a killer.

Flora's face went tight and hard.

'Graham,' Jason said, standing stiffly. He looked across at Monica, feeling his breathing stumble. 'Mrs Noble,' he added quietly.

'You've arrested the wrong man,' Monica said flatly. Then glanced at Graham. 'We've got to be quick. Graham, I'm worried.'

Jason felt a moment of anger — after all, no copper liked being told he'd made a mistake — but then the urgency and fear in her voice had a cold fist of fear clenching around his own innards.

'Chief Inspector,' Graham said, his voice quiet and calm, but carrying the same tense urgency as his wife's. 'Can we please go up to the Bryces' room? We're . . . well, we need to make sure that everything's all right up there.'

Jason had two choices. Demand an explanation before he did any such thing, which might take time that he suddenly felt sure that they didn't have, or take immediate action. It didn't take him a second to make up his mind.

'Follow me,' he said tersely. 'Flora, their room number?'

Flora hastily consulted her memory, since all the notes were gone, and came up empty. 'The register, sir,' she said instead.

Together, like a tense little war party, they filed into the hall, and Jason enquired of the receptionist about the room occupied by the Bryces.

'The Bryces are in room twenty-two, sir,' she said, her eyes alive with curiosity and resentment. With Sir Andrew in jail, nobody who worked at the manor house was inclined to be friendly to the police.

Rather than take the lift, Jason strode for the stairs. Only Graham was able to keep up with him easily, matching him stride for stride. The two women, though, were nearly running as they followed them along the corridor to room twenty-two.

Jason knocked, his knuckles rapping peremptorily on the wood. Two other doors opened and heads looked out enquiringly, then, seeing the blond-haired chief inspector, were hastily withdrawn again.

Throughout the big house, conference-goers were packing. But not, it seemed, in the Bryces' room. Jason opened the door, but as he'd half expected, the room was empty.

He looked questioningly at Graham.

Graham looked at Monica, who said quickly, 'We need to find Jessica. Jessica Taylor. She's staying in room twenty-eight. I remember her telling me.'

Once again they strode quickly down the corridor. Once again they knocked. Once again nobody answered.

Monica gnawed her lip worriedly. 'Graham!' she said urgently.

'I know,' her husband said, then hesitated as a maid turned the corner, a pile of towels in her arm. 'I say, miss, you don't happen to know where we can find Bishop Bryce do you? The good-looking blond one,' he added, and watched the girl's face immediately clear.

'Oh, him!' she said, and giggled. 'He was out on the lawns just now. A whole group of them are out there drinking Pimm's.'

Graham thought that mid-morning was hardly the time for Pimm's, then wondered what on earth that could possibly matter now.

Jason was beginning to get a little tired of all this, but already the Nobles were heading quickly for the stairs.

'Sir,' Flora said, sounding peeved.

206

Jason shrugged helplessly and set off in pursuit.

They found Arthur Bryce, not in the Pimm's-drinking party, but just walking away from it. He saw the group hurrying towards him and, his eyebrows going up, he met them halfway.

'Hello, you all look rather hot and bothered and—'

'We need to speak to you, Your Grace,' Graham interrupted rudely, something in both his tone and manner making the bishop give him a quick double take. 'Is there somewhere we could talk?'

'We can go back to the office,' Jason said, giving Arthur Bryce no option but to obey.

Once inside the office, the bishop from Yorkshire looked from Graham to the chief inspector, then to Monica. Monica's presence seemed to trouble him most of all, but it was Monica who spoke first.

'Your Grace, I know this may sound very impudent, and I'm sure your first instinct will be to deny everything, but please tell us the truth and as quickly as possible. Did you have an affair with Jessica Taylor's best friend?'

Jason, who'd been wondering for some time now what she'd come up with, hadn't expected this.

Arthur Bryce gaped at her. He was wearing his purple-fronted best shirt and the dog collar looked very white under his chin. 'I'm sorry? What did you say?' he asked tightly.

His eyes flitted quickly to the chief inspector then away again.

Monica took a deep breath. 'Please, Your Grace, we may be running out of time. Where's your wife?' she asked sharply.

'Chloe?' Arthur was obviously startled. 'Upstairs packing.'

'No she isn't,' Jason said flatly.

Arthur opened his mouth, then shut it again.

'Mrs Noble,' Jason said, 'I've been very patient so far, and I'm sure even you'll admit, more than co-operative. Now I want to know what's going on.'

Monica looked at him, then at Graham, who nodded. 'I think . . . I think Chloe Bryce killed Celia Gordon,' she said flatly.

'What?' it was Arthur Bryce's voice that split the deep, sudden silence. 'You can't be . . . That's ridiculous. Why on earth should Chloe want to kill that awful woman?' He sounded both genuinely angry and almost amused. 'You're out of your mind! Look here . . .' He turned to Graham, obviously about to order him to keep his wife under control, but Monica interrupted.

'You're quite right,' Monica said, aware that every head save her husband's had turned to look at her in astonishment. 'Your wife had no reason to kill Celia Gordon. But then, it wasn't Celia Gordon she'd meant to kill. It was Jessica Taylor.'

Jason motioned impatiently to his gobsmacked sergeant to start taking notes.

'I think you'd better start from the beginning,' Jason told Monica icily.

'But we've got to find her before she can have another go at it!' Monica demanded impatiently, leaning forward urgently in her seat, frustrated worry visible in every taut line of her.

Jason shook his head. 'Then make it quick. Convince me.'

Monica shot a look at Arthur Bryce, who'd gone amazingly quiet. 'You don't seem so surprised that she might want to kill Jessica Taylor, Your Grace,' she accused softly.

Arthur blinked. 'Now look here, there's nothing going on between me and Reverend Taylor, if that's what you're implying . . .'

'It's not,' Monica said flatly. 'But you're probably aware that there have been rumours circulating about you, and that they state that sometime last year you had an affair with one of your parishioners. If I'm right, that parishioner was a good friend of Jessica Taylor's. Is that so?'

Arthur blinked again. He was so obviously trying to think of the right route to take, the least embarrassing or compromising, that Jason barked thunderously, 'Well, yes or no, Bryce? Is the lady right or isn't she? Come on, man, this is a murder investigation. Another person's life might depend on it. Now's not the time to be worrying about your PR.'

Arthur's face, if anything, went even tighter.

'Your Grace,' Graham said, his voice as quiet as this-tledown after Jason's bark, but somehow more compelling. 'You're a man of God,' he said simply.

Arthur, bishop and one-time hopeful archbishop, looked at the humble country parson and took a long, slow breath. 'Her name was Debbie,' he said quietly. 'Debbie Rogers. But it's all over now. Debbie moved to Portugal. She decided it was no good, couldn't face the scandal if we'd been found out. She ended it, months and months ago. I haven't seen her since. It was Jessica who told me that she'd gone abroad. Debbie had written her a letter saying that . . . well, that it was best. She wanted to get right away from her past sins. Debbie was a very devout Christian, you know. Oh, I know that sounds strange but . . .' his voice wavered a little with emotion.

'I don't understand,' Jason put in, when it was obvious that Arthur Bryce wasn't going to say any more. 'How does Celia Gordon come into all this?'

'She doesn't,' Monica said wearily. 'That's what's been misleading us all this time. The way it must have happened went something like this. Everyone I've spoken to told me what Celia said at breakfast about being allergic to nuts, but Chloe Bryce wasn't present at the time. Is that right?' Monica, rather surprisingly, turned to Flora for help, raising one eye-brow questioningly.

Flora nodded promptly. 'Yes, that's right. We know that there was talk about how fond Celia was of oranges, and that Jessica Taylor said that she had a fondness for cake. And although most of the people we questioned didn't mention knowing about the peanut allergy — worried I guess, given the rumours — we've got reliable information that Chloe had left the room before the talk turned to Celia's nut allergy.'

Monica let out a long breath. 'I knew that's how it must have happened, or else how would Chloe know which dessert Jessica was likely to choose? And, of course, because of what happened later on, at the shop.'

'The shop?' Jason prompted, totally lost.

'Yes. When I went in — and this is the Saturday morning that I'm talking about — Jessica was there and we got talking to one of the village mums. Phyllis was listening, of course, and Jessica was espousing working mums' rights. And, well, the upshot of it was, she didn't make herself very popular with some of the more . . . traditional male clerics who were also at the shop.'

'We've been told about that, sir,' Flora added in an undertone. 'At the time, it hardly seemed relevant.'

'Yes, but when I went into the shop later, Phyllis said how sad it was that the woman who'd made all the fuss about women's rights had been killed. It didn't really mean anything to me at the time,' Monica confessed, 'and all I did was tell Phyllis that she'd made a mistake. That it wasn't Jessica who was dead, but someone else.'

'I still don't—' Flora began, but Monica quickly held up her hand.

'No, wait. I went back to the shop this morning to speak to Phyllis. I asked her why she thought it was Jessica who'd died, and she said the rumour was that it was the . . . how did she put it . . . that it was "the loud-mouthed women's-libber vicar" who'd died. Obviously after listening to Jessica championing women's rights and urging a mother-and-baby group for the village community, she thought that it was Jessica they were talking about. In reality of course, they were talking about Celia. But the thing is, Phyllis told me that after Jessica left, the Bryces came into the shop. And that the men outside were still full of it, and were grumbling.'

It was Jason who caught on first, and he quickly looked at the bishop, who sat slumped in his chair. 'Bishop Bryce, did you and your wife discuss anything in the shop that morning? More specifically, did you think, when you'd heard that a woman vicar had been there before you stirring up trouble . . . did you think they were talking about Celia Gordon?'

'Well, of course I did,' Arthur said rather huffily. 'That's a natural mistake for me to have made, surely?'

'Yes it is,' Monica said. 'But, Your Grace, did you mention to your wife that the woman they were talking about had a peanut allergy?'

Arthur Bryce went very pale. 'I . . . I can't remember,' he said, unconvincingly. 'I guess I may have mentioned the incident with the cornflakes to her.'

'Of course you did. You thought they were all talking about Celia Gordon, too,' Jason said flatly. 'A woman you had no particular affection for, since you were both competing for the chairmanship of an important committee. Oh yes, I know all about that.'

'The point is,' Monica said, agonizingly aware that time was passing far too quickly, 'that Chloe Bryce, knowing that the mother-and-baby thing was Jessica Taylor's particular area of expertise, thought, quite rightly, that the woman who'd made the old boys rumble and grumble was Jessica Taylor. She'd even seen her walking away from the shop with me. But you thought everyone was talking about Celia. So when you told your wife that "she" had a peanut allergy and was making a fuss at breakfast . . .'

'She thought you were talking about Jessica,' Flora finished triumphantly.

'But why did she want Jessica Taylor dead?' Jason put his finger on the whole crux of the matter. 'Just because she was a friend of her husband's one-time mistress? That just won't wash . . .'

'Oh no,' Monica said. 'I don't think that was the reason at all. It was because of what Jessica said at dinner that very first night. On Friday.'

Jason and Flora both leaned forward.

'She said,' Monica said quietly, 'that she was going to search for her friend who'd gone missing in Portugal. That she was going to get advice from the authorities to ask for their help in locating her. Isn't that right?'

Jason stared at Monica flatly. 'But why would that throw Chloe Bryce into a murderous frenzy?'

'Because I don't think Debbie is in Portugal,' Monica said quietly. 'I don't think Debbie ever went to Portugal. If she had, she'd have kept in touch with her best friend and vicar. She was a devout Christian, remember? She'd feel the need for Jessica's Christian guidance. But she didn't.' Monica repeated, with emphasis, 'She didn't.'

'Because she couldn't,' Flora breathed. 'She was dead. Oh my . . .'

Arthur Bryce jerked upright. 'What? What are you talking about?'

'I'm sorry, but I think it's true,' Monica said to him helplessly. 'And when she failed to kill Jessica with her first attempt, she tried again.'

'At the swimming party,' Graham said grimly. And to Jason, who hadn't yet heard about it, he recited the details briefly.

'Yes,' Monica carried on. 'When we arrived at the river, I realized that Jessica and I were wearing a very similar costume — oh, they were shaped differently, but they were both one pieces, and both the same bright shade of turquoise. And to anyone swimming underwater, it would have been easy to confuse us. I think Chloe wrapped her hands in river weed and pulled me under first before realising her mistake. I closed my eyes the moment I went under, so I didn't see her. And I expect Jessica did the same thing. But Carol-Ann, who likes swimming underwater, had her eyes open, and when she dived down to look for Jessica, Chloe had no other choice but to break off the attack and swim away.'

'You were all very lucky,' Graham said, with feeling. When he thought of how close he'd come to losing his wife, he felt sick.

'Yes. But luckily, Carol-Ann was able to save Jessica, and with the two of us on either side of her, Chloe didn't dare try again. But the point is, whoever tried to drown her had to be a good swimmer, being both strong and at home in the water. To be that confident, and to be able to stay underwater as long as the killer must have — well, it struck me that the average person wouldn't have been able to do it. That's when I remembered that silver medallion Chloe wore that had a figure of a swimming female figure on it. Your Grace,' she turned to Bishop Bryce. 'Is your wife a champion swimmer?'

'Yes. Yes she is,' Arthur Bryce confirmed, his voice hollow and hoarse.

Jason got up. His face was shuttered and grim. 'We've got to find Chloe. Or Jessica. Sergeant, have the men still here rounded up and then call for reinforcements. I want them found. NOW!'

CHAPTER 16

They found a prelate in the conservatory who told them that he'd heard Jessica Taylor saying to one of the staff that she was going for a walk by the river before packing.

Bishop Arthur Bryce retired to the bar, where he began to drink heavily. The thought that Debbie Rogers might be dead had seemed to take all the life out of him. The barman kept him supplied with whisky, and gloomily wished that he could join him. With Sir Andrew arrested he wasn't sure how long he'd have his job.

The police teams outside had already divided into pairs and were setting out to search, sectioning the village in neat squares.

Jason was unhappily aware that he was in a tricky position. Monica Noble's theory might well be right, but they would need reliable proof and solid evidence before his superiors would charge the wife of a bishop. Still, he wasn't going to take any risks with another person's life.

Flora, Jason, Monica and Graham were walking in a tight-knit group towards the manor's big double gates. 'We'll try the river,' Jason said, indicating himself and Flora. 'Would you two please go home and stay there.'

Monica opened her mouth rebelliously to say they'd do no such thing, but Graham nodded and murmured, 'Of course.'

He slipped his hand into Monica's, both as a warning and as a comforting gesture, and Monica felt her tension slowly subside. Graham was right. There was no reason for them to be mixed up in this anymore. It was up to Jason now.

* * *

Jessica Taylor had found her walk along the banks of the river wonderful. It was a warm morning and she'd seen the dippers, so beloved of one of her fellow clerics, as well as a pair of pretty yellow and grey wagtails. The grass was dry, and the smell, sights and sounds of a glorious English summer had put her in a good mood.

She came to a narrow footbridge, and crossing it, fetched up in a narrow lane. Slightly lost, she turned right and, to her surprise, found herself back in the village square. She contemplated the shop, but there was nothing she really wanted in there. She noticed several villagers watching her surreptitiously, and headed back towards Church Lane. She could understand their unfriendly scrutiny, of course.

Everyone at the manor had been stunned to learn of the arrest of Sir Andrew Courtenay. Obviously, there was a lot of talk about it, but no one had yet come up with any reason why the squire, of all people, should have been taken in. Still, it meant that it was over, and Jessica, for one, would be glad to get back to Birmingham and her husband and kids, and the duties and routines of her church.

Next year, she'd give the conference a miss.

As she passed the entrance to the big old vicarage, now turned into twelve flats, Jessica smiled and veered inside. It would be nice to say goodbye to Monica and Graham.

* * *

Chloe Bryce watched from the bend in the wall as Jessica Taylor walked towards her. She carefully stepped back onto the grass verge bordering the road and pressed her back tightly against the stone wall that marked the boundaries of the old vicarage. Clutched tightly in her hand was a small but deadly paring knife. Her knuckles were white.

This time there would be no mistake. This time another woman wouldn't die in her place. This time there would be no mother-and-daughter rescuers to save her.

She strained her ears for the sound of her victim's foot-steps, but could no longer hear them. She glanced around but there was no passing traffic and, so far, not a soul in sight.

But where was Jessica?

Chloe, dressed in a svelte slate-grey skirt and neat white blouse, risked a quick glance down the road.

It was empty.

* * *

Monica and Graham passed through the manor gates, heading down Church Road and the entrance to their own home. Behind them came a gasping voice. 'Er, vicar . . . Reverend Noble.'

They turned and saw one of the gardeners, employed full-time at the manor, hurrying to catch them up. His normally content and well-fed face had a shocked, haggard look. 'Is it true, Mr Noble, about Sir Andrew?' he asked anxiously.

Monica, sensing that now would be a good time to leave the two men alone and let her husband do what he did best — namely soothing and reassuring — briefly touched Graham's hand and whispered, 'I'll go and put the kettle on.'

Graham nodded and turned to the old man. He reached out and put a steadying hand on his shoulder.

* * *

Jessica turned away from the door to flat one feeling a keen sense of disappointment. There'd been no answer, and she was reluctant to leave, but she had nothing on her with which to write even a little goodbye note. She sighed and turned away from the door, hearing a rustle in the laurel bushes down the pathway in front of her, no doubt caused by a blackbird or some other creature, turning over the dead leaves that always accumulated under such shrubbery.

She began to walk back down the gravel path towards the gate.

Hidden in the dense evergreens, Chloe Bryce watched her coming closer. It was going to be crude — very crude. And risky. A stabbing, in broad daylight! But luck was with her.

When she'd discovered the empty road it had been obvious that there was only one place that Jessica could have gone: into the grounds of the old vicarage. These were off the road and hidden behind walls and greenery. It couldn't have been better. There was not a sound to be heard anywhere, except Jessica Taylor's shoes, step, step, stepping, closer and closer.

Chloe felt a wild sob build up inside her and ruthlessly pushed it back. It was all Jessica's fault anyway. Why hadn't she forgotten all about that worthless friend of hers and let it rest?

Then none of this would be happening now.

But no. She'd had to go digging around. Threatening to rouse the authorities in Portugal, looking for a woman who'd never even crossed their borders. How soon then would suspicions have been raised? And how long before they realized that a woman was missing, and had been since last February? And once the authorities started asking questions the trail would lead them straight back to the Bryce household. To Arthur. And herself . . .

The steps were closer now, almost on top of her, and through the foliage she could see the salmon-pink of the light-weight jersey that Jessica was wearing. The moment was upon her. It had to be done now.

She felt her heart leap, and quickly raised the knife . . .

Monica turned into the gate and heard the crunching of gravel. Looking up she was just in time to see Jessica rounding the bend. Jessica saw her at the same time, and a relieved smile lit up her face. She was just about to call out a greeting, to say how glad she was that she hadn't missed her after all, when suddenly something erupted from the bushes.

Jessica just had time to see a blob of white and grey hurtle into her peripheral vision before something hit her, knocking her to the ground.

Monica, after one horrified, frozen second, screamed at the top of her lungs, 'Chloe, NO!'

She dashed forward, startling the bishop's wife, who was standing over the stunned Jessica, the knife raised in her hand, for all the world a caricature of Norman Bates, knife raised and poised as in the infamous shower scene from *Psycho*.

Chloe spun around. Her mouth and eyes were open wide in surprise.

Out in the street, both Graham and old Tom heard an indistinct cry, but Graham at least had no difficulty in recognizing his wife's voice. He started to sprint for the vicarage, thinking just in time to call over his shoulder to the startled gardener, 'Get the police!'

Lying sprawled halfway on the path, halfway on the lawn, Jessica looked up at the vengeful figure standing over her and gasped. She was vaguely aware of the stickiness and warmth of her own blood running down her side.

Had she been stabbed?

Shocked, stumbling for answers, her eyes went to the knife in Chloe's hand. It looked shockingly red.

But Chloe was stood with her face turned away from Jessica, zeroed in instead on the woman running towards them. Chloe thought she vaguely recognised the dark-haired, blue-eyed woman, but what . . . ?

'Chloe, put the knife down,' Monica panted, drawing to a near comical, staggering stop just a few yards away. Her first instinct had been to help Jessica, but now fear for her own safety lanced through her. She tried to tell herself not to be a coward, but Monica was very well aware of how suddenly, sickeningly afraid she felt. Chloe was looking at her with such a wild look in her eye.

218

'No, you won't stop me this time,' Chloe suddenly hissed. And moved. She almost tripped over Jessica's foot, which only sent her staggering that much faster towards Monica, who instinctively raised a hand to her face, trying to ward off the blow.

And she screamed the first and only thought that came into her head.

'Graham!'

* * *

Jason and Flora, having found no sign of Jessica Taylor at the river, had returned to the manor to see if any of the others had reported in. But they hadn't even reached the big impressive front doors before the sight of an old man, running towards them with a hand raised in appeal and such a look of fright on his old face, had them tearing down the pathway to meet him.

Tom was so out of breath he could barely get the words out. 'Vicarage. Hurry. Someone . . . trouble,' he gasped.

Flora and Jason didn't wait to hear any more.

* * *

Graham was just rounding the bend of laurels when he heard his wife's terror-stricken scream. The sound of his shrieked name made the blood turn cold in his veins, even as he rounded the bend and saw . . .

His wife and Chloe Bryce, struggling together, the flashing silver glint of a knife flickering between them as they seemed to dance together in some macabre waltz. Monica had managed to reach out and halt the downward slice of the knife as Chloe had lunged at her, but now she couldn't let go.

Chloe was snarling and cursing, very low under her breath, for all the world like some kind of animal, instead of a rational human being. Except of course, she wasn't rational. She wasn't rational at all.

Jessica Taylor was trying to get to her feet in order to help her friend, but her injured arm was hampering her, as was a frightening, creeping kind of lassitude. She knew that she was losing blood and going into shock, and that she had to get up . . . but she couldn't.

'Monica,' she called desperately.

Graham was almost on top of them before Jessica saw him and collapsed back against the grass in relief.

Monica's back, though, was to her husband, and the first she knew of his presence was when she felt Chloe's fiercely squirming weight and appalling strength suddenly lessen. Then, miraculously, she heard her husband's voice and saw his hand reach out beside her.

'Let go of it,' Graham yelled, his own hand now on Chloe's wrist, just above Monica's own, adding his strength to hers; he tightened his grip painfully. Chloe screamed in frustration, but still, maniacally, refused to let go of the knife.

Jason, who'd gained a few good yards of advantage on Flora, sprinted up the path, taking in the scenario at once.

Monica, shunted and shoved in the three-sided struggle, fell away onto the grass, leaving Graham grappling with a fierce madwoman on his own.

Chloe began to screech, a sound so inhuman that it made Jessica want to clamp her hands over her ears. But it seemed to be coming from so far away now . . .

'Chloe, stop it,' Graham said desperately, beginning to pant. When he'd seen her and Monica together, his sole thought had been to save Monica. Now he knew that he had to stop the struggling woman before someone else got hurt. But he was hampered by his reluctance to hurt a woman physically. He couldn't just hit her.

'Chloe, let go . . .'

Then, suddenly Jason was there, and Chloe's knife-arm was ruthlessly clenched and thrust back up and behind her. Chloe screamed in pain and instantly released the knife.

Flora, panting and fumbling for her handcuffs, appeared beside her boss and, between them, and with some considerable difficulty, the two police officers managed to get the cuffs on the screaming, abusive, sobbing, wild Chloe Bryce.

Monica stared at the woman in amazement for a moment. It was incredible. Her cool outfit was blood-spattered and creased, her chic hair a wild tangle, her face contorted, her make-up running . . . She looked like something out of a Victorian horror show. There was something almost primitively frightening in watching a well-groomed, elegant woman turn into such a monster.

Then she saw Jessica, who was lying weakly on the ground, and crawled across to her. The amount of blood seeping into the ground scared her. 'I'll call for an ambulance,' she told the pale-faced woman, who nodded feebly.

Monica scrambled towards her handbag, which had been discarded in the struggle, and reached for her mobile.

* * *

It was evening before Monica and Graham drove back from the headquarters of the Thames Valley Police, where they'd given a full statement.

Jessica Taylor had been rushed to the John Radcliffe Hospital, having been given a blood transfusion in the ambulance on the way. She'd been operated on, and was going to be fine. They'd got to her just in time. Her husband had arrived from Birmingham, and was staying the night at her bedside.

Chloe Bryce had been booked and charged, primarily with assault and causing grievous bodily harm. It was an easily provable charge, given the witnesses and circumstances, and would give the police the time and leverage they needed to hold her and build up a case against her on other, more serious charges.

The clock in the hall was chiming eight when the doorbell rang. The Nobles were sitting in the kitchen, exhausted, a mostly untouched meal of salad and cold ham in front of them.

'I'll get it,' Graham said wearily, and came back a few moments later with Jason.

The chief inspector looked as tired as they did, but there was an edge of satisfaction in his voice and manner that was lacking in his companions.

'Well, she's confessed to everything,' he said, his words bringing a palpable sense of relief and closure to the room. 'And you were right on all counts.'

As Graham put on the kettle for more tea, Jason sat at the table. The top two buttons on his shirt were undone, his tie was stuffed into one pocket, his hair was tousled and a sheen of gold on his chin indicated that he needed a shave. He looked fantastic.

'She killed Debbie Rogers all right, sometime in February. She was almost triumphant about it. She'd heard the rumours and knew all about her husband's affair, apparently. To hear her talk, it was the crime of the century,' Jason said disgustedly. 'I don't know what outraged her the most — that Arthur Bryce would risk his career and his shot at becoming an archbishop all for the sake of a paltry little affair, or that he should choose someone so . . . how did she put it? "Ordinary and dirty."' He shook his head helplessly.

Wordlessly, Graham put a mug of tea down in front of him, and took a seat next to Monica.

'How did she do it?' Monica asked, wanting to know, even whilst she felt sick inside.

'She gained access to Debbie's house and turned on the gas.'

'But surely the police must have suspected . . .' Graham began, then shook his head. 'No, I'm not thinking straight. They never even found her body, right?'

'No. Chloe was too clever for that,' Jason said. 'She faked a letter on the victim's own computer, supposedly from Debbie to her best friend Jessica Taylor. Chloe had certainly done her homework on Debbie. Reverend Taylor, of course, knew all about the affair and had been trying to talk Debbie into ending it for some time. So of course she was quite glad when she got a letter, supposedly from her friend, saying that she was getting away from all her past sins by moving to Portugal.'

'It's hard to think Chloe could get away with something like that,' Graham said. 'Surely someone was bound to question it?'

Jason shrugged. 'Debbie had no family. The house was rented on a month-by-month basis. Her own sense of guilt seemed to have turned her into something of a recluse, it seems. None of the neighbours commented much on her sudden absence. A sign of the times, I'm afraid,' Jason said grimly. 'Men and women disappear in this country all the time.'

Monica shivered. 'Did Chloe say what she did with the body?'

'Oh yes. She told us she went back into the house once the gas had done its work. She turned off the gas, and only opened an upstairs window for ventilation, then tidied the house and packed the victim's belongings, which she later disposed of. She's a very fit woman, you know, and surprisingly strong. And from what we've learned about Debbie from Arthur Bryce, she was a petite sort of woman, and very lean. Chloe told us she drove to a disused canal near Bristol and weighted the body down and dumped it. We'll get divers out there first thing in the morning, but I've no doubt that she was telling the truth. They do that sometimes. Get caught, and then can't wait to boast about it. She keeps referring to Debbie Rogers as "the whore" or "the enemy," never by her name. It's part of the dehumanizing that killers practise on their victims . . .'

Monica shuddered and held up a hand. 'Enough,' she said quietly.

Graham reached for her raised hand and curled his fingers around it, pulling it back down onto his lap.

Jason went white and took a shuddering breath. 'I'm sorry. I forget sometimes . . .' He took a sip of his tea and ran a tired hand across his forehead.

'Did Jessica and Chloe know each other?' Monica asked, more to break the sudden awkwardness than anything else.

'No,' Jason said, 'Chloe had no real idea who Jessica Taylor was until the first night of the conference. That was when Jessica began talking about her friend, who'd gone to Portugal, and seemed to have disappeared. A rather big coincidence for Chloe to swallow.' Jason leaned forward tiredly on the chair. 'You have to remember that there was no reason for Jessica and Chloe ever to have met. Jessica didn't approve of her friend's affair, and saw Chloe as the wronged wife. She'd learned a lot about her, but it was all second-hand, from both Arthur and Debbie.'

'So Arthur knew Jessica?' Graham put in.

'Oh yes,' Jason confirmed. 'Debbie had introduced them. Of course, Arthur wasn't keen on his mistress being best friends with a female vicar, you can be sure of that!' Jason snorted. 'And he told us that on the first night at the conference, he'd tried to talk to Jessica in her room. He wanted to be sure she was going to keep quiet about everything. Chloe admitted she'd seen him knocking on her door, which was all the confirmation she'd needed that the Jessica Taylor who was at the conference was the same Jessica Taylor that she'd sent Debbie's forged letter to. But Chloe would have had no reason to fear for her safety, even then, if Jessica hadn't made it clear that she wasn't going to let Debbie's disappearance rest. It must have come as quite a shock to her that first night to find someone so dangerous right on her doorstep. Given the state of her mind, it was no wonder Chloe tried to kill her.'

'And poisoned Celia Gordon by mistake instead,' Monica said. 'What a waste. What a pointless, stupid waste . . .'

Jason said nothing. There was nothing to say. 'Well,' he finished his tea and pushed the mug to one side. 'I just thought you'd want to know the details. Oh, and we've released Sir Andrew of course,' he added with a smile, wanting to leave them on a much happier note.

What he didn't tell them was what Sir Andrew had confessed to before all this had broken about Chloe Bryce. Namely that he and Matthew Pierrepont had hatched up a scheme between them, not to kill Celia Gordon, but to ruin her.

Sir Andrew had purchased a small amount of heroin and was going to plant it in Celia's room. He would then have given an anonymous tip-off to the police. Meanwhile, Sir Matthew had been trying to get his journalistic buddies to record the story. It would have been, Sir Andrew had told them bitterly, poetic justice.

They could have charged him for various offences relating to this scheme, but had decided not to. For one thing, Sir Andrew had sworn that he'd tossed the drugs into the river so they'd never find them. It would therefore be hard to prove anything. And since they hadn't actually carried out their plan . . .

Still, Jason knew that his superiors were going to have a strong word with Sir Matthew Pierrepont's bishop, and that soon the archdeacon was going to find himself living in a nursing home, and not before very long. Which was the best place for him, as far as Jason was concerned.

As for Sir Andrew . . . it was agreed that nothing would be accomplished by trying to make any charges against him stick. And for that, Jason was rather grateful. The man had surely suffered enough.

He let Monica and Graham walk him to the door. There was an awkward moment as he stepped outside and turned to look at them, nobody quite sure what to say. Then he nodded briefly at Graham, who had become one of the few men that he truly respected. And finally, he turned to look at Monica. His lips twisted in a wry smile. 'Well, yet again, you've come up trumps,' he said, his voice perhaps more annoyed than he'd meant it to sound. 'I hope . . .' he tried again, but then trailed off.

He shrugged instead and smiled. 'Well, so long,' he finally said briskly, nodded once, then turned and forced himself to walk away.

Monica watched him go, a tall, blond, handsome man who belonged in another world.

Then she looked up at Graham and smiled gently. 'Are you tired?' she asked. And when he nodded ruefully, she reached up and kissed him. 'Then let's go to bed,' she said softly.

THE END

THE END

THE JOFFE BOOKS STORY

We began in 2014 when Jasper agreed to publish his mum's much-rejected romance novel and it became a bestseller.

Since then we've grown into the largest independent publisher in the UK. We're extremely proud to publish some of the very best writers in the world, including Joy Ellis, Faith Martin, Caro Ramsay, Helen Forrester, Simon Brett and Robert Goddard. Everyone at Joffe Books loves reading and we never forget that it all begins with the magic of an author telling a story.

We are proud to publish talented first-time authors, as well as established writers whose books we love introducing to a new generation of readers.

We won Trade Publisher of the Year at the Independent Publishing Awards in 2023. We have been shortlisted for Independent Publisher of the Year at the British Book Awards for the last four years, and were shortlisted for the Diversity and Inclusivity Award at the 2022 Independent Publishing Awards. In 2023 we were shortlisted for Publisher of the Year at the RNA Industry Awards.

We built this company with your help, and we love to hear from you, so please email us about absolutely anything bookish at feedback@joffebooks.com

If you want to receive free books every Friday and hear about all our new releases, join our mailing list: www.joffebooks. com/contact

And when you tell your friends about us, just remember: it's pronounced Joffe as in coffee or toffee!

Milton Keynes UK
Ingram Content Group UK Ltd.
UKHW042124211024
450028UK00010B/84

9 781835 267455